FATE
THE WINX SAGA

The Fairies' Path

By Ava Corrigan

Scholastic Inc.

Fate The Winx Saga™ © 2021 Rainbow S.p.A. All Rights Reserved.
© 2021 Netflix. Used with permission.

The publisher does not have any control over and does not assume any responsibility for author or third-party websites or their content.

This book is a work of fiction. Names, characters, places, and incidents are either the product of the author's imagination or are used fictitiously, and any resemblance to actual persons, living or dead, business establishments, events, or locales is entirely coincidental.

ISBN 978-1-338-69226-6

1 2020

Printed in the U.S.A. 23
First printing 2021

Book design by Katie Fitch

The Beginning of the Fairy Tale

Bloom Peters pulled her grubby sleeping bag up to her chin, shivered on the deflating air mattress laid on the cold floor, and wished for home.

No kindly fairy godmother came to grant her wish.

The warehouse where she spent her nights was a space that could give you nightmares, and Bloom didn't need any help in the nightmare department. There was detritus heaped in the corners of the cavernous space, and sometimes Bloom heard weird rustling coming from that direction—rustling that she'd firmly decided *not* to investigate. Moonlight sent shafts of cold illumination down through the apertures in the roof, like alien spaceships searching for an abductee.

Luckily for Bloom, her nightmares were about burning homes and not chilly warehouses. And she couldn't have nightmares if she never slept.

She sat up in her makeshift bed and reached for her note-pad, using her phone to light the top page.

Bloom's list of ideas was titled *What the hell is happening to me?*

Pyrokinesis?

Mutations?

Superpowers?

Fireproof?

Under her list of ideas, she'd written the results of her experiments.

July 6th—candles—no burns.

July 8th—camping stove—no burns.

July 10th—blowtorch—no burns.

Experimenting on herself had been scary, but not as scary as the memory of her home burning. Every night, she relived the fight she'd had with her mom, and then the moment she'd woken to find her house in flames. She'd known that somehow, she'd done this. She'd charged through her burning house into her parents' bedroom to find the bed, the curtains, the whole room a seething inferno. Even the ceiling was a sea of flame. Bloom remembered her dad coughing desperately on the floor, her mom wrapped in a blanket and covered in burns. As though the fire had lunged to swallow her mom, when Bloom would never . . .

Bloom would never. Only she had.

Every night, she crept out of her nice, normal bedroom in her nice, normal, being-reconstructed-from-fire-damage home. She came here and huddled on the floor and tried to think her way out of this. Bloom considered herself a fighter, but she was the one who'd hurt her mom. She didn't know how to fight herself.

Another rustle came, this one much louder. Bloom's head jerked up. She couldn't see much through the grime-smeared windows. If someone had seen a teenage girl sneak into the abandoned warehouse, they might get all kinds of ideas.

Bloom put down her phone and her notebook. Let them try to come at her. She'd hurt her own mother. She wouldn't hesitate to go scorched-earth on a creep. Literally.

There was another sound, an echoing footstep. Bloom's hands clenched into fists. She felt an itch in the center of each palm, like heat building.

The sound of the footstep hadn't come from the direction of the door.

Bloom spun around to see the woman.

This was no ordinary intruder.

This woman was clearly extraordinary. There was no question about that. She was tall, a middle-aged white woman in conservative clothes with an ash-blonde mane severely pinned up, dark decided eyebrows, and an air of immense dignity. Her presence seemed to transform the grubby warehouse into a stateroom.

Also, the wall behind the woman had opened into a shimmering portal of light. Just another clue that something unusual was going on.

"Bloom Peters?" said the stranger. "I'm Farah Dowling. Please try to forget my first name immediately. If you come to my school, you won't be using it. Headmistresses don't have first names."

Bloom's first shock was fading.

"If I come . . . to your school," said Bloom. A jagged laugh erupted from her throat. "Oh, a mysterious stranger has come to tell me about her school for wizards?"

"Not wizards," said the woman.

Bloom waved this off. "Is this the part where you tell me I'm magic now?"

"You always were, Bloom," said Headmistress Dowling. "You just didn't know it yet."

That was enough. She might have mysterious powers that were out of control, the world might be going mad, but her parents hadn't raised her to listen to strange adults who approached in the dead of night with what sounded like a cult recruitment speech. Bloom snorted, abandoned her sleeping bag, and made for the door.

The woman's voice stopped her at the mouth of the warehouse.

"I know about the fire, Bloom."

Bloom trembled like a candle flame in a gust of wind. Slowly, she turned around. The woman was watching her with a steady gaze, keen but not unkind.

"Where are you going? You can't go home. You're too afraid you'll hurt your parents again."

Headmistress Dowling was right. Bloom shivered. Even in California, the nights could get cold.

Dowling moved toward Bloom, and Bloom held still, caught by a mixture of fear and hope.

"You're looking for answers. I'm a teacher. That means I have all the answers. Or at least, I'll tell you that I do."

Bloom wanted to go home even more than she wanted answers, but she couldn't find a safe path. Not on her own.

So when the woman spoke, Bloom listened.

FAIRY TALE #1

Come away, O human child!
To the waters and the wild . . .
—W. B. Yeats

FIRE

I had only just arrived at the castle, and honestly, I was in shock.

Chill, Bloom, I kept repeating in my mind, but it was hard to be chill in fairyland. I hadn't expected my new fairy school to look like the castle in an illustration from the book of fairy tales I used to treasure. Once upon a time, it was my favorite possession, the fanciest book I owned, with golden swirls on the cover. But I'd grown up and packed the book into my old toy chest along with my teddy bears. I'd thought I was long past fairy tales.

That was before I used magic to burn down my house. My toy chest and my fairy-tale book had burned, too.

Even as a kid, I'd never expected to actually step into a fairy tale. The whole landscape was like this. Verdant rolling hills that looked soft as green velvet, dark deep forests, and now a castle surrounded by gates and gardens.

There were domed towers on either side of the castle, and the roof was speckled with turrets. The walls seemed to be granite, but smoother somehow, like granite turned to glass or given a magic gloss. Maybe fairies could do that.

I had no idea what fairies could do. Yet apparently, I was one.

My book of fairy tales hadn't included a swarm of kids around my age. One long-legged, capable-looking African American chick strode by, wearing a denim jacket and carrying a bag full of athletic gear. Wait, she wasn't African American. Fairies didn't have Africa or America. I didn't know the name of the fairy realm I was currently in. Also, I hadn't pictured fairies being into extreme sports.

Another girl, pale with a cloud of brown hair, was clutching several plants to her bosom as she hurried across the courtyard. A third sauntered by, vaguely punk rock and olive-skinned and wearing enormous headphones that buzzed faintly on her ears. I hadn't pictured fairies rocking out, either.

There was a rangy guy with skinny jeans, overly sardonic eyebrows, and a knife-bridge nose. California had plenty of white boy edgelords, but this edgelord had an

7

actual knife. Oh no, *actual knife!* I wasn't interested in getting to know Knife Boy better.

A stunning blonde girl with porcelain skin was taking a selfie with a group of overawed younger students. A luminous wisp floated in the air, making her glossy hair shine. Talk about a beauty angle. Seemingly, fairies could create their own beauty lighting.

I checked my phone. Headmistress Dowling had told me an older girl called Stella would meet me and show me the ropes. Stella was late, and I was tired of waiting. I could find my way on my own.

I started forward, hesitated and redirected, and then started forward again. Boldness was everything.

"Wow," said a voice. "You are so lost."

Some guy was talking to me. Thankfully, not Knife Guy, but . . . sorry, Some Guy, I don't have time for you.

Some Guy continued, his voice thoughtful. "The issue is you overcommitted. I mean, you're essentially running. And now that I'm here, you can't possibly give me the satisfaction of turning around."

I sneaked a look at him and grinned. His hair had coiffed peaks like a gold helmet and his shirt was pink, which I liked because gender stereotypes were for the weak. He even had a summer tan that fishbelly-pale redheaded me could only dream of. But no matter how cute he was, I wasn't going to encourage him.

"I guess that means we have to do this forever. There are worse things, but—"

I stopped and turned to him. "I don't need help, but thanks."

Now I was looking at him properly, Some Guy was *very* cute, with a hero jawline and a confident air. Some Guy might be cute, but I was the independent type.

Some Guy teased: "Don't remember offering it. So presumptuous. You must be a fairy."

Well, that's what Headmistress Dowling had told me. I took a deep breath, and said it out loud for the first time. "Yes. I am a fairy."

The castle and the cute boy went hazy around me for a minute. I continued bantering, but I wasn't doing a great job at hiding how overwhelmed I was. He guessed I wasn't from around here, and his gaze softened as though he felt bad for me.

Back in California, I hadn't fit in. Could I here? This boy seemed so completely at home, in a castle, in a world where fairies were real. Part of me wanted to keep smiling at him, and part of me wanted to find my own way.

"Dude! Quit perving on the first years."

Cute Guy turned around at the voice, which belonged to Knife Boy. Oh, hell no. I was out of here.

I made my way toward the staircase while the pair brohugged. Knife Boy was apparently called "Riv." Well. My name was Bloom. I shouldn't judge.

The blonde with the magic beauty lighting caught up with me at the staircase. She would've been even more beautiful if she hadn't been wearing an expression suggesting she smelled something bad.

9

"Bloom?"

I guessed that something was me.

"You must be Stella. Hi. I've been waiting. I just kinda got impatient."

Stella didn't seem impressed by my impatience, but she led the way through the castle, waving an airy hand around at the impressive surroundings. Some of the chandeliers in this place were so dainty and delicate, they looked like stars suspended on gilt ribbons. The rooms were large and bright, with sunbeams dyed by stained-glass windows that were as intricate as the embroidery on a princess's hem. Much of the stained glass was different shades of green, subtly coloring the air around us as though we were in a world made of jade and emerald.

Stella wasn't impressed, but she was totally impressive herself. She wore her hair in a cool looping braid, a trench-coat with a *haute couture* air, and awesome red boots. I was a boots girl myself, plus I wore red and pink because red-heads weren't supposed to and I liked breaking rules. All my dresses-and-boots ensembles would pale compared to Stella, though. Even Stella's hand was decorated. I nodded toward her ornate jewelry. "That is a lot of ring."

"Family heirloom," said Stella. "A gateway ring. The only thing that keeps me sane in this place is the ability to leave it."

She continued talking, full of ennui about the fairy-tale castle, while I sneaked another look at her ring. "If you ever want to go back," Stella said as she deliberately flashed it at me. She was making some kind of power play, and I didn't know why.

This girl Stella didn't know how badly I wanted to go back home. But I couldn't. That woman, Headmistress Dowling, had promised me answers.

I let Stella lead me upstairs to the set of rooms in the fairy-tale castle that she referred to as the Winx suite. I dumped my bags, but I didn't pay much attention to what Stella was saying. I was focused on answers.

My first order of business was finding Headmistress Dowling again.

FIRE

A fairy who seemed mostly interested in her phone directed me to the headmistress's office. Once there, I only found more questions. There was a globe in the office that showed realms instead of continents. There was a realm called Eraklyon, which sounded like a dragon clearing its throat. Apparently, the realm I was currently in was called Solaria.

The fairy school Alfea. The fairy realm Solaria. Worlds away from California, and home.

And Headmistress Dowling, the woman with the answers. My only hope. She fit in here against the background of books and ornate stained glass, her globe of the realms and her shining desk. She stood at her desk, elaborately carved chair and circular mosaic windows of green glass behind her, telling me I was a Fire Fairy.

"That much I know," I said dryly, and then asked my first question. "So. When do we start?"

Ms. Dowling answered in a measured tone. "Classes begin tomorrow. You'll start with the basics. Learn to use your magic slowly, but safely."

It stung. I thought, since she came to get me herself, that she might be giving me special lessons. But no, I was just another student at fairy school. Fine with me. My mission was to get out of here as quickly as possible.

Thus, one word she'd used concerned me. "When you say *slowly* . . ."

"I mean it. Magic can be dangerous, as you well know. Our curriculum is designed with that in mind. Trust the process."

With an edge in my voice, I said: "The . . . slow . . . process."

"Alfea's graduates have ruled realms and led armies. They've forged powerful relics and rediscovered long-lost magic. They shape the Otherworld. If you succeed here, you will, too."

Her voice was soft, serious, and compelling. Her words unrolled in front of me like another map of strange realms. Ms. Dowling gave a great recruitment speech, but I wasn't looking to be recruited.

"This place . . . the Otherworld, Alfea? Honestly, it seems"—*like a storybook come to life*—"amazing. But it isn't my home," I told her. "I don't need to rule a realm or lead an army. I'm here because you promised you'd teach me control."

I didn't want to beg for reassurance. She provided none.

Ms. Dowling met my beseeching gaze with her own cool, level stare. Her voice drew a line under the conversation. "No, Bloom. You're here because you knew you had no other choice."

I almost hated her for not helping me, but she was right. This was the place I could learn control. My parents deserved better than a child gone wild as a forest fire. I was doing this for them.

FIRE

I'd do anything for my parents, including lie to them about my new boarding school in Definitely Switzerland. My afternoon video chat with them was slightly awkward, especially when Mom and Dad hinted about seeing the view from the window. If only fairyland had ski slopes!

Mom and I used to play pretend that I was a princess, back in the days when she thought I'd grow up to be a cheerleader and maybe prom queen. We'd get dressed up and she'd play me cheerleader-type music. I remembered one chant that went *Close your eyes and open your heart!* The cheesy brainwashing hadn't worked. I never much cared about frilly princess gowns, but I liked the idea of being at home in my princess castle.

In my fairy-tale castle daydreams, the princess got a room of her own.

In what beautiful blonde Stella had called the Winx suite—a bright series of rooms with tall windows and a view I couldn't allow my parents to see—only one person got a room of their own. To my total lack of surprise, that person was Stella.

The second room was occupied by Musa, the girl with the buzzing headphones I'd spotted earlier, and Terra, who was even now bustling through the rooms placing plants on every available surface. I was sharing a room with a girl called Aisha. I'd noticed her athletic bag earlier, but now Aisha's impressive array of sports medals on her dresser were shining more brightly than the mirror. I didn't know where Aisha herself was. She moved fast, loping through our rooms with terrifying grace and speed.

She seemed nice, but I didn't envision myself being bosom buddies with a supreme jock.

When Mom, always waiting for my transformation into Ms. Popular, asked about the other girls, I shrugged. "Honestly, it's five girls in an enclosed space, so . . . it's only a matter of time before we descend into a *Lord of the Flies* situation and kill one another."

My mother didn't love that answer. After our usual back and forth, my parents asked to see the Alps again. I stared around in panic. I couldn't provide my parents with a socially successful daughter *or* the Alps.

On my nightstand, a light bulb went off. Then on. Then off again.

Aisha's calm voice said: "All right. Lights out. Phones off."

I told my parents I loved them and signed off. Then I was free to express my everlasting gratitude to Aisha.

She smiled faintly, but I thought there was warmth there. "Do I want to know why they think you're in the Alps?"

"My parents are both human. They're apparently not allowed to know anything about this place, so they think Alfea is an international boarding school in Switzerland."

Aisha sounded startled. "Human parents, fairy daughter?"

I'd been hoping that wasn't as unusual as Aisha's tone said it was. She didn't seem the type to startle easily.

I busied myself with unpacking to hide my discomfort. "Ms. Dowling said there's a fairy somewhere in my family tree? A long-dormant magical bloodline?" I sighed. "One day I will get used to how ridiculous all this sounds."

Aisha's surprise became wry amusement. "Oh my God. Have I just met the one person in the universe who's never read Harry Potter?"

"How dare you. If you knew how many hours I have wasted taking online Sorting Hat quizzes . . ."

"Ravenclaw?"

"Sometimes Slytherin," I admitted.

Sometimes I cheated so I wouldn't get Slytherin. I worried that made me more Slytherin than ever.

"That explains the lies, then," Aisha said mildly. For the first time, I noticed that Aisha had cool cobalt blue streaks running through her box braids.

"Gryffindor?" I shot back. "Explains the judgment."

Aisha and I both grinned. Then I grabbed my makeup bag and headed for the bathroom. So far, I kinda liked my new roommate. If we did all end up murdering one another, maybe I'd kill Aisha last.

That still left the spot for who I'd kill first wide open.

I passed Stella's room to see her studying the glittery and silvery outfits laid out on her bed like a general planning a campaign.

"May I help you?" Stella asked, without a glance at me.

Headmistress Dowling said Stella was supposed to be my mentor. Though she'd shown little interest in helping me so far.

"You're changing?" I asked.

"I am."

"I thought the orientation party was a casual thing?"

"It is."

Just to clarify, I said: "A casual thing you're changing for."

"People have seen me in this outfit. They'll expect something different."

Stella said this as if it were obvious. She contemplated a different skirt with the intensity of a thousand suns.

I blinked. "People expect you to wear multiple outfits a day?"

"People expect me to care how I look."

Stella's eyes flicked to my very casual outfit. She glided over to her mirror without another word. As she gazed at her reflection, her eyes glowed a sudden umber yellow, startling as car headlights in a girl's face. Another shimmering magical light appeared. Casually, Stella plucked the magic light from the air, placing it at an angle to illuminate her outfit.

I froze, caught like a rabbit in the headlights of magic.

"Something else?" Stella sounded bored.

"That light. It's magic, right? How exactly do you . . ."

"I'm a mentor," Stella said firmly. "Not a tutor."

Okay, Stella, message received.

Stella relented. "This is something you'll learn your first day in class, but fairy magic is linked to emotion. Could be good thoughts, could be bad. Love, hatred, fear. The stronger the emotion, the stronger the magic."

"So do you hate me or fear me?" I teased. "You were staring at me when you did that spell. And I'm pretty sure you don't love me."

I was kidding, but Stella seemed to take me seriously.

"I don't know you," she answered. "I'm sure once I do I'll find . . . something to love."

The way she looked at me said she wasn't so sure. At the same time, it was kind of nice that Stella wasn't discounting the idea. There were times I looked in the mirror and didn't see much to love.

I wondered if any of my new suitemates ever felt that way. Happy bustling Terra, cool girl Musa, glamorous Stella, and Aisha who seemed so grounded. Somehow, I suspected not.

MIND

Five girls. Forty-eight plants. The Winx suite was crowded. For Musa, everywhere was crowded: buzzing with other people's intrusive feelings, slipped under her door like a constant stream of messages she'd never asked for.

Musa wished passionately that at least she'd gotten a room of her own. But no. Into their shared bedroom came Terra, drooping because queen bee Stella had told her to take her plants elsewhere.

Terra seemed to be easily hurt. Her pain rang in Musa's head like a gong, and Musa set her teeth.

"She seems lovely," Musa observed.

Stella's emotions were anything but lovely. But then, in Musa's experience, most people's feelings weren't lovely.

Terra's super sweet voice revved into overdrive, picking up speed and frantic pleasantness on the way. "She's just having fun. And I know it's a lot. Shocker, Earth Fairy named Terra likes plants. It's a family thing. I've got a cousin named Flora. My mom's name is Rose, and my dad works in the greenhouse here. That's why I know a lot of the second years. I grew up around Alfea, and—"

A lot of the second years, like Stella, Terra meant. That felt wrong. It pinged around Musa's head, like noticing a book missing on a bookshelf.

"Stella's a second year? Why is she in a suite full of first years?"

"Oh yeah. Actually . . . I don't know. Some administrative thing last year? I mean, I think . . ."

I think you're lying, thought Musa. She turned her back and dipped her power toward Terra, getting a faint sense that . . .

No, she shouldn't pursue it. Lots of people lied. Terra must not be encouraged, that was clear. She was already filling their room with plants and Musa's head with way too much information Musa had never asked for.

"You know what?" Musa decided. "It's actually not a big deal." She reached for her headphones like a drowning person reaching for a life raft.

Terra rattled on. "Also, like, I wouldn't bring it up to her. Let's just . . . all of us . . . blanket statement: Who cares?"

"Weirdly enough, that's my motto in life. So we are golden." Musa meant this as a way to kindly but firmly disengage. Terra the Terror didn't get it.

"Do you want a succulent? They're hip. Low maintenance. Very you. Not that I really know you, but—"

"If I take it, will you stop talking?" Musa snapped, and then instantly felt bad. "Terra. I'm just having fun."

Musa took the plant, giving Terra exactly what she wanted, and was rewarded when Terra turned away. Relieved, Musa quickly slid on her headphones.

Then, disaster. Because Terra didn't really want Musa to take a plant. She wanted Musa to engage, to be interested, to be overwhelmed by Terra's jumbled rush of emotions. To drown in them.

"Actually, this one might be—"

Musa turned her back so Terra couldn't see her face. She hoped desperately that Terra would give up and leave her alone.

There was a knock on the door. Musa glanced toward it, guessing this was calm-waters Aisha, or firebrand Bloom. Stella was so clearly not the knocking type.

Aisha popped her head in. "Did you say you grew up at Alfea?"

Sports fiend Aisha wanted to find a pool to swim in, because she had to swim twice a day every day or perish, apparently. Terra burst into a totally unhelpful torrent of information about the pond where the Specialists trained. According to her, the military division of the school took turns tipping each other into the water while they sparred.

Musa left Aisha to deal with Terra.

Get used to disappointment, Musa thought, about Aisha and Terra both. Aisha wasn't getting a pool, and Terra wasn't making any friends here.

Terra was clearly the type who wanted everyone to like her. The more that type tried, the less people liked her— which made her try even harder. That was the Try–Hard Catch-22.

It made Musa feel lousy to see Terra trying so hard . . . but it didn't make Musa like her. Musa guessed that reaction was part of Terra's problem.

Whatever. Musa had her own problems. She didn't care about Fire Fairies, Light Fairies, Earth Fairies, Water Fairies, or Specialists. She focused on trying to tune everything and everyone out.

SPECIALIST

It was another beautiful day in Alfea, in which the mighty Specialists trained to defend their magical realms. Trainees sparred on the platforms spanning the pond, a large rectangle of water that reflected the gray stone walls, a tree-lined path on one side and a swathe of green lawn on the other. Some chump had just gotten knocked into the water.

Riven smirked and swung his sword. After a long summer off, it was cool to have a blade in hand again. Less cool was Sky, Riven's super annoying best friend in the whole world, who was rattling on about the ginger girl from the human world he'd met yesterday. Riven was sure she was crazy. He knew this because crazy was what Sky looked for in a woman.

Also uncool, but not unexpected: Sky was beating Riven hollow in their sparring session.

"You got slow this summer," Sky laughed.

Riven bared his teeth. "Correction: I got high this summer."

There was no real point trying to beat Sky. He was the best. Anyone in Alfea could tell you that . . . right after they told you Riven was the worst.

There was no real point, but Riven kept trying to beat Sky, anyway. Hey, nobody ever said Riven was smart.

Sky's dad was Andreas of Eraklyon, the dead legendary hero, slayer of the Burned Ones. Sky's dad-substitute was

Specialist Headmaster Silva, their fearless leader with the cold blue eyes and passion for early morning runs. Riven cast a wary look around. He had a problem with authority, and his problem was the part where anyone had authority over him. Riven was certain Silva would be along shortly to explain that all the baby first-year Specialists should look up to Sky and copy him and be just like him but never as good.

Kill me, Riven thought. *I'm off to the woods to get high.*

He made his way toward the forest, blowing off Sky's protests. As he did, he noted one of the baby Specialists watching him go. Don? No, Dane. Riven considered giving the staring guy the finger, but he couldn't be bothered.

He passed the blue, shimmering Barrier and went into the deep, dark woods. He could almost hear Silva's voice now, telling the first years that the Barrier was their magical shield against the Burned Ones. Beware those merciless monsters with their inhuman strength and speed, never mind that nobody's seen one in sixteen years, *woo woo*, so scary.

Riven was allergic to inspirational speeches.

He had just sat down on some mossy rocks when he heard the noise: A deep, low rattle, like bones being dragged across bones, A strange sharp snapping.

It was coming from the trees. The forest looked the same as always, curving branches heaped with green leaves, dappled sunlight shimmering through. It was a sound that made every nerve ending Riven possessed twinge, chills running under his skin despite the sunlight.

He scanned his surroundings and used every bit of training he could remember to stay alert, to be prepared.

Nothing could have prepared Riven for the sight that lay beyond the leaves. It was the mangled corpse of an old man. The corpse barely had a head left, the skin of his cheek torn like paper, but what remained of his face told a story of terror and pain beyond imagining. The body had been pulled apart into rags and tatters. In the depths of the deepest, most jagged wounds, Riven glimpsed charred darkness.

Riven took one long look at the ruined fragments of what had once been a man. He tried to be a soldier, to be brave. Then he ran, stumbling over tree roots and rushing headlong back through the deep, dark woods toward the Barrier and safety. He screamed for Sky. For Silva. For help.

EARTH

There were lights strung over the courtyard. There was music playing. Terra was finally a student at Alfea, attending the orientation party just like she'd always dreamed. After years of being the professor's kid daughter who hung around the greenhouse too much, she was finally a full-fledged student.

But when Terra had pictured this scene, she'd never imagined that everyone would be talking about murder. She didn't particularly care for party gossip focused on corpses.

Apparently, Riven had found a body in the woods. There were whispers that the old man might have been killed by a Burned One, but people always whispered about Burned Ones. Terra knew it couldn't be true.

Riven must be so upset, Terra thought, but she certainly didn't care about that. She was hanging out with her new suitemates at a party. Their suite was called the Winx suite, which was such a cool name. Maybe they could call themselves the Winx Club?

Terra, Aisha, and Musa were just getting food together, having a good time, talking about . . . murder.

"Maybe he was just old," Terra said uneasily. "People get old. Die. We all die."

That sounded okay. Not too scary.

Terra's new roommate, Musa, who was too cool for school and certainly too cool for Terra, said: "Yeah. That old-age decapitation really sneaks up on you."

Terra bit her lip. Musa must think she was really dumb.

Aisha was building a magnificent cookie tower on a napkin. The Leaning Tower of Cookies. Terra nervously eyed the food laid out on the tables before them. Sometimes she felt as if food might bite her before she bit into it. She couldn't take cookies. All the other girls in the Winx suite were so skinny and pretty. If Terra ate a bunch of cookies, people would say, "No wonder she looks like that." But if

Terra got a plate full of carrots, people would say, "Who does she think she's kidding, when she looks like that?" It was hard to know what to do.

Musa and Aisha were joking around about how many cookies Aisha was eating. It looked as though Musa actually did know how to smile.

Musa nodded at the cookies. "No judgment, but—"

"I eat a million calories a day. If I didn't swim, I'd be massive." Aisha sounded amused as she spoke. She looked and moved like a lean, mean, beautiful machine. Of course she found the idea of being massive hilarious.

"I used to dance," said Musa. "I get it."

They really seemed to understand each other. They really seemed to be getting along.

"And on that note . . ." Aisha rose in quest of more cookies.

Musa teased, "Second round. Damn. Twice a day. Every day. You weren't kidding."

Aisha laughed and headed off. Musa moved to put her headphones back on now that Aisha wasn't there to have fun with.

Terra spoke more sharply than she'd meant to. "So you heard her earlier?"

Musa said, "What?"

Terra knew she shouldn't push it. She already had a sick sensation in the pit of her stomach, and she knew this would only make her feel worse, but she couldn't help it. "In the room. 'Cause I remember you had your headphones on. And . . . you ignored me like you couldn't hear me. But you could hear Aisha?"

Musa was clearly choosing her words carefully. "Sometimes I wear my headphones when I don't feel like talking."

"Yeah," said Terra. "I just noticed you wear them a lot around me."

As the lights twinkled and the music played, Terra watched her new roommate struggle with how to respond. *Musa was a nice person,* Terra thought bleakly. She didn't want to hurt Terra. She just didn't *like* Terra.

After a pause, Musa claimed, "It's a me thing. It's not—"

"It's fine," Terra told her, abruptly sick of herself. "No need to explain. You've said enough. And I've said too much."

She did Musa the only favor she could and walked away, leaving Musa in peace and Terra alone at her first party at Alfea.

She spotted her dad moving through the party with an especially purposeful air. A couple of students called out, "Hey, Professor Harvey!" as he went, which he hardly seemed to hear. Even Terra's dad was more popular than Terra.

Her dad was currently her only hope.

Terra tried to speak to him brightly. "Hey, Dad! You headed to the greenhouse? Something you need help with?"

It couldn't be anything to do with . . . with the body. No, Terra was sure the new crying crocuses had come in.

Her dad twinkled benevolently down at her, and Terra's heart sank. "Not gonna happen, love. It's your first day. No hiding in the greenhouse. You've wanted to go to Alfea your entire life. You're here now. Mingle. Be *you.*"

Being me is the problem, Terra thought. *I wish I could be someone else.*

She wasn't going to hunt for her annoying brother. She couldn't go back to Musa and Aisha. The mere idea of going to find Stella was both hilarious and very, very terrifying. And Terra wasn't even sure if Bloom was coming to the party. The redheaded girl from the human world—just as slim and lovely as all their other suitemates—seemed distracted whenever you spoke to her. As though she were very focused on something else and didn't have time for you.

It was time to admit it. Her suitemates clearly all thought Terra was dull as dirt. *The thing was,* Terra thought, *dirt was really interesting.* Unfortunately, nobody else agreed with her.

She just wanted one person to hang out with, to do fun things like compost. Just one. A friend.

Deserted even by her dad, Terra let her eyes drift over to the tables full of discarded food. At least Terra could make herself useful. Somebody had to clean up this mess.

FIRE

I scanned the courtyard of my fairy school, searching for my Winx suitemates. Enough writing in my notebook about fire and thinking of my parents, I'd decided. I was here at Alfea until I learned enough to go home. I had to make the best of this.

But there were a lot of people here at the party. Fairies.

Weird fairy people, in this weird fairy place. I'd been at this party two minutes, and I needed a breather.

Instead of a suitemate, I spotted Cute Guy from before. I headed for him, thankful for a familiar face.

"This is a lot of people," I told him, to explain my possibly frazzled air.

"What, you don't have parties in . . ." Cute Guy paused, weighing it, then took the risk. *"California?"*

I paused in mock surprise. "He remembers!"

Cute Guy gave me a smile. "Impressed?"

That he'd gone to the trouble, maybe. I liked the careful way he said *California* as though he were pronouncing a foreign word. He'd done so correctly, but with the anxiety of uncertainty behind it.

I still needed a breather. "Where can I go that's the opposite of this? What's outside?"

Cute Guy looked alarmed. "Past the Barrier? Depending on the rumors, bears or wolves or something much scarier."

"But no people?" I asked. "Perfect. Thanks."

That sounded like the warehouse I'd hid out in back home. Essentially harmless, but creepy, so others would avoid it and I could find refuge there. I started for the gates, and Cute Guy started to say I shouldn't go alone. He offered to accompany me, and I scoffed. Such a line.

He said, "It wasn't a line. Trust me."

I thought about Stella saying once she knew me, she'd find something to love about me.

It made me smile. Or maybe it was the boy in front of me who made me smile. "Maybe someday, I will."

He was so cute, and he was clearly making an effort, and he was a boy who thought California was an alien concept. The fact I had never fit in there wouldn't matter to him. Maybe I should let him come along.

As if I'd conjured her by thinking about her, Stella's voice rang out. "Hey, Sky. Can we talk?"

Stella was wearing her flawless new outfit and holding two drinks. Every twinkly light in the courtyard caught gold in her hair. She was looking right at Cute Guy, whose name was apparently Sky. From Sky's expression, he knew Stella pretty well.

Wow, this was none of my business. I left them to it. All around me people were talking excitedly about some horror movie with guts everywhere. I wasn't here to make friends, or to trust anyone, or to love anyone. Soon enough, I was going home.

I headed past what Sky called the Barrier. To be alone, where it was safe.

EARTH

Terra was passing busily through the party carrying food trays when a scene of horrible injustice caught her eye.

Oh, for the love of . . . Riven was menace-flirting at

29

some poor Specialist boy. This was Riven's typical behavior when he felt off balance. Terra had once witnessed Riven looming at a fern in a way that suggested he either wanted to prune viciously or make out.

At the time, she'd thought: *Bless this mess.* These days, she was more of the opinion that this mess needed composting.

The poor boy must be a first year. Terra didn't recognize him from last year. Riven had an arm around him and was making him drink something that Terra highly suspected was alcoholic.

The new boy's eyes said *help me.* So Terra did.

"Really? Bullying the new kid? Be more obvious."

Riven smirked, because of course he did. "Can't bully the willing. Right?"

There was something loaded about Riven's tone.

"I don't know what that means!" the new boy said sharply.

The new boy was clearly feeling uncomfortable. Terra sympathized. The poor thing mustn't take Riven's terrible personality personally.

"Ignore him," she said, indicating Riven. "He thinks he's some badass; you should've seen him last year. He's just a tragic nerd in disguise."

Riven's eyes narrowed. "And she's just three people in disguise."

There was a silence ringing amid the noise of this party where Terra didn't fit in. The new boy gave her a guilty look, silently offering to do something, which was so nice of him but not necessary.

Terra told the sweet boy, "I got it. But thanks." She let her chipper tone drop as she stepped up to Riven. *What a relief,* she thought distantly. No need to fake nice at Mr. Skinny Jeans Sociopath. Terra could just wreck him.

"See, people always think they can treat big girls like crap. We're nice. Harmless. We should be happy you're even talking to us."

The vines on the castle wall behind Riven started to writhe and move, like friendly green snakes.

"But sometimes we've had a bad day, and a scrawny little twerp says the wrong thing at the wrong time," Terra purred. "And all of a sudden, we're not happy you're talking to us. And we're not nice. And most of all, we're not harmless."

The vines coiled around Riven's neck. It happened so fast, he didn't have the time to use his Specialist skills to dodge. The vines were suffocating him so he couldn't even talk. It was so nice and peaceful.

Terra smiled sweetly. "What's that, Riv? I'm sure it's clever. I just can't hear you."

His face turned red. He was about to pass out, Terra noted, still with that feeling of cheery distance. She shouldn't actually let him faint. Riven would hate that.

The vines receded. Riven took a huge gasp of air.

"You could've killed me, you freak," he spat out, as if he was the one who'd been betrayed.

Riven bolted. Terra called after him, a pleasant trill coming naturally for once: "Missed you, too!"

Then she abruptly realized how she'd behaved in front of

the new boy, and turned around in a state of total mortification.

"Hi," she gushed. "Sorry. I'm Terra, and that was not my ideal first impression."

The new boy smiled at her. It was a weak smile, but Terra appreciated him making the effort.

"Is it better or worse than throwing up after a single drink?"

The new Specialist boy, Terra noted, was very cute. Which was impressive for someone about to throw up. He had lovely forest-deep black curls, close cropped with shaved sides. His eyes were deep chocolate brown, like rich, new-turned earth, and he had great arms and great everything, muscles rippling beneath his smooth dark brown skin. His teeth were white, but his smile was faltering.

Appreciate the cute later, help the new boy first. He was holding it in, but Terra judged he wouldn't be for long. Terra should get him somewhere private, and maybe fetch him a cool flannel.

"I'm Dane," the boy told her as she led him off.

All Terra knew was this: Here was someone who needed her. At last.

FIRE

It was beautiful and peaceful in the forest, just as I'd hoped. There were multicolored swarms of tiny insects among the trees, jewel bright against the shadowy green.

This mystical forest was the perfect place to practice my magic. *Magic worked through feelings*, Stella had said. Like love. I pulled out my phone and looked through pictures of my family. Okay, Bloom, good thoughts! You can do it!

The burning house. My mother, so still.

No, Bloom, not those thoughts . . .

Running toward my parents as they screamed, knowing I'd be too late . . .

Oh hell. I was feeling something. Surely that would work. I *felt* as though this might work. I focused on that feeling, instead of my memories. I was starting to feel warm all over.

As the glow rose within me, a small fire grew in my right hand. Then my left hand ignited as well. When fire sprang up in my hand, I was glad I didn't melt my phone.

I stared down at the twin flames in my palms, dancing, bewitching. Beautiful. I was starting to feel pretty great.

I played with the flames as though they were juggling balls, watching their starlight brightness lick against the air. The flames were burning hotter, higher, their intensity spreading. My hands were dripping flame.

Panic began to rise along with the fire.

I tried to throw the flames away, and only realized how stupid that was when the sparks fell from my hands and the forest floor caught fire.

Over the crackle of flame, I heard Aisha's quiet voice saying my name.

I stared, embarrassment fighting panic, as she stepped

forward, her blue clothes a bright contrast to the green leaves and earth of the forest. Her long braids of dark hair were still wet from a river swim, and she'd used a cloth headband to keep them off her face. As she approached me, she kept talking, in her calm, soothing way, but I was in no mood to be soothed.

"You shouldn't be out here," I snarled.

"Neither should you," said Aisha. "You're out of control."

My frustration was an inferno inside me.

"I know that."

I knew that better than anyone else.

"Calm down," Aisha urged. "If you get angry at me—"

"Just go away!"

The frustrated scream burst out of me, manifesting into the flames at my feet. Suddenly, I stood in a fire, as though I was a witch being burned, but the flames didn't hurt me. They erupted toward Aisha, rushing to envelop her the way they'd rushed toward my mom.

I was a forest fire in the shape of a girl. Everyone should stay away.

"Run, Aisha!" I screamed. *"Run."*

But Aisha didn't. Instead, she faced the flames racing toward her. She crouched to the ground, and her eyes glowed brilliant blue as she summoned the water to her. Water burst from the ground at her feet in droplets cascading upward, as though Aisha had made the earth the sky, and then made it rain. Water struck the fire like a blue sword, and halted my destruction.

WATER

Aisha wasn't used to Alfea, but she was used to being part of a team. She was glad she had suitemates, and even gladder she had a roommate rather than being alone like Stella. She'd liked Bloom right away, too, appreciating Bloom's directness and her easy humor.

Bloom setting fire to the woods was a drawback, but Aisha was trying to deal. If she could make the girls in the Winx suite feel as though they were her team, then she knew she could take anything Alfea threw at her.

Aisha had hoped for something from her brand-new roommate. Not an explanation, necessarily, but possibly a "sorry for almost setting you on fire"?

But Bloom didn't say anything. Instead, she ran out of the forest and back to the castle.

Aisha chased Bloom into the courtyard, trying to explain how reckless she'd been. "You were a runaway train, Bloom! You had no idea what you were doing!"

"Which is why I was out there *alone*, trying to figure it out."

"Brilliant idea," Aisha said. It was the dumbest idea she'd ever heard in her whole life.

Bloom snapped, "I didn't grow up here. I don't have fairy parents. I've done magic once in my life. And it was . . ."

"What? Terrible?" Aisha asked wryly. "I'm shocked. I

flooded my entire secondary school after I failed a math test. Taps, sprinklers . . . *toilets*. Have you ever waded through human excrement? I have. Not pleasant. But sometimes being a fairy means you have to deal with crap."

It was meant to be a funny story, one that would make Bloom laugh. One that would help them bond, turn them into a team. When Bloom stopped and turned around, looking into Aisha's eyes, Aisha thought for a moment Bloom would share a dumb story of her own, and they could laugh together.

"We're roommates, Bloom," Aisha murmured encouragingly. "We have to be open with each other."

Aisha and Bloom were walking down a passageway, Bloom looking off the balcony to one side. Then Bloom went to sit on a bench. She took a deep breath and told her story. How her mother and Bloom had been fighting about her social life, and how Bloom would rather fix old lamps than cheerlead. How Bloom had slammed a door, so her mother had said, "Slam your door, lose your door."

Bloom's parents had taken her door off its hinges, and apparently Bloom had gone unhinged.

"That night, I couldn't sleep. Every time I closed my eyes, I could feel the rage building. And that's when it happened. The fire." Bloom stopped for a minute, glancing over to see if Aisha understood.

Aisha did. She stared at Bloom in quiet horror. Bloom's red hair stood out against the black sky like fire itself.

"It was almost like the fire had a life of its own," Bloom

went on. "I don't remember how long I let it burn. I just remember their screams."

When Bloom finished the story, she was clearly fighting back tears. A subtle, weary tremor went through her frame, like a runner past her endurance. It seemed like Bloom had been fighting for a long time.

"My mom was covered in third-degree burns," Bloom said. "Because of me. And if I hadn't gone in there to stop it? To stop what I started?" She looked completely burned out.

"Every night after that, I sneaked out. I was so scared I'd hurt them again that I slept in this creepy-ass warehouse near home. Until Ms. Dowling found me and . . ."

She trailed off, shivering a little with no fire to warm her or destroy anything else. This wasn't the fun sharing of secrets Aisha had imagined. Bloom's already withdrawing body language suggested she was sure Aisha would walk away from her now.

Instead, Aisha went and sat next to her roommate. "All right," she murmured. "Fire story beats crap story. You win."

At last, Aisha had succeeded in making Bloom smile.

"And your parents had no idea what happened?" Aisha asked. "No idea it was you?"

"Not sure how distant my fairy ancestors are, but the most mystical thing my parents believe in is knocking on wood."

Aisha frowned. That didn't make any sense.

Bloom picked up on her doubt right away. "What?"

Aisha hesitated. "It's just odd. You drew on a great deal of magic without even trying. It's hard to believe you're from a dormant bloodline. Is there . . . any chance you're adopted?"

From the way Bloom's eyes were boring into Aisha, there was no chance in hell, or fairyland.

"I've heard the story of my birth a million times." Bloom's tone brooked no argument. "Miracle baby. There was a problem with my heart in the womb, but the day after I was born, it was gone."

Aisha went cold. "Oh God," she breathed. "You're a changeling."

"What's that?"

Aisha fell silent. She wanted her new roommate to like her, wanted them to get along. She didn't want to be the one to crush everything Bloom believed in.

"Aisha. What's a changeling?" Bloom pursued and persisted in the face of more silence. "We're roommates. We have to be open with each other, remember?"

Aisha drew in a deep breath. "A changeling is a fairy baby that's switched with a human one at birth."

The whole world seemed to tremble around them, as though it was a candle flame about to go out.

"Wait," Bloom said shakily. "What?"

"It's barbaric, and it barely ever happens anymore, but . . ."

"That's not possible!"

Aisha tried to speak reasonably, to make Bloom

understand and come closer to acceptance. "You're clearly very powerful, Bloom. You have to be pure-blooded."

"I would know," Bloom said, struggling to keep her voice even, "if my parents weren't my parents."

Aisha surrendered immediately. "Okay. Okay. You're right."

Accusation turned Bloom's voice sharp. "Why would you even say that?"

"I'm just trying to help," Aisha said helplessly.

Bloom got up from the bench.

"Well," Bloom told Aisha coldly, "you're not."

She turned her back on Aisha as though it was her fault. As though she blamed her, hated her.

And why wouldn't Bloom hate her? Aisha had effectively told Bloom she could never go home. That Bloom didn't belong there.

Bonding with her new roommate was not going great.

MIND

Musa liked Aisha. She liked Aisha's general aura of unruffled waters. So she was trying to soothe the worry and guilt pouring out of Aisha as they walked to the Winx suite together, on their way back from the welcome gathering.

"She's blanking my texts," Aisha fretted about Bloom.

"Strange. I wonder if it's because she poured her heart out to you and you told her she was a freak?" Musa asked.

Aisha did not seem soothed. *Right*, Musa thought. *Whoops.*

"Have you seen Bloom?" Aisha demanded, running past Stella into the bedroom and then out again.

Stella, lying on the sofa taking selfies, drawled: "Not recently."

Stella's tone gave Musa pause. Plus, Musa could tell Aisha was really upset. Deliberately, she let her powers turn on, and faced Stella with her eyes glowing.

"Your face looks so calm, but you are wracked with guilt," she informed Stella.

Aisha gave Musa a look. Musa was familiar with the look.

"You're a Mind Fairy," Aisha observed, but there was no other judgment.

Aisha turned to Stella just as Terra came out of her and Musa's room.

"A Mind Fairy?" Terra repeated sharply. "What's your connection? Memories, thoughts—"

"Not a great time," Musa pointed out.

Terra's gaze traveled from each of her suitemates to the other. "Everything okay?"

Aisha sighed. "Not really. I'm looking for Bloom, and for some reason, Stella's feeling guilty about it."

Stella gave a sigh, as though overcome by tedium.

"Could everyone please save the drama for drama club?"

Stella was determined to pass this off, Musa realized. And

Musa wasn't going to fight her on it, not now that Terra knew what Musa could do, too. Musa knew how that would turn out, could already sense the horror Terra would feel coming toward her. Musa was suddenly and unutterably weary. Stella could keep her secrets.

Only Terra was moving toward Stella, and the way she moved wasn't Terra's usual going-nowhere happy bustle. The way Terra moved was that of a woman on the warpath.

Musa was almost impressed.

"She was talking to Sky, wasn't she?" Terra demanded.

"And?" Stella demanded haughtily in return.

Terra pursued: "And I know what happened to the last person who *talked* to Sky. I was here last year, remember?"

A crack appeared in Stella's veneer as she shot back, "You don't know the full story!"

Didn't seem like Terra cared. "Ricki was your best friend, then she talked to Sky. Now she's not here anymore. Why is that again?"

A threat hung in the air between them.

"Where is Bloom, Stella?" Terra demanded.

Stella visibly decided she wasn't winning this battle.

"She was homesick," Stella explained. "So I did a nice thing, and let her borrow my ring."

Stella's magic ring allowed fairies to travel between the realms.

Terra asked, "Doesn't your ring only work *outside* the Barrier?"

Outside the Barrier, where a man had been murdered.

Musa had been trying not to hear the thoughts about what had been done to the old man's body all evening.

FIRE

There was even more rustling than usual in the detritus piled in the warehouse corners, but I didn't care. I ran out of there all the way to my parents' house. I was going to run through the door of home, and never leave, and . . .

There was a tarp over part of the house, still. There was the rubble of construction. The porch light was a beacon, lighting my way home.

And what would I do, once I was home? Burn it down again? Kill my parents?

I stopped moving forward. I took out my phone and called my parents, staring through the window, as I spoke to them and lied that I was jet-lagged when they asked if I was okay.

"You don't have to be okay," Mom assured me. "You're only sixteen. Being that far away is a huge deal."

Dad said gently, "I couldn't have done it when I was your age. Be thankful you got your mom's bravery."

But now I knew that wasn't true. I didn't get anything from my mom. No wonder I was always such a disappointment to her.

Only I could see Mom through the kitchen window. She didn't seem disappointed. She looked so happy just to be talking to me. How could I ever tell her what I did to her? How could I ever tell her what I was?

Mom was right. Even though I was so close, I couldn't be farther away. And it *was* so hard.

My parents told me they loved me. I knew I loved them. And I knew I didn't belong here. Maybe I never had.

I slunk back to the warehouse, where I'd spent so many weary nights. Once I was there, it was like I'd never left, never seen Alfea. Like I was stuck here, confused and helpless.

I heard faint whispers. Sibilant. Strange.

Through the dusty windows, all illumination was fading away.

My head jerked up, and in the sole spotlight provided by the skylight, I saw a silhouette.

Even at first glance, I could tell everything about it was wrong, from its elongated limbs to its grotesquely crooked posture. It took a lurching step toward me.

Whatever it was, it wasn't human.

I staggered backward, falling, and Stella's ring rolled right out of my pocket. I watched the gleaming thing roll into the slats of a floor grate. *Oh no.*

I crawled to it, reaching out my hand to grab the ring. But it was out of reach. I kept trying, when I heard the rasp. Distant. Growing louder.

The inhuman creature was coming closer and closer. I

reached desperately for the ring again, flattening myself against the wall under the window, trembling as I held my breath.

Inches away from me, staring through the dirty window, I saw its monstrous face.

It was covered in charred flesh, with hollowed eye sockets. But deep within them, its black eyes were sharp. As though it saw me, and seeing me, it knew what to do.

The window shattered, glass flying everywhere. I pulled up the grate and dived into it, squeezing my body through and then crawling into the tiny space. Steam obscured my vision. Then I saw it, only a few feet away: Stella's ring. On the other side of a vertical mesh barrier. I headed toward the shine of the ring, but then came a slamming sound that made my head echo.

The monster was on the grate above me.

I crawled as fast as I could. The ring was on the other side of the mesh, but there was a hole just big enough for my hand to get through. I reached for the ring, almost had it.

But in the crawl space in front of me, past the barrier, the shadow of the creature passed on top of the grate. The monster bashed frantically at the grate. Once. Twice. Until with a ringing metallic crash, the monster fell into the claustrophobic space with me.

I made one last grab for the ring, but the monster slammed its hand down on it.

I decided on a new plan. I called it plan B: Run like hell.

I crawled hastily out of the grate and ran for the

warehouse's emergency exit. Behind me, I heard the creature coming after me. I didn't dare look back. I didn't have to. I could tell it was coming fast.

Then Headmistress Dowling stepped out from behind a beam with that particularly serious expression on her face.

"This way," Headmistress Dowling said coolly.

She stepped aside, revealing a framed doorway, and light. It was another magical portal. I stepped through.

From the other side, I turned as Ms. Dowling stepped between the monster and the doorway. She put her hand up, and the door slammed. After the slam came only silence.

I was left staring, stunned and saved.

Behind me, Aisha's voice asked, "Are you okay?"

I turned and found, to my amazement, Aisha, Terra, and Musa all waiting for me. From the looks on their faces, they had seen the monster on the other side of the door.

"I think so? What the hell was that thing?"

Terra said in a fearful voice, "I'm pretty sure it's called a Burned One."

I couldn't believe they had all come here, for me. There was only one of my suitemates missing.

"Wait. Where's Stella?"

"I don't know," Aisha answered. "Why?"

I said numbly, "That thing took her ring."

SPECIALIST

Sky couldn't get California girl Bloom out of his head. He was thinking about her while he was in the shower.

Oh no, Sky corrected himself in dismay, as his inner Riven made a comment about that one. Not like that. Just . . . how pretty she was, her red hair bright as a new copper penny, in the sunlight streaming through the courtyard. How funny she was. She'd looked so lost, trying to find her way around a strange castle, and that had drawn Sky to her like a moth to a Fire Fairy.

Sky had already done something a little bit sketch. At the orientation party, he'd found Terra Harvey, Professor Harvey's daughter. Sky had an in there. Terra was drifting around looking happy and dreamy-eyed.

"Hey," he'd said to her. "Terra, right?"

Terra blinked at him. "Yes."

"Sorry if this is awkward," Sky said. "But I was wondering . . . Bloom's your suitemate, right? And I assume . . . you have her number . . . ?"

Terra lit up like a light bulb. "And you'd like me to give you her number!" she exclaimed.

"Not if you think it's weird," Sky said hastily. "Or aggressive."

"I don't think it's weird, Sky," Terra assured him. "I think it's beautiful. Love is beautiful!"

"Uh," said Sky. "I don't know about . . . I was just thinking, I'd, you know . . . text her . . ."

Terra had given Sky Bloom's number, but Sky was still worried it was weird. Terra meant well, but she wasn't socially adept.

Sky didn't know how to ask someone out on a date. He'd been with Stella forever. She clung to him, because of her mom. She clung to him so tightly, it seemed like they must fit together. But then there had been the whole mess last year, and Stella had dumped him, and hadn't spoken to him all summer. *They were done*, Sky told himself firmly.

He was single. He could potentially date someone new.

If he could just figure out what to text Bloom.

He was wandering around the room in his towel, composing a text to Bloom, when Stella came through the door. And immediately tried to get under his towel.

Sky felt obliged to point out, "*You* broke up with *me*."

Stella pulled back. "I know."

"I didn't hear from you all summer, then I say two words to a first year, and here you are."

"I said I know, okay. I'm sorry."

An apology was unusual enough, coming from Stella. When she said *sorry*, she meant it. Sky felt himself waver. He knew Stella, well enough to see she was truly upset.

"What are you doing here?" Sky asked more gently.

"I got jealous," Stella burst out. "I know I'm not allowed to, but I did. Then I did something stupid and . . . They think I'm a monster."

"Stel," Sky murmured, stricken.

"I can't sleep there. In a room where everyone hates me.

So can I please just stay here tonight? Next to somebody who doesn't? Hate me? I hope?"

Sky moved toward her, and brushed her golden hair out of her perfect face.

"You're better than you think you are, Stella," he murmured.

He pulled her close, wrapping her in his arms. Letting Stella collapse into him.

Beautiful new girl Bloom had looked lost, trying to find her way through Alfea, but she didn't look as though she'd *stay* lost.

She didn't need Sky, not really. And no matter how alluring the idea of someone independent and shining-new might be, it was Sky's duty as a soldier to go where he was needed.

FIRE

Late that night, I got ready for bed. None of us knew what to do about the ring. None of my roommates seemed to know what to say to me. I sure didn't know what to say to them. I appreciated that they'd come for me, but we weren't friends.

Maybe tomorrow, things would be more clear. I'd understand what it meant to be a changeling, and what was going on with those monsters called the Burned Ones.

I suspected not.

Aisha was lying in bed, watching me with worried eyes. She'd been nothing but kind to me, telling me that Ms. Dowling would deal with the Burned One—whatever nightmare thing that was—and that my parents were safe. She'd even tried complimenting the old lamp with the ruby-red wing pattern I'd salvaged and restored and brought from the human world to Alfea.

My mom never understood why I wanted to fix up old junk. Maybe it was because I always knew there was something broken in me. That someday, I would have to learn how to fix myself.

"I always felt it," I told Aisha. "That there was something off inside me."

Aisha said, "There's nothing *off* with being a fairy, Bloom."

"What about being a changeling?" I demanded. "I saw the way you looked at me. Why would a fairy do that? Leave its baby in the human world?"

"I told you. They don't anymore."

Lucky me. I was the exception.

"But they did. I did a pretty deep Google search, and changelings pop up in a bunch of cultures. If they're not defective fairy babies or sacrifices to the devil, they're just a mean joke on an unsuspecting human family. You know what they never are? A good thing."

Aisha said gently, "I'm not sure Google is the best source for fairy lore."

"You're right." I looked directly at her. "A fairy is. Which is why I'm asking: *What am I?*"

49

Even before I saw the sorrow in her steady, dark eyes, I knew I was asking too much of her. She couldn't be my salvation, any more than Ms. Dowling could.

"I don't know, Bloom," Aisha whispered. "I'm sorry."

That was really all there was to say, wasn't it? And I was sorry, too. I climbed into my bed, fighting the urge to pull the blankets over my head and cry for my mother. Mom couldn't get to me, and I couldn't go to her.

Here I was, surrounded by fairies and monsters, and I was still the freak.

Lying awake, curled in my cold bed, I knew I was trapped at Alfea. I had no control over my powers and no way to tell my parents the truth. There was no going back. And I didn't see how this castle could ever feel like home.

SPECIALIST

What a garbage start to Riven's second year this was. He'd hoped for hooking up with hotties and possibly leveling up his knifework. Not horribly mangled corpses and Terra trying to murder him with a plant. Okay, he knew he was an awful person, but there was no need to be a psychopath about it!

Everyone thought Terra was so sweet, but Riven knew better. A truly nice girl would've been concerned about Riven's traumatic experience and brought him a cup of tea and a blanket. Not that Riven wanted anything like that, because that would be pathetic.

And now he couldn't even go back to his room tonight, because Sky was in there with Stella. Princess Deranged Ex herself. Stella must have gone to Sky's room and thrown some poor-pity-me, I'm-so-fragile-but-also-beautiful tantrum. Sky always fell for it. He was such a sucker.

Riven had taken one look at Sky tenderly cuddling Stella in bed, resisted the urge to throw up, and walked right back out.

Whatever. It wasn't as if Riven was getting to sleep anytime soon.

Every time he closed his eyes, he saw those blackened wounds and the torn, bloodstained mask that had been an old man's face. But it was fine! He had a plan, and his plan was to get high.

He lit up, and as he did so, he noticed a very cute new girl crossing the courtyard carrying a stack of books. She had cute little pigtail braids and a short little skirt.

Riven spoke to her immediately, because she was hot, and he was a simple man. "Burning the midnight oil?"

Mystery Girl said, with a sly look that in no way diminished her attractiveness: "Snorting the midnight Adderall is more like it. I'll need sleep eventually."

Riven offered the joint to her. She smiled, which made her even more sexy.

"Hands are a bit full."

He smiled back. *Oho*. He took a long hit. She got close,

so he could better appreciate her wicked dark eyes and the very appealing cleft in her chin. Their lips an inch apart, he let the smoke filter into her mouth. She held it in, nonchalant. Riven was impressed.

"You a first year?"

She blew the smoke back in his face. In a sexy way. Her eyes danced with a strange, dark gleam.

"I'm a lot of things."

The girl turned and walked away, putting a little swing in her step.

Thunder rolled. Riven had the feeling thunder had rolled a six.

Okay, the school year had started off lousy, but maybe something was finally going his way. Somebody thought Riven was cute.

Actually . . . Riven remembered baby Specialist Dane, and cracked a smile. Two people thought Riven was cute. And they were right.

THE HEART
GROWS OLD

Farah Dowling stood alone in her office, staring out the window at the gathering storm, swirling black and silver behind the glass. The students were all safe in bed, she hoped. She'd sent off her secretary Callum hours ago, despite Callum's propensity to lurk. She could take a moment in her sanctuary and reflect on the magnitude of what had happened today.

She had a Burned One imprisoned on school grounds.

Only then Silva stalked in, stormy as the world outside the window. He thought she should have killed the Burned One.

Dowling demurred. "I need to get in its head. We need to know if this is an isolated incident, or something more."

"Something more? Like what?"

"I found a changeling in the First World," she admitted.

Silva's voice sharpened, questioning. "A changeling? I haven't heard of one of those in centuries."

"Yet there she was," said Farah. "Left *sixteen* years ago, right around the time the last Burned One was spotted."

They had known each other a long time, she and Saúl Silva. They had been young together, visionaries together, soldiers and rebels together. That felt like another life, but sometimes it still seemed as though he could read her mind, with magic that came not from fairy power but from being part of a team.

Silva said slowly, "You think it's all connected."

She did.

FAIRY TALE #2

No strangers here, only friends
you have not yet met.
—attributed to W. B. Yeats

EARTH

From the other room, Terra could hear Aisha's chipper morning clarion call. "Chug some coffee and get the hell up. Be excited. Today you get to learn to use your magic!"

Poor Bloom. Terra couldn't imagine she was excited. She'd been chased around by a terrifying monster last night.

Everyone was having roommate troubles this morning. Terra herself was faced with a dilemma. *Can't go to school in floral jammies. Can't get dressed in front of scary mind-reading roommate.*

Terra fled to the bathroom. She was halfway into a shirt

55

when Aisha came all the way into the room, chattering blithely, and sat down to . . .

Oh. Oh dear.

". . . you're peeing in front of me. Okay. That's new. And fine!" Terra added hastily.

Terra was cool. She could hang.

Aisha was magnificently indifferent. "Oh. That weird? Not used to caring. Swim team and all. Were you going to take a shower?"

Aisha flushed the toilet, and stood. She turned on the shower and Terra wondered for a frantic moment if Aisha was suggesting a nonchalant lady shower of togetherness. Terra didn't know if they would both fit, and she wasn't interested in learning.

"No, I, uh . . . I was gonna change, but . . ." A brainwave struck. "I forgot my bra."

Aisha pointed to the bra on top of Terra's pile of clothes. "That one?"

Terra gabbled excuses—this bra was too small, it was maybe on fire, she'd never seen this bra before in her life— as Aisha started stripping for her shower.

To change the subject, Terra asked: "Have you seen Stella? I don't think she came back last night."

Stella had probably been with Sky. But would Sky really get back together with Stella, after last year . . .?

Nonchalant about this as about all else, Aisha shrugged. These were Terra's longed-for Winx roommates. Staying out all night with boys. Getting super naked. Each one of them cooler than Terra would ever be.

Terra grabbed her clothes and fled.

FIRE

First day of classes, I thought. Time to learn, and not think about being a changeling, or burned monsters chasing me. Happy thoughts, just like in *Peter Pan*! That's how you fly.

Not literally, because fairies didn't have wings anymore. Emotionally. Emotionally, I would fly. No bad thoughts.

Through my open bedroom door, Musa's voice filtered. "I didn't even think those things were real, but we all saw it. It was creepy as hell. It looked like it wanted to kill her—"

Even Musa's detached voice sounded worried. How could I stop thinking about burned monsters if people wouldn't stop talking about them? I willed Musa to quit killing the flying vibe.

"What about my ring?" Stella demanded.

What was mortal danger compared with jewelry? Stella's priorities rocked my world.

No. She'd been kind, to loan me the ring. I was responsible. I didn't want to run away from any responsibility.

Chin up, I stepped out into the common room.

It was a bright beautiful space, filled with comfortable chairs and sunlight. There was a light shaped like a fluffy cloud. The common room looked made for a different, nicer conversation.

"That burned thing . . . took it," I admitted.

Stella snapped, *"What?"*

Musa drawled, "Calm down, Princess."

Stella drew herself up in a temper. "Do not tell me to calm down, and do not use my title as an insult."

It was my turn to say *What?* But I did it in the privacy of my own head. I blurted out, "You're actually a princess?"

Stella glared. "The ring you *lost* is one of the crown jewels of Solaria. That might not mean much to a First Worlder, so feel free to ask your suitemates how big of a screwup that is."

On cue, Aisha emerged from the bathroom. My savior, towel-drying her hair. "Almost as big as giving it to her in the first place," she told Stella calmly. "Dowling has the creature locked up. Which you'd know if you were here last night when she gave us an earful."

I was still dazed and amazed by the princess news. Solaria, I knew from Dowling's map, was the realm we were in right now. Stella was the royal princess of this land.

"Quality walk of shame, though," Musa commented.

Musa and Aisha had my back. I appreciated it, even as I wondered where Stella had been last night. With Sky? They'd talked at the party, but talking was one thing, and hopping into bed was another.

I'd kind of got the vibe Sky liked me. I was surprised

by how much I wanted Stella to have spent the night with someone else.

Aisha continued on the subject of Ms. Dowling. "And as luck would have it, she wants to keep last night a secret, so you didn't get in trouble."

Musa shook her head. "If anyone knew there was a Burned One in the First World? Even temporarily? Disaster."

The way Musa said "Burned One" sounded like the fairy name for those creatures, as if the name had ominous capital letters. But Ms. Dowling had saved me from the monster. Perhaps she would help us again.

I offered, "I didn't tell her I lost the ring, but I'm sure if we do . . ."

Stella replied, the lash in her voice making everyone jump: "We will do no such thing. I'll figure it out after class. But for now? Nobody tells anyone anything. And will somebody please make sure Terra knows that? She can never keep her mouth shut."

On that pleasant note, Stella opened the door to her bedroom. For some reason, Terra was changing in there. She'd clearly heard everything, and looked absolutely mortified.

I was too dazed to spare much pity for Terra. It shouldn't have mattered, compared with magic arson and monsters, but I couldn't get over the fact that Stella was the literal princess of a fairy tale. Golden-haired, walking in light, to the castle born.

She was so the heroine of this story.

FIRE

Class today was being held in an ancient stone circle. The stones were gray, some slightly broken and chipped, like the teeth of a vast and long-dead giant. They were placed at regular intervals from each other, in a clearly deliberate pattern in the long green grass. The sense of history, past memory, had me feeling overawed. This circle had stood for centuries before I was born, and would stand for centuries after I was gone. Surely, I couldn't be a part of this.

The subject of our lesson appeared to be a bowl, ancient tarnished iron or possibly even bronze, with an embellished rim and covered with intricate looping designs that looked Celtic. Terra whispered that it was called the Vessel. The bowl stood on a plinth in the circle of stones, and I stood with the other first years in a ring around it. Each one of us was waiting our turn, to show everybody what we could do.

With flaming torches and a tumbling waterfall behind her, blond hair pinned up and navy trenchcoat flaring around her, Headmistress Dowling was at the very center of the stone circle. She fit in here, in a way nobody else did. Her dignity gave this lesson a sense of ceremony, her serious voice intoning the words loaned the lesson an air of ritual.

"Magic lives in the very fabric of nature. And here in our circle of stones, it is magnified. The Vessel tests your ability to channel that magic. A baseline to start your training. Down the road, you may learn to connect with other elements. But your first year is all about the element you were born with."

She began calling elements, as though she was taking attendance.

"Earth. The soil, sand, rock, and all manner of plant life."

No surprise, Terra advanced, placing her hands on the Vessel. Instantly her eyes glowed green and delicate tendrils of ivy sprang from the stone bowl.

Dowling continued: "Water. The lakes and oceans of the world, or the molecules that exist in organisms all around us."

Aisha took her turn at the Vessel. Her eyes glowed blue, and inside the Vessel a tiny whirlpool started.

"The mind. The connection to memories, thoughts, dreams, or emotions of all living beings . . ."

As soon as Musa touched the Vessel, her eyes glowed purple, and electric ripples like sound waves cut across the bowl. There was a flash of crimson in the Vessel, the color of heart's blood.

"Or air. Its speed, temperature, moisture; its sound and electrical properties . . ."

A girl I didn't know, with dark mischievous eyes and a cleft chin, stepped up to the Vessel. Suddenly, her eyes glowed gray, and arcs of lightning zapped around the bowl. She slanted a confident smile over at Ms. Dowling.

Ms. Dowling continued as if she hadn't seen the girl's almost-taunting smile. "Whatever your element, the emotions underlying it are the same for all fairies."

Ms. Dowling hadn't given the other girl a glance, but she

nodded at me as I approached the Vessel. I tried to take regular breaths and cover my nerves with swagger. I laid my fingertips on the stone loops and curls covering the Vessel.

The steady voice of Ms. Dowling urged me on. "Open yourself up to the magic of the world around you."

I tried.

I stared at the bowl.

Nothing was happening.

"Focus on clear, positive feelings," Ms. Dowling encouraged.

"Yep," I said.

Happy thoughts. Flying feelings. Come on, dammit.

"There's an emotional wellspring that lives deep inside you. Find it. Step into it. Push through your doubts."

Even Ms. Dowling was starting to sound doubtful. Time stretched on, and the Vessel stayed humiliatingly unresponsive to my touch. The other first years were murmuring behind my back, their whispers filling the stone circle like fog.

Very quietly, I heard Musa say: "This is a disaster."

And I knew she was right.

FIRE

After class, the other first years were still gossiping about me, and Ms. Dowling drew me aside under the trees. Even the green leaves above seemed to be whispering mockery.

"It's only the first day," she reminded me, but I wasn't in the mood for a pep talk.

I resented her, standing there eating an apple like someone with knowledge she wouldn't share. I reminded her of some facts, too. "I'm either on the verge of killing everyone, or I can barely light a match."

"You need a clear mind," Ms. Dowling advised. "Distraction can cause magic to be erratic."

I wondered what could possibly be distracting me. I could think of about only a thousand things.

I didn't know I was going to ask the question before I did.

"Am I a changeling?"

I saw that hit Ms. Dowling harder than I'd anticipated. Clearly, she hadn't expected me to find out so fast. I wondered how long she'd planned to keep it from me. I wondered what else she was keeping from me.

"Where did you hear that?" Ms. Dowling asked carefully.

"My roommate saw me lose control in the forest yesterday. Had a tough time believing I was from a long-dormant fairy bloodline."

I repeated the lies she'd told me, the lies I'd swallowed so easily, with bitterness.

"Bloom . . ."

Ms. Dowling drew in a breath. From a woman as poised as her, it was as good as an admission of guilt.

My voice went sharp. "Would it have been so hard to tell me my parents weren't my parents?"

"I didn't want to burden you with too much, too quickly."

Oh sure. She'd lied to me for my own good.

"So instead you let me learn from teenagers, the most gentle and reliable sources of information."

Ms. Dowling almost winced. "I will admit. It was not ideal."

I snorted. "Ya think?"

"*Tone*," snapped Ms. Dowling, and I knew I'd pushed her too far.

I didn't want to push her away. I wanted her to help me.

"Do you even know who they are?" I asked softly. "My . . . real parents?"

I saw the negative in her eyes before she spoke. "I don't. Which is another reason I didn't tell you."

Abruptly, I lost my grip on anger. I was so tired, all my hopes for the day already crushed.

"So . . . what am I supposed to do?"

I just wanted answers. But nobody would give them to me.

"You come to class every day," Ms. Dowling said. "You focus. You learn. You grow. Eventually, the answers will come."

The answers wouldn't come from Ms. Dowling. That much was obvious.

"Cryptic and vague," I said bitterly. "Just like everything else in this place."

I barely knew this woman. I didn't know why I kept looking to her for aid. She'd lied to me, and now she was telling me to come embarrass myself in class day after day. She didn't care about me. Asking Ms. Dowling for help was worse than useless.

I turned away.

SPECIALIST

On the platforms spanning the lake, two baby Specialists were sparring. Kat was a badass. New boy Dane decidedly wasn't.

Sky called out helpful suggestions. Riven, on the bench next to Sky, called out unhelpful suggestions and mockery.

As he did so, he watched intently as new boy Dane's phone buzzed over and over again. With what appeared to be five thousand messages from Terra. Wow, Riven guessed they were besties now. Or Terra liked Dane. Did Terra like Dane? Barking up the wrong tree there, Terra!

Riven had the urge to mock Terra, but then Terra might strangle him with vines again. He snickered as Kat tackled Dane to the mat.

"Could you try being fifty percent less of a jerk?" asked Saint Sky.

Riven smirked. "That's fifty percent less fun."

Dane headed over to get his phone, presumably so he could read his many messages. He was avoiding eye contact with Riven.

Sky said mildly, "Remember what a lost cause you were last year? Two black eyes and a sprained ankle. Day one."

No, Riven didn't need reminding of last year, and he didn't see why Sky and Terra had to keep doing it. Yeah, he got that Sky had taken pity on him, taken Riven under his wing. Riven just didn't like thinking about how pathetic Sky must have found him. How he'd been hero Sky's charity case.

Riven made a scandalous suggestion about how he might express his deep gratitude for Sky's benevolence, adding, "Thought my friendship was reward enough—"

Sky tipped back his head and laughed. Riven was aware Sky mainly kept him around for the amusement value. That was better than Sky feeling sorry for him.

Then Sky spotted Stella, princess of Crazytown, lingering at the edge of the field. Sky immediately headed toward Her Insane Highness.

Riven turned his attention to Dane. "Get off your phone."

"And I'd listen to you because . . .?"

At least the new guy had some spirit.

Riven threw down the gauntlet. "Because you full creeped on my Insta last night and I'm not telling anyone."

He'd been amused when he noted Dane liking an old picture of him. It wasn't even a particularly hot picture. Obviously, Dane disagreed.

A hot red flush crept up under Dane's clear brown skin. "I was just curious about all the second years, and then my finger slipped, and—"

Riven scoffed. "Your finger slipped? That's what you're going with? I'm feeling generous. I won't feel that way much longer."

As Dane put his phone down, Riven leaned forward to observe the long stream of texts between New Boy and

Terra. Yeah, it appeared they had a real dialogue going. Riven shook his head.

Okay, he decided. He could be like Sky. Do a good deed. Take Dane under his wing.

Yeah, Riven was feeling benevolent. And if that annoyed Miss Terra and all her vine friends, too bad. Riven was virtuously devoted to helping the new kid, who flushed deeper under Riven's continued attention.

"First piece of advice? Pick your friends carefully this year. Second? Focus. Get your mind in it. You fought Kat with your limbs and you lost. Being a good Specialist is not about how big you are. It's about strategy." He called out: "Hey, Mikey! Let's do this."

Dane eyed Mikey with alarm. Probably because Mikey was huge, and Dane was worried Riven's pretty face would get messed up.

Mikey lumbered across to the sparring mat, where Riven walked to meet him. Mikey came at Riven hard. Riven parried two crushing punches. Then he launched himself and took Mikey to the floor in a choke hold.

Riven glanced up to see if Dane was watching. Of course Dane was.

First lesson. That's how you win, new kid. No mercy. Not for anyone.

Good deed for the day done, Riven strolled away from the training area to find some of his friends. The universe gave him a reward for his virtue when Mystery Girl zipped over to his side.

She couldn't stay away, Riven thought.

"Lurky stoner guy, right?" asked Mystery Girl.

"Or Riven," Riven suggested.

She made a face. In the sunlight, she was even cuter. He could reach out and press a fingertip against the cleft of her chin.

"Your name is *Riven*? Really?"

Riven asked, "Can I help you?"

She purred, "You can."

She entwined her arm in his, leading him away from his friends. He let her do so with a vague feeling of triumph. He'd known she was into him.

"You seem like a proper delinquent."

"Depends who's asking," said Riven.

She twinkled up at him. "The person who wants to break into Dowling's office. Thought you might wanna help."

"And why," Riven inquired, "do you think that?"

"Because you're a guy, and I'm hot." The new girl locked eyes with him. "Or did I misread the depth of your character?"

Turned out the sexy criminal's name was Beatrix.

MIND

Once people knew you could read feelings, and that your mind magic was strong, they wanted you to read everyone around them. And they never wanted you to read them.

Even Aisha, much as Musa liked her, started questioning Musa as they got lunch.

Musa tried, but she didn't even know how to explain her magic. She worried about scaring Aisha off. She worried about Aisha feeling sorry for her.

And it was difficult for words to encompass the endless chaos that surrounded Musa at all times, pressing in on her from all sides. The lunch lady's back hurt. A new Specialist kid called Dane was feeling frantic and trapped. Terra's dad, the professor, was feeling nervous about something, possibly that dead body, and Musa's words stumbled as she tried to tell Aisha all this and attempted to cope.

And then Musa stopped midsentence, hit by something she'd never felt before. Silence, after so much noise had made silence seem unimaginable. A calm in Musa's emotional hurricane.

The new sensation was coming from a guy in a green jacket, leaving the room. Musa only caught a glimpse of his back, and then he was gone.

"What just happened?" Aisha asked, beside her.

"Not entirely sure," Musa answered distantly.

She didn't know what had happened, but she knew how she'd felt.

Peace at last.

LIGHT

Stella had planned to share a room with her best friend the whole time they were at Alfea together. That hadn't worked out. Now she had to share a suite with first years, and the worst first year of all had gone and lost Stella's ring. Sure, why would anyone be careful with the crown jewels?

Bloom from California clearly believed she could have anything that caught her eye. Stella's ring. Stella's boyfriend. But Stella was keeping Sky, and she intended to get her ring back, too.

Bloom had already somehow won the loyalty of all their suitemates. Terra, Musa, and Aisha were having lunch with her right now. Aisha the perfect roommate was in the midst of explaining her scheme to help poor pitiful Bloom.

"So here's what we should do. Maybe you can make a list of emotional triggers, and we can go through . . ."

"Aisha, I appreciate what you're doing," said Bloom, clearly not appreciating it at all, "but I can figure this out myself."

"I'm sure." Aisha didn't sound sure at all. "I just think you're in your head about the changeling stuff, and maybe overthinking?"

The *changeling* stuff? Oh, that was interesting. No wonder Bloom thought she could grab other people's things. She'd grabbed a human child's whole life and kept it for her own. Stella was getting the full story on that, and soon.

Voice sharp with alarm, Bloom said: "So they all know? About me being—"

"Oh, is that why you were weirding out at the Vessel?" Terra asked. She rattled on: "That makes so much more sense, 'cause it's the easiest assignment we'll have and—"

Musa put a hand on her arm.

"I'm making it worse," Terra realized out loud.

Terra always made things worse. The girl was totally socially inept. She should be confined to the greenhouse for her own good.

Stella took this awkward silence as her cue to stroll up to the table, Sky at her side where he belonged, a map in hand.

"So we have a plan," Stella announced. She spread her map out at the end of the table.

"What is this?" asked Musa, while Terra looked gleeful at the sight of a map.

"Hey. Stella told me what happened last night. Are you okay?" Sky sat down close to Bloom, almost touching. His voice was gentle.

That wasn't part of the plan. Stella appreciated Sky's soft heart, but she wasn't loaning it out. She was holding on to it for herself.

"What do you think?" Bloom asked tiredly.

Sky looked at Bloom with kind, wise eyes. "I think you're freaking out, but pretending that you're not."

"That obvious?" Bloom asked.

"Nah," Sky said easily. "I'm just really good."

71

Bloom smiled, charmed against her will, her hackles going down.

"Sky?" Stella said sharply.

She stared down her nose at the girl from California. Bloom's hackles went right back up.

"Where do you think they're keeping it again?" Stella asked.

Sky got up from his seat and moved to the map as everyone began to plan how to find the monster Dowling had trapped and reclaim the ring. Finally, people were concentrating on the important things: Stella's jewelry.

As he leaned over the map, Stella put her hand on Sky's back. Scratching gently. Tracing. Marking her territory. Apparently, Bloom talked to her mother every night and got showered in praise and affection, but Stella's mother had taught Stella more important things. Such as how to stake a royal claim.

Sky began pointing things out on the map with soldierly precision. He was a knight aiding the princess.

"There's only a few buildings outside the Barrier where they could secure a creature like that. And I'm pretty sure I saw Silva heading in from the east this morning, so." His strong fingers traced the map. "There's a barn and a mill—"

"Barn is my bet," Terra piped up. "My dad fortified the beams to chain a wounded horse when I was little. I still remember sneaking in and—"

Stella cut her off. Somebody had to stop Terra's incessant

chattering. It was a mercy for Terra, and certainly a mercy for anyone who had to listen to Terra. It was a public service Stella was undertaking for her people. "So we just have to sneak out there to the barn and get my ring."

"Strange how casually you're tossing about the word *we*," Aisha remarked.

Funny how Aisha was so eager to help Bloom and so reluctant to help Stella. She'd chosen her side pretty fast.

Musa chimed in, "Seems like more of a *you* kinda deal."

Apparently, all the suitemates had.

"Except *I* didn't lose it." Stella gazed at Bloom significantly.

Message received. "When do we go?" Bloom asked.

Everyone exchanged apprehensive looks. Naturally, Aisha the interferer was the one who spoke up to protect her precious roommate.

"Gonna be blunt here. Sorry. Bloom, you have zero control over your magic. That is if you manage to channel it. Bad idea."

"I lost the ring," Bloom snapped. "I'm gonna get it back. I'm fine."

Bloom was talking sense. She knew what was due to Stella. She wasn't flirting with Sky, Stella had to admit. Maybe the changeling girl wasn't so bad. It sounded as though she was having problems with her magic, and Stella knew all about handling problems with magic. If Bloom knew her place, they could help each other.

Stella's newborn approval of Bloom faded as Sky looked at Bloom like he knew she wasn't fine. But he didn't. He didn't know this new girl at all, and he shouldn't be so concerned about her feelings.

Hesitantly, he said: "Maybe we should take a second to—"

Stella ignored her knight. "Everyone is making this a bigger deal than it needs to be. You said the Burned One is locked up, right?"

"Oh, and subdued," contributed Terra. When everyone blinked at her, she explained, "I'm pretty sure my dad has been distilling this oil that calms it down. It's called Zanbaq."

Terra glanced over at the faculty table, where her father the professor was sitting with Ms. Dowling and Specialist Headmaster Silva.

Terra offered, in a small voice: "I can probably make some more . . ."

Terra might actually be rather sweet, if she stopped talking so much, or at least kept saying useful things. Stella showed her royal favor. "Thank you, Terra, for being helpful. And thank you, Bloom, for taking responsibility. And thank you to everyone else for . . . nothing. I guess thanks for nothing."

She eyed Aisha and Musa with royal disfavor. She didn't care that they all preferred Bloom. Their feelings were of no interest to Stella whatsoever. She was getting what she wanted.

Hold on to what's yours, she'd learned as a child. *Or you'll have nothing.*

Bloom climbed to her feet and addressed Stella alone. "Let me know when you want to do it."

FIRE

Escaping a Specialist wasn't so easy. Sky caught me down by the pond, his face earnest and troubled, his hair ruffled in the breeze. He really did look like the perfect knight. But he couldn't save every damsel he met. He had to pick one.

"You don't have to go along with what Stella wants," he told me as he jogged to my side. "There are other options. Don't do it just because she has a . . . strong personality."

My voice was flat. "I lost the ring. Helping her get it back is the right thing to do. End of story."

Sky conceded, "Two strong personalities. Got it."

I looked him dead in the eye. "Clearly, you have a type."

There was a pause. I didn't regret saying it. He'd been flirting a little with me yesterday, and then he'd spent the night with Stella. I hadn't made things awkward. I'd just pointed out where the awkwardness was.

After a silence, Sky offered, "So, yesterday . . . when I was . . . when we were talking . . . I hadn't talked to Stella in months. Yes, we dated last year. But we had kind of a rough breakup, and . . ."

And they'd only talked last night? And they'd decided to just be friends?

"And what?" I asked.

Miserably, Sky said: "I just don't want you to think I'm *that guy*—"

I cut him off. "Sky. We just met yesterday. I don't think anything about you."

What mattered wasn't what I thought. What mattered was whether he was *being* that guy. Or not.

"Okay. That's fair," said Sky.

I caught his eye. I liked that he seemed to really listen to me. I did feel a spark when our eyes met: a spark of possibility, of potential.

I chose my words carefully. "Your deal with Stella seems . . . complicated. And right now, my life could use less complication. Not more."

So, that was that. Goodbye, fairy-tale knight. The princess could have him.

SPECIALIST

Headmistress Dowling kept good booze in her office. Riven helped himself, lounging in a desk chair as his foxy new acquaintance Beatrix prowled around the books. They bantered while Riven kept an eye on his phone. Dowling took half an hour for lunch. Her assistant Callum got fifteen minutes, so the timing was tight. Riven had posted a lookout, since Callum could get sneaky.

Riven was sneakier. He'd pulled the hood of his hoodie up, since they were sneaking around. "What are you after, anyway? Test answers?"

Beatrix made a disdainful face. "Please. The tests they give now might as well be written in crayon."

She was fun to watch in her little blue tartan dress. Better yet, she was fun to listen to.

"The history of this place is a lot darker than Dowling and the rest of the faculty want us to know." Beatrix turned from the carved stone bookcase back to Riven with a predatory glint in her eye. "I want the truth. Don't you?"

Riven wanted something, all right. He teased her about being a hot nerd.

She got closer to him as she purred, "Why? Is that a confusing archetype for you?"

Things seemed about to get really interesting when Riven's phone buzzed with a text from Dane, telling him Callum was en route. Baby Specialist Dane was coming in useful. Riven was glad he'd decided to become a mentor.

Riven and Beatrix left in a hurry. Riven never noticed the electric sparks playing along the surface of the stone bookcase, revealing the outline of a secret door.

He did notice Beatrix's self-satisfied smile as they hurried along, but he misinterpreted that. He assumed it was all about him.

FIRE

The stone circle at sunset was beautiful. The glow of the setting sun gave every stone a halo. It seemed like at any moment in this space, magic might happen.

But magic wasn't happening. I kept trying, and failing.

"I hear you're broken," said Princess Stella, strolling into the circle.

And now Stella had come to be tactful to me. Great.

I tried to ignore her taunting and insisted: "I'm still gonna help you."

"And I'm thrilled," Stella drawled, "but I'd prefer we wait until you aren't completely useless. What's the damage?"

I wasn't sure Stella was the best person to let in, but she was the one who was here.

"I . . . don't know," I admitted. "And the more I try to figure it all out, the harder it gets."

I made a frustrated gesture to my notebook. Stella eyed the book with even more disdain than she usually exhibited.

"That thing is your problem. You can't think your way into magic."

I sighed. "I know. It's all about clear and positive emotions. There's a page dedicated to them."

"Wait. You made a list?"

Embarrassed, I started to put my notebook away.

"What's on it? Your favorite ice-cream flavors? Otters holding hands?"

Look, otters holding hands were very cute! The princess shouldn't judge. I stuffed my belongings into my bag while Stella listed ideas she found hilarious, including the notion of my mom being proud of me.

"Wait," said Stella. "Probably not that last one anymore, right? Considering she's not your actual mom."

I stopped putting my things away. I turned to Stella. She'd better not push it.

Stella pushed it. "Am I wrong? Do you still care what your not-mom says? Even though you're a changeling? Who tried to kill her?"

My fist clenched.

I spoke through my teeth. "If you say one more thing—"

Stella's voice cut across mine, authoritative in a way perhaps only a future ruler could be. "Put your hands on the Vessel."

"What?"

Stella's eyes were gleaming in the sunset. Her voice in my ear was almost sinister, almost intimate. "The strongest magic comes from the worst emotions: anger and rage. So put your worthless changeling hands on that bowl and *feel* it."

Uneasily, I looked up at Stella. Her expression was strained with rage, and I saw something there I recognized. I felt something inside me shift, as though I was moving to lower but safer ground.

I put my hands on the Vessel, and flame erupted from the bowl. A hungry leap of a flame, rising to consume something—or someone. Quickly, I pulled my hands off. The fire extinguished.

"What? You think you're done?" Stella demanded.

Her face was painted by the dying sun, alight with fierce triumph. I recognized that feeling, too. I wanted more of it.

I heard a roar like fire in my ears. I realized I was just getting started.

MIND

"I don't like what Stella is teaching her," said Aisha.

Musa was barely listening. Aisha fretting about Bloom was becoming a regular thing, like Aisha's constant swimming. Musa was busy looking around for the guy in the green jacket, the one who exuded peace. Like a white noise machine of a person.

She kept catching snatches of that peace, but whenever she whipped around, she saw nobody there. She was starting to fear the boy could turn himself invisible and she would never find him.

Even though she wasn't listening, Musa could pick up the emotion Aisha was broadcasting, loud and clear.

"Jealous much? Why's a friendship with Bloom so important to you?"

"Aren't roommates supposed to be friends?"

Oh, sweet Aisha. Musa thought of Terra the Terror, and sighed. "I am not the right person to comment on that."

Aisha wasn't just concerned about Bloom. She regarded Musa sympathetically, and asked about the hunt for Mr. Green Jacket.

Musa poured out her frustration. "I'll feel him around a corner, but whenever I try and track him down? He's never there."

Musa felt another ripple of that sweet, tantalizing peace. At this point, she felt too tired even to whip around and be disappointed once more.

"There he is again. Behind me."

As expected, Aisha said: "There's no one behind—"

Then Aisha's big brown eyes widened. Musa realized that Aisha's gaze was tracking someone, over Musa's shoulder. Mr. Green Jacket might finally be located.

"Mystery solved. He's been walking through walls. An Earth Fairy!"

That was why he'd seemed to keep disappearing. But he hadn't vanished now. Aisha was actually seeing him. Musa didn't dare turn around, but she did have a question.

Musa spoke in a low voice. "I'm not superficial, but . . . is he cute?"

Then Aisha, a lady who was wildly out of control, called out: "Hey. What's your name?"

No. No!

"What are you doing?" Musa asked in an agonized whisper. "Aisha, *do not*!"

Musa wasn't good at that thing where people interacted and spoke to each other. She needed time to plan her strategy, and hide her headphones, not be weird. She couldn't do this now.

Only it was too late. A boy's voice, pleasant, relaxed, and slightly puzzled, said: "Um . . . I'm Sam. What's up?"

"I'm Aisha," announced Aisha, that vile traitor. "And this is Musa."

Aisha turned to Musa, in a *we're-all-friends-here* gesture. Funny, because Musa was going to hate her forever.

Sam of the Green Jacket was extremely cute, with soft brown hair and clear white skin and a jawline it would be a pleasure to run her fingers along. It was a shame that Musa was going to have to crawl under her bed, live there, and never see him again.

Musa spoke quietly to Aisha: "I hate you. I will always hate you. I will hate your children and your children's children and—"

Aisha, apparently rendered deaf, told Sam: "Musa has been stalking you."

Musa could barely get out a threat, only a one-word promise of what she would do to Aisha. "Dead . . ."

Then all words died in Musa's throat as she met Sam's eyes. What must he think of her? Some freak, clutching her headphones, following him around desperate for a chance at quiet in the chaos.

The last rays of sunshine in the courtyard caught the light

in Sam's brown hair. He had smile crinkles around his eyes and his mouth. And Aisha had just said Musa was *stalking* him—

Beautiful, peaceful Sam looked at Musa, and murmured, "Lucky me."

EARTH

The setting sun shone through the opaque panes of glass in the greenhouse, onto winding vines and vivid flowers. Some were classified as magical. Some were not. It didn't matter. Every flower was magic to Terra.

Set at intervals amid the greenery were black lab tables, where they could perform the wonders of science amid the beauty of nature.

Terra was always happy here, and she'd never been happier than she was at this moment. In her special place. With Dane, who was taking an interest in her chemistry equipment and pretending he didn't know what a pipette was. He got her to say the word five times.

She tossed a dead leaf at him. "Do it again and this whole flowerpot's coming at ya."

Dane grinned. *He was so, so cute*, Terra thought. This was just like last year, being happy in the greenhouse, having someone to hang out with.

Except this was way better than last year, because Dane

was a wonderful, adorable person. And Terra was almost sure Dane liked her back.

She touched a plant, and made it bloom into a sunset-orange flower. Just for him.

Dane smiled, teeth white and bright, looking truly impressed.

Then his phone buzzed. Dane texted back, then returned his attention to Terra and asked what they were making.

Terra replied eagerly, "It's an oil. Well, technically an unguent. But thin for an unguent."

She and her suitemates were on a secret mission, to save Stella's royal ring from the Burned One. Stella had thanked Terra personally for helping.

"Ah," said Dane. "An un . . . guent."

Maybe Dane didn't understand what a cool thing they were doing.

"It's protection. From the Burned One—in case you didn't hear."

"I did," Dane replied. "Mental that they're back."

Dane's phone buzzed again. Dane took it out again, then put it away, but soon after he mumbled that he had to run and hurried off. Maybe a friend of his was in trouble? Maybe he needed to go train.

Before his phone started buzzing, Dane really had seemed to be enjoying spending time with her.

Whoever was texting Dane, Terra thought, *they were super annoying.*

SPECIALIST

Riven stopped texting Dane and smirked to himself.

Beatrix was sitting on his bedroom floor, going over a textbook with a highlighter. Smart was sexy.

She raised an eyebrow at Riven's phone and his hilarious messages. "You're gonna help him by making him feel bad about himself? A well-intentioned bully?"

"That's the plan," Riven drawled. "Why? Is that a confusing archetype for you?"

Beatrix slanted a smile at him, this one a little startled as well as impressed. *That's right*, Riven thought. *I'm not just your piece of meat. Though I'm fully willing to also be that.*

Sadly, he couldn't invite Beatrix to despoil his nubile body, as right then Riven's roommate walked in and clocked the *Beatrix-on-the-floor-getting-high* situation.

"Hello," said Sky, all disapproval.

"Hi," said Beatrix, not bothered.

Sky looked at her. Then at Riven. Then back at her. Like Sky hadn't had a girl in their room last night.

Beatrix offered Sky the vape she was holding.

"No, thank you," Sky said primly. "Daytime's not smart, Riv. Silva catches her up here—"

"Beatrix," said Beatrix. "Not *her*. Beatrix."

You tell him, girl.

Riven pointed out: "And Silva left. Kinda snooped to

85

make sure. Something about meeting up with a military detachment from Solaria? Ask your girlfriend."

Sky just wasn't as great at sneaking around gathering information as Riven. It was the good intentions and the inner nobility. Those majorly got in the way.

Beatrix started mocking Sky for dating Stella. Truly, Riven might have found his soul mate.

Sky ignored her. He'd gone all tense. Even tenser than normal.

"If the Solarians are coming . . ."

Sky appeared to be thinking hard.

Riven finished the thought for him. "Means the rumors are true. They captured a Burned One. The Solarian prison is no joke. Guess they're gonna transfer it."

Seemed like a great idea to Riven. Get the murderous monster far away? A big win for the team!

"Upshot is . . ." Riven stretched luxuriously. "We got nowhere to be."

Everyone else seemed to disagree. Suddenly, Beatrix needed to go the library at once, and Sky needed to talk to Stella urgently. And Dane was off in the greenhouse, having fun and being pathetic with Terra.

Riven had been totally abandoned. Typical.

WATER

Sky had told Stella the Burned One was being moved. It was now or never. It was time for Bloom, Stella, Musa, Terra, and Aisha to act as a team. Finally.

So it would be great if Stella could stop sniping at her, Aisha thought, *and Bloom would listen to Aisha's warnings about Stella's training.* This wasn't the spirit of teamwork.

Aisha eyed the back of Stella's hunting green coat. "So what's the plan, Army Barbie?"

"Did you ask Aisha to come with us?" Stella wondered aloud as the team headed away from Alfea and toward the woods by night.

Bloom kept silent, and Aisha appreciated it. Bloom might be annoyed with Aisha, but she wasn't gonna play Stella's game.

Stella continued, "I don't think you did. And if you didn't ask Aisha to come, and I didn't ask Aisha to come . . . It's official. No one asked Aisha to come."

"This is idiotic," Aisha snapped. "You need me. What are you going to do, Stella, dazzle it with light? While Bloom struggles to light a fire?"

Bloom snarled, "I'm right here."

Stella claimed: "I fixed her."

Like Bloom was one of the broken lamps or clocks Bloom had told Aisha she liked to fix. Only Aisha didn't trust Stella to fix anything.

It was so clear Stella wasn't a team player. There was no *I* in *team*, but there was an *I* in *ring*. Getting her costume jewelry back was all Stella cared about.

"Negative emotions are unstable," Aisha argued. "They have limits. Your method won't help her in the long run."

"Neither of you are helping right now! Can we just do this?" Bloom's snarl echoed through the trees.

From behind them came Musa's detached voice. "Oh good. Everyone is calm and collected. Perfect."

Terra and Musa came toward them, Terra waving a vial. Apparently, Musa had helped Terra make the oil that would control the Burned One. And Terra knew where the Burned One was being kept. Terra and Musa were both team players.

The mission was a go.

Silence reigned at last between the five girls. As they moved through the trees, the only sound was the soft crackle of twigs and undergrowth beneath their feet.

The scene was wreathed in fog. Utterly quiet. A set piece for a horror story waiting to happen.

They emerged from the trees and stopped short at the sight of the derelict barn. Bloom took a deep breath and forged ahead.

Aisha heard the breathing of the others quicken as they approached the broken-down old structure.

The door of the barn was hanging, already open.

Bloom advanced, so Aisha went with her and Stella came in pursuit of her ring. But even before they entered the gray echoing space, Aisha was afraid of what they would find. Nothing.

The team spread out, Aisha stopping by a pair of manacles, unlocked and open.

"They've taken it already."

They were too late, she thought, distantly despairing. Then Bloom's head swung in the direction of the back door of the barn, which was standing open.

There was a tiny sound. Perhaps it was only the creak of a hinge, but it made Bloom move instantly forward, as though on a hunt for prey. There it was again. Not a creak, or a rustle, but a rasp.

Instinctively, Aisha was about to follow in Bloom's footsteps. Then the screaming began.

EARTH

Terra was just about to enter the barn when she noted Musa going the other way. Musa's eyes were glowing an unsettling violet, and she was stumbling like a sleepwalker in the direction of the creek. Roommates should stick together. Terra changed course.

"You okay, Musa?"

Musa barely seemed to hear her, mumbling as she walked, oblivious to everything.

Until she doubled over, moaning: "It *hurts.*"

Terra moved to help Musa, but Musa's eyes were fixed on the creek.

So Terra's gaze moved to the creek as well.

"Guys!" Terra shouted for her suitemates. "We have a problem!"

It was carnage.

There was a black jeep overturned. A truck, askew against a poor wounded tree. Four dead soldiers, hacked apart into hideous pieces. And the lone survivor, Mr. Silva.

The Specialists' commander was sitting slumped against a tree. There was a gash in his side. Cuts on his arms and neck. Blood running from a wound on his scalp.

Terra's eyes cataloged the list of injuries, knowing what this must mean. "The Burned One," she said out loud.

It didn't seem as though transporting the Burned One to a Solarian prison had been a huge success.

"It's still here somewhere," Stella breathed.

At least they were all together, Terra thought. They could figure out what to do as a team.

Then Aisha said, "Wait, where's Bloom? *Bloom!"*

There was an edge of panic, even in Aisha's voice. Stella looked as though she was about to take flight. This was ridiculous. Bloom could get eaten by the Burned One. Mr. Silva could die.

Terra took charge. "We'll help Mr. Silva. You and Aisha go find Bloom," she commanded Stella, and Stella nodded.

Terra moved forward to Mr. Silva, who appeared

semiconscious. Musa tried to keep up with Terra, but she was clearly in a bad way, too. Mr. Silva's pain and fear must be an onslaught, bringing down all poor Musa's defenses.

"I can't," Musa whimpered.

"I'll help you," Terra promised. "Come on."

Mr. Silva's eyes snapped all the way open. They were black. His sword was suddenly pointed at them, his mouth locked in a snarl.

To a soldier, it must be terribly disorienting to feel the urge to react as though your friends were enemies. Terra's father had warned her of the effects of a Burned One's attack.

"Be careful, he's not in control," Terra warned Musa. She explained to Mr. Silva, as kindly and steadily as she could: "The Burned One cut you. You're infected. We're going to help you."

She summoned magic to bind Silva's arms with vines so that his nasty sword wasn't pointed at them. Mr. Silva struggled violently against the restraints, and when he tried to lunge, Musa froze.

Panicking wasn't going to help anybody.

"I have Zanbaq for you," Terra assured Mr. Silva. "It'll calm the infection, and we can get you back to the school."

She turned to Musa. "I'm going to hold his head, but I need you to pour it in his mouth."

Musa hesitated. Terra understood that Musa must feel awful right now, but that didn't change what needed to be done.

"Musa," Terra said firmly. "He's scared. I'm not. Focus on me."

After a moment, Musa's eyes met Terra's, and held. She nodded.

FIRE

I was lost in the forest, chasing the sound of the Burned One, but no matter how deep into the woods I went I couldn't find the sound again.

Until I did. The faint rasp sound. Behind me. I turned to face the monster.

Shrouded in fog, the Burned One was staring across the clearing right at me. The monster took a step toward me, and I took a moment. Willing my magic to work. The Burned One charged, barreling down on me. I stood firm and flung up one of my hands.

A line of fire erupted across the forest floor toward the Burned One.

My fire hit head-on, lighting up the night. The Burned One staggered back, writhing as the flames engulfed it, and I found myself smiling. *Gotcha.*

But then, the Burned One stopped staggering. Stood upright. Regained its composure—and charged at me again.

Still on fire.

It was possible I'd really screwed myself here.

The monster that was no longer burned, but burning, leaped right for me.

I felt rooted to the ground. Fortunately, its leap was cut off midair by a powerful blast of water. The monster was sent flying, tumbling into the cradle of the upturned roots of a tree. One tree root pierced it, and the body lay crumpled and unmoving.

I turned slowly, already knowing who I would see.

Water to cool my fire.

Aisha.

The kingfisher-blue shimmer of water power already fading from her eyes, she asked: "You okay?"

I nodded, and we looked toward the Burned One.

"Is it . . .?" Aisha whispered, as if worried she might wake it.

"I think so. You hit it pretty hard."

Aisha grinned, and nudged me, sharing the victory. "And I'll admit, you had more control than I thought you would."

I grinned back. "Hang on. Is that a . . . compliment? Are you complimenting me right now?"

Aisha rolled her eyes, but she was smiling.

"Let's just get Stella's ring," Aisha said, but I was already full-on beaming.

I stopped beaming as we examined the Burned One. My fire magic and Aisha's water magic had not improved its appearance.

Aisha squinted. "Where is it?"

"There. It looks like it stuck . . . inside itself . . .?"

The ring was barely a glint in the creature's arm. The ring seemed embedded in its charred skin.

"So . . . Do you wanna?" I asked Aisha, hoping against hope.

She widened her eyes. "Me? Oh no. I did my part. Did you forget? Water cannon?"

"No. It was *so* impressive that I thought you'd wanna finish the job."

I gave Aisha a beseeching look. She stared back at me.

"Didn't you . . .? Who actually lost the ring, again? I forget."

Point taken. I took a deep breath, then I dug my fingers into the charred flesh.

"This is the most disgusting thing I've ever seen," Aisha murmured.

It was the most disgusting thing I'd ever felt. But finally, I got it out.

Aisha cheered. "But she does it!"

My eyes met Aisha's. My heart was pounding fast with victory. My smile woke hers, and I opened my mouth to tell her thank you. For coming after me. For believing in me.

Then the Burned One lurched upright.

Aisha and I ran for our lives.

EARTH

Terra had always been slightly afraid of Mr. Silva. He was so stern looking, with his buzzed hair and cold eyes.

Now she had her arm around him, supporting him as he hobbled toward Alfea. Mr. Silva was being so brave, not stopping to rest, though she could tell every breath and every step cost him. Musa was smaller than Terra, and not as solidly built. Terra had to take most of Silva's weight, but she could do it.

As they walked into the courtyard, Terra's eyes scanned the terrain for assistance.

There was Sky on the balcony and thus too far away to help, his arms around a shaken-looking Stella. Terra caught a snatch of conversation: Apparently, Stella had gotten lost in the woods. Really, Stella wasn't good in a crisis. Terra had to trust Aisha would find Bloom.

"Is that Silva?" Sky demanded from above, as though he couldn't believe it.

Oh no, Terra remembered. Sky was really close to Silva. Her dad said Silva was like a father to Sky. It must be horrible for Sky to see Silva like this.

She'd feel sorry for Sky later. Right now she needed someone she could rely on, to help her in this emergency. "I need a med kit from the Bastion!" Terra shouted out the order.

Riven ran to obey.

The sly-looking Air Fairy, Beatrix, offered to get the headmistress. Musa was helping support Silva, Riven was getting medicine, and Terra needed more assistance. She noticed Dane was there.

"Can you help us get him to the greenhouse?" Silva made a low wounded noise and Terra soothed: "Almost there, Mr. Silva."

It was a relief to spot her annoying brother. He was coming toward her and Musa, moving fast.

"Sam!" said Terra. "Get Dad."

Musa said, in a small horrified voice, "Dad?"

"Yeah," Terra told her absently. "That's my brother."

She wondered why Musa looked so stunned. Had Musa not realized that Terra's dad was a professor here? Or had Sam annoyed Musa somehow?

If Sam was bothering Terra's roommate, Terra would tell him off later.

For now she had to concentrate on helping Silva. He was clearly in agony, though he was pretending not to be. When Terra got Silva to the greenhouse and her father, Sky was following hot on their heels.

"How bad is it?" Sky demanded tensely. "Can you help him?"

"I'll be fine, Sky. If you'd let Professor Harvey work," Silva joked.

Terra believed it was pride for an instant, but then Sky stepped back. Once out of Sky's sight line, Silva's face twisted, and she realized what was actually going on. Silva was trying to spare Sky, who was frantic with worry. And all Terra could do to help them was prepare the medications to ease Silva's pain.

When her father had a moment to breathe, he told Terra that she'd saved Silva's life.

Terra felt happier than she had in months, until Headmistress Dowling ran in with none of her usual dignity. She and Terra's dad and Sky's dad and Mr. Silva used to fight the Burned Ones all together, when they were young. Before Sky's dad died. Ms. Dowling always looked so calm, but now she looked terrified.

Mr. Silva must not be safe yet.

Terra's father had praised her, and made Terra so happy. But Sky's dad was dead, and the man who was as good as Sky's father might be dying.

FIRE

I felt almost giddy with victory. I'd controlled my magic successfully and brought down a monster with a friend. Terra had texted to say Silva was being treated.

If only Stella didn't have to snipe at us. I would've thought that getting her ring back would improve Her Highness's mood.

"You have no idea what I had to do to get this," I informed her. "It was—"

"How about we never talk about this night ever again?" Stella demanded.

Then the door to the suite opened, and Sky came in. His head was bowed, and he moved toward Stella as though he was tempted to cling. Stella's demeanor softened instantly.

She led the way into her room. Just before he went, Sky looked back at me.

But he went into the bedroom after her. I was left outside alone.

Only then Aisha came back from the bathroom. *I wasn't alone*, I thought as Aisha began to turn down her bed. A roommate meant you were almost never alone.

And maybe that was great.

Aisha said cautiously, "So . . . at the risk of making you hate me again . . ."

"I never hated you. Everything that's happened to me has been out of my control. I just . . ."

"Needed to do it your way," Aisha supplied, with ready understanding. "Why do you think I swim? The lane markings don't tell me what to do. Best friends a girl can have."

Lane markings actually were there to indicate what someone should do, but Aisha was trying. Having Aisha try to understand me made it suddenly easy to understand her, too.

"You were just trying to help."

Aisha admitted, "It was only partly about helping you. This, here—it's new for me." She indicated the room, and our beds. "Just want it to go well."

I smiled. "Same."

"Okay, so . . . Why did you wander off, at the barn?"

"I don't actually know," I confessed. "Which is strange. I felt something. Like I had a connection to that thing."

"Weird."

Aisha had a gift for understatement. But tonight, I felt too good to let the weirdness get me down.

"I'm realizing I just have to live with weird. I'm not going to understand it all. The thinking side of my brain has limits. But opening up emotionally? I can feel it. The magic is all around me. It's new and kinda scary, but . . ."

And our bedroom, Aisha, my new feeling of hope, were all telescoped away. I could hear Aisha calling my name, but she seemed very far away.

Instead, there was a woman leaning over a table toward me, blocking the light. She was in her sixties, wearing a military-style coat. She had long, honey blonde hair and striking features, stress lines carved deep into her skin, and the kind of sunken steel-blue eyes that come from years of no sleep and hours of staring at horrors.

Suddenly, those eyes glowed.

My vision of a mystery woman whispered, "When the time comes . . . find me."

And I wanted to. But I didn't have the first idea where to look.

FAIRY TALE #3

But seek alone to hear the strange things
said . . . to the bright hearts of those
long dead . . .
—W. B. Yeats

FIRE

My vision was of a human hospital room, and it was more sound than sight. I heard the erratic beeping of a heart monitor. Then the flatline.

A doctor's voice said, quietly urgent, "We're losing her. Come on. *Come on.*"

The flatline cut off. The only sound left was silence, and a sigh.

The doctor's voice said wearily, "I have to go tell the parents."

A new sound came, a new set of footsteps, and then—

The doctor said, "Excuse me, ma'am? You can't be in—"

The doctor's voice cut off, and there was only silence again. And a soft light that turned blinding.

A human hospital room, with two fairies in it. Me, as a baby, and the woman with glowing eyes and the military coat.

I really was a changeling. My parents' real daughter had died on the surgical table in my vision. And I'd been placed in that room for them instead. A cuckoo in the nest, and they never even suspected.

The image of the woman was so clear. She burned in my vision . . . until she reached out a hand, and there was only darkness.

The darkness was replaced by Aisha's face. I was back in my bedroom, and Aisha looked frantic with worry for me.

"What the hell just happened?"

I took a deep breath, and answered: "I think I saw the fairy who left me in the human world."

I'd been looking to Ms. Dowling for answers, but this woman was the one who actually had them. She was too old to be my mom, but she must know where I'd come from. She wanted to tell me. She wanted me to find her. And somehow, I would.

SPECIALIST

Riven was giving Sky a run for his money at swordplay on the training grounds today, so maybe Sky was off his game. Or maybe Riven was just getting more awesome!

As Specialist Headmaster Silva approached, Sky glanced Silva's way. Silva was looking pretty rough these days. Concern flickered across Sky's face every time Silva so much as shifted his weight. Riven took advantage of Sky's distraction and almost got a jab in.

Silva, whose sharp cold eye never missed a thing, spotted it and called out: "Sky, watch your footwork. Riven, when he favors his left—"

Riven knew what Silva was saying. He made a strike at Sky's right side. Sky hit the mat.

"Nicely done, Riven," Silva said, and Riven did his best not to grin like an idiot.

Riven offered Sky a hand up, and they headed over to the benches. Sky's girlfriend was there. She didn't appear concerned that her guy had taken a fall. She was, in fact, texting.

Sky was frowning.

If Stella was Riven's girlfriend, he would be frowning every day, and also he would cut his own head off. But Riven suspected this wasn't about Stella.

"Does he seem worse to you?" Sky asked quietly.

No need to ask who "he" was.

"Riven gets a compliment, and all of a sudden Silva's got brain damage . . ." Riven grumbled.

Okay, he got it. No need to rub it in. Sky was the most awesome, and Silva would always like him best.

Sky's frown only deepened. "It's been a week since he got infected by the Burned One, and—"

They reached Stella at the benches. Riven started to untape his hands and get changed. He didn't love wearing the Specialist symbol emblazoned across his chest.

Sky turned to question Stella about his all-absorbing topic of interest. "What do you think?"

"About what?"

"Silva," Sky answered tensely. "How does he look to you?"

Stella barely glanced in Silva's direction. "Fine."

"Dr. Stella, coming through with the zero-effort diagnosis!" Riven cheered with mock enthusiasm.

Stella ignored him. What else was new? Fine by Riven. He'd rather have poison ivy than Stella's attention.

"Are you training later or are we hanging out before the party?" Stella asked Sky.

Sky didn't respond. He was still focused on Silva.

"Sky?" Stella prompted. "He's *fine*. Professor Harvey still has him on the Zanbaq, right?"

"That just manages his symptoms," Sky fretted. "He won't be better until they kill the Burned One that attacked him."

"And there are people out there looking for it. It's not going to get away from every fairy and Specialist in the Otherworld."

But Sky didn't seem convinced. There was a look in Sky's eyes that Riven had never seen before. He'd never imagined his best friend, the hero of Alfea, actually looking vulnerable. It freaked Riven out.

Clearly, it freaked out Stella as well. She stood up hastily.

"I have class. Stop worrying."

As if it was as easy as that. Stella kissed him swiftly on the cheek, then hurried off.

Poor Sky. Where was he meant to get, like, emotional support? With a girlfriend like Stella. And a best friend like Riven.

Since Riven couldn't provide emotional support, he tried to get to the bottom of the mystery of why Sky had started up with Stella again.

Since Riven wasn't a gentleman, he made a suggestion of a salacious nature about what Stella might permit in the boudoir.

Sky shoved him clear off the bench. Riven landed, sprawling, and then got up laughing. He was hoping Sky would laugh, too. Riven could usually get him to do that, at least.

But Sky wasn't laughing. Riven looked at Sky's tense unhappy face and felt a weird pang in his chest like something small getting broken or going soft. It had been decent of Sky to take Riven under his wing last year. Sometimes he was patronizing and that stung, but Sky was the best guy Riven knew, and he did try to be kind. Someone should be kind to Sky in return. And Stella wasn't stepping up.

This wasn't actually about Riven's feelings. This was about how Sky felt. Sky looked up to Silva so much. Riven lived in constant fear that Sky would copy Silva's sketchy facial hair.

"Well, I'd blame her for your terrible sparring the last week, but . . ." He tried to make his voice gentle, though he was pretty sure his voice didn't do that. "I know how close you and Silva are. I'm around if you want to, like . . ."

Riven swallowed, trying to find the words. Talk? Cry on my shoulder? Have me say "it's gonna be all right, man, I'm here"?

Sky's head turned to track Silva's movements. Silva seemed to be trying to slip unobtrusively away from his students.

"I gotta run, okay?" said Sky.

Riven nodded, with a smile that wanted to twist in on itself. It had been a dumb idea to reach out, anyway. Given the choice, he wouldn't choose himself to talk to, either.

WATER

Bloom had to wait to solve her mystery. Aisha dragged her to magic class, where Bloom was presented with a pile of kindling on a table. Aisha sat down next to Bloom and devoted her attention to a bowl of water.

Aisha was actually a little excited for class. Now was the time to hone their skills and build their team.

"I think it's actually impossible," Bloom announced. "Maybe it's a trick assignment."

Aisha, focused on her bowl, muttered, "Maybe it's all the talking."

Dowling prowled by and interjected, "A fire that lays waste to everything in its path is instinctual and impulsive. What about when you need that fire to stop?"

Bloom didn't respond. Aisha feared that hit too close to home.

Dowling continued severely, "Can you light a *single* piece of kindling and leave the others untouched?"

Bloom focused, and saw one tiny piece of wood start to smoke. She made a clear effort to hold it, keep it going. And then she began to smile big. *Holy crap*—she'd done it.

Dowling nodded, which was high praise coming from her. Aisha was a tiny bit jealous. Dowling had the stern aspect of a coach Aisha had had once, who everyone had resented for being a hardass . . . until she led them to victory. Aisha wished she would get a nod, but she hadn't even made a ripple on the water's surface yet.

Then Dowling turned to another student. An Air Fairy whose eyes glowed gray as she used what Aisha figured was something like static electricity to lift single grains of rice out of a pile.

Dowling said, "Impressive, Beatrix. Keep it up."

"Got it, Miss D," said Beatrix the Air Fairy.

Dowling shot her a look.

"Headmistress Dowling," said Beatrix.

Ms. Dowling moved away.

Under her breath, Beatrix intoned dramatically, *"Your Grace."*

Bloom stifled a laugh. Beatrix shot her a smile, conspiratorial and friendly, shared between two people whose class was going great. Maybe Beatrix and Bloom would be friends, easy as that.

Trying to make friends with Bloom had been pretty tough for Aisha. Now Aisha was sitting in class, the only one whose magic was failing her.

Aisha made a small frustrated noise. She was aware of Dowling hovering near her, breathing down her neck. Before Dowling could speak, Aisha snapped, "Yes. Control. I get the idea. I mean, I can do this."

She concentrated so hard she felt her brain bend and her eyes glow. All the water sloshed to the center of the bowl, forming a perfect sphere. She hoped Dowling would be just a little impressed.

"Good, Aisha. However, a mass of water is persistent and reliable. Consider the individual elements that combine to form the whole."

Dowling's eyes glowed. A single drop separated from the sphere.

"A drop of water is unpredictable. Vague. Amorphous. Can

you isolate it? Can you maintain that which fights form?"

Aisha focused harder. Suddenly, the water splashed right out of the bowl and onto her desk. She'd accomplished nothing but making a mess.

"Something yet to be learned," Ms. Dowling said dryly. Then she addressed the class. "That's all for today."

Everyone packed up, but Aisha took a moment to clench her jaw and try to work through the frustration. She'd been thinking of magic as a team effort, but if she wasn't any good at magic, nobody would want her on their team.

"You cool?" Bloom sounded concerned.

"Just . . . tired," Aisha claimed.

EARTH

Terra was only trying to have a nice lunch. A potentially romantic lunch with the boy she really, really liked. It was tricky enough, trying to entertain Dane with witty conversation and ultimately get him to like her back.

But Terra couldn't have a nice lunch because Riven spoiled everything. He cut in line to get lunch, which was so rude that Terra despaired.

Now Riven was sharing an apple with the Air Fairy in the short skirt. Strange. Unsanitary. A whole apple was too much for either of them to handle?

"She's so weird," said Terra. Who couldn't eat a piece of fruit by herself? Also, who could ever like Riven? Terra felt Riven's weirdness went without saying.

"Apparently, she's also a huge nerd," Dane contributed, offering details about Beatrix's interest in fairy history and a hard-partying lifestyle that Terra certainly wasn't interested in, thank you very much.

She sniffed. "Riven has questionable taste."

Beatrix's questionable taste also went without saying. Dane sent a look Beatrix and Riven's way that almost seemed admiring, but surely not. Surely, Dane was just too nice for his own good.

On the other hand, Terra bet Beatrix was the kind of girl every guy liked. Terra abruptly felt too sick to eat even a single bite of apple.

"Maybe . . ." said Dane. "But I kinda think they're not terrible? Plus, they invited me to the party tonight, so—"

"Wait, what?"

"The Senior Specialists party?" said Dane.

"Yeah. I know what it is. They do it every year. It's a mess."

"Does that mean you're not going?"

Terra abruptly realized she was being very uncool, and she badly wanted for Dane to think she was cool. She tried to play it off.

"Maybe," Terra said. "Gonna see what the vibe is."

There! That was a cool thing to say, right?

Dane smiled. "Then maybe I'll see you tonight."

Was that a signal? Was Dane trying to tell her to come to the party? Did Terra really have to go to a party? Especially a party like that . . .

Terra had grown up here. She'd heard the rumors about the Senior Specialists party.

Oh, what had she done?

FIRE

Having lunch with Musa was nice, but Aisha's performance in class was still bothering me.

"It's just strange seeing Aisha not get something right away," I fretted.

"Agree. Not sure why that makes you feel so obnoxiously guilty, though."

Musa shot me a smile. But I couldn't help bristling.

"I know you have to feel everyone's emotions, but here's a thought: You don't have to broadcast them." I sighed, and tried to explain the guilt. "Aisha's tired. My parents think Alfea is in Switzerland, so they Skype me at nine a.m. Switzerland time. Every morning. Which is . . ."

"Two a.m. our time?" Musa sighed. "Yes, we all hear."

Oh good, more guilt.

"Am I loud? I'm trying to be quiet."

"Like every old lady unwrapping hard candy in a theater.

But I'm doing fine in class," Musa assured me. "And so is Terra . . ."

Musa trailed off, now distracted. Her eyes glowed purple as she scanned the room, eventually landing on what she was looking for.

"Where'd you go?"

I followed Musa's sight line to find that boy Sam weaving through a few students. His gaze found Musa's, and he gave her a brief, warm smile.

"My turn to broadcast your emotions?" I asked Musa.

Musa grinned. "They're still developing. Plus, there's a complication. So do me a favor and don't broadcast them in front of—"

Terra arrived, dumping her lunch tray on the table with a resounding clang.

"Here's a question," she said abruptly. "When did being a nerd become cool?"

Musa and I exchanged a look. A patented Terra-style rant loomed on the horizon like a thundercloud.

"Don't get me wrong," Terra raged. "It's great. So amazing. Power to the nerds. But suddenly it's cool to talk about fairy history?"

"Um," I said. "What?"

Terra ranted on. "I like school. I like good grades. I like reading alone with a cup of chamomile . . . But nobody is sharing a freaking apple with me. Even though, *gross.*"

Musa said slowly, "We're gonna need so much more context for this."

"Beatrix." Terra said the name with loathing. That was new. "I don't really get what the difference is. Between her and me. Why for her it's . . . working."

Musa and I exchanged a look while Terra pushed her food around. Who exactly was ready to tackle *that* remark?

Then Musa's guy held up two Popsicles to her, across the way. A clear bribe. As if Musa needed any bribe.

Musa began to pack up. "Actually. Gotta run. Sorry." She didn't sound sorry.

As Musa headed out, I stared at Terra helplessly. This must be about Dane. Did Dane like Beatrix? But I'd heard that Beatrix was running around with Riven. Terra had spoken at length of Dane and her longing to drown in the chocolate pools of his eyes. She'd also spoken at length of Riven and her longing to drown him in the Specialists' lake.

I hoped Dane didn't like Beatrix. I hoped he liked Terra. She deserved that. And she deserved a friend who knew what to say to her.

Terra sighed. "It's okay. I know the reason. She smokes and she drinks and she looks like her. And I . . ."

I look like me.

The sentence hung in the air between us.

Before I could say anything, Terra shook her head and firmly redirected herself away from self-pity.

"How are you doing? How's your search for the memory lady?"

"Stalling," I answered honestly. "Does your dad happen to have any old yearbooks?"

That had been Aisha's bright idea.

"Probably, but I'll have to check myself. He's been so busy with Silva, I don't want to bother him."

I'd been trying to avoid thinking of Silva. Whenever I thought of Silva, I thought of Sky.

"How is Silva?" I asked guiltily.

"My dad has been pretty down, so I don't think it's looking good."

Now I'd started thinking about Sky, I couldn't stop. I barely knew him, but I'd never felt such a strong connection to someone so quickly. Thinking of him felt like my fire magic: dangerously close to being out of control.

"I can't imagine how hard this must be for Sky. I know they're close. Have you seen him today? Sky?"

Terra eyed me, her expression saying she was fully aware of what was happening.

"Sky is a great guy, Bloom. Legit one of the good ones, but Stella . . ."

Terra's gaze skipped a few tables over, where Stella sat with a bunch of second years.

"I'm just worried about him, Terra," I said. Too quickly.

Terra gave in, but her face stayed skeptical. Clearly, she didn't buy it.

I didn't blame her.

EARTH

After listening to Bloom worry at lunch, Terra darted off to intercept her dad on his way out of the greenhouse, where she knew he was treating Mr. Silva. The moment before he saw her, Terra saw her father's face. There were lines graven around his mouth, worry so deep it made him look years older.

Oh, poor Silva, Terra thought. *Poor Sky.*

She didn't know Sky well, but last year she'd been thankful to him for taking care of Riven. It had been so nice of Sky to reach out and help someone. Not many guys would've done it. Especially not sons of famous heroes.

Sky was patient enough to put up with Riven and Stella, too. There were so few kind people in the world. Sky didn't deserve this.

"How is he?" Terra asked nervously. "Headmaster Silva?"

Dad's frown of concern was instantly replaced with a smile. *Pacifying, and . . .* Terra thought uncertainly . . . *a bit patronizing.*

"He'll be fine, love. Let me worry about that."

In other words, *Don't worry your pretty little head about it, Terra.* "Oh yeah. Obviously. But . . . Musa and I did bring him back, remember?"

You said you were proud of me then, Dad, Terra thought. *Remember.*

Dad said, in his *my-little-girl* voice, "And I'm sure that was very scary."

"No," Terra told him flatly. "I mean you can tell me what's going on. I'm not a kid anymore."

Dad kissed her on the top of her head before he moved on. "Of course you aren't."

Yup, Dad, very convincing. Terra sighed. She did have faith in her father. Maybe she should let him handle this and concentrate on the terrifying prospect of going to a party. Still, it hurt.

Dad believed Terra was a little kid who couldn't be trusted with the truth. And Terra believed Silva was dying.

WATER

Bloom was sitting on her bed, poring over a stack of yearbooks. Aisha was working on a hopeless mission of her own. She was at her desk with a bowl of water, laboring over her magic. Not a single droplet had risen from the bowl since she sat down.

Bloom flipped back and forth between the pages of the yearbooks so they rustled like wind through the trees in a storm. Aisha's eyes darted over to her in silent inquiry.

"The memory is starting to fade," Bloom admitted. "It's getting harder and harder to tell who it could be."

She closed the yearbook as a new idea formed. "But I was thinking . . . I had the memory after I used magic to fight the Burned One. A *lot* of magic. Maybe wherever she is, she could sense it. Or it opened a magic gate in my head or—something. So what if I go to the stone circle and draw on as much magic as—"

Aisha looked at Bloom with grave concern. "Please do not tell me I have to explain why that's a terrible idea."

Aisha felt they had enough problems without Bloom causing a full-on forest fire.

"A few weeks ago, I'd agree with you. But you saw me in class, right?" Bloom's eyes shone. "I'm way better."

Aisha stared down at her bowl. "Yep," she told her roommate flatly. "You're killin' it."

The awkward moment was interrupted by Terra, calling out desperately for help.

"Does anyone know how to do a good cat eye?"

They found Terra in the bathroom, standing in front of a mess of makeup. A cat-eye attempt had been made. *Attempt* was the operative word.

Glad to have something to fix, Aisha dived in to help Terra immediately. She wielded the eyeliner as if flourishing a sword.

Bloom lingered at the door. Aisha knew Bloom wasn't much of a party girl, but she hoped Bloom would stick around. Strength in numbers was clearly called for at this critical juncture.

116

Musa peeped into the bathroom. "This is weird. What's happening in here is weird."

Musa was even less of a party person than Bloom was, and Aisha knew Musa had her reservations about her roommate.

"Get changed," Terra ordered Musa. "We're all going to this party. And we're gonna show . . . people . . . that we're cool and fun and—"

Obviously, Terra was thinking about that Beatrix girl again. Her voice went higher and more rapid as she spoke, clearly about to launch into a full-fledged rant.

Then Aisha moved away from Terra's eye, and showed her in the mirror. Aisha couldn't fix her own magic, but she'd fixed Terra's makeup.

Aisha was pleased to see Musa smile at Terra in the mirror.

"Hot," Musa told her reassuringly.

That was when Aisha knew they were all headed to this party.

SPECIALIST

Stella's makeup junk was spread out all over Sky's desk. Even Saint Sky, coming into his and Riven's room, couldn't repress a twitch of irritation. Riven's twitching had become a steady vibration of irritation some time ago.

"Sorry," Stella told Sky airily. "But four first years getting ready for their first party is a nightmare inside a nightmare."

Riven sneered, "Fun fact, if everyone around you is a nightmare . . . *It's not them.*"

She'd been complaining about Terra's annoying attempts to do a cat eye for some time.

Undoubtedly, Terra was panicking in a hilarious manner about actually attending a party, and Riven would also have made fun of her, but he didn't see why Stella thought she could do it.

Sky turned to face Riven, who was carefully pouring vodka into his flask. Everyone got party-ready in their own way. Riven was dressed for the party and excited for trouble.

"You're already drinking?" Sky raised his eyebrows.

Riven explained the situation. "She's been here an hour. So I've been drinking for an hour."

Riven was not the one who'd invited Stella back into their room and their lives. Riven was a martyr to Sky's terrible girlfriend decisions.

"Can you take it slow tonight? Last year you vomited in no less than five places."

And what, Sky wanted Riven to be a quitter? He didn't believe he could beat his own record? Riven gave him a disappointed look. Like, have a little faith here, buddy.

Then Stella said that Marco, one of the most badass Specialists in the business, was on the hunt for the Burned One. She was sure that the monster would be taken down and Silva saved soon.

Finally, Stella came in useful. Finally, Sky could relax and have a good time.

But Sky still said he wasn't gonna drink. Riven was all out of ideas. He had no clue what would make Sky feel better.

EARTH

The abandoned East Wing, with its cracked stone and dark corners, was anything but abandoned tonight. Beer was spilling over plastic cups. A bonfire burned and music played. The room was suffused with purple light, as though Musa's magic was filling the air and people's thoughts were painting the walls. Fairies in jeans and sexy tops were shaking their feet in a ring, tossing their arms in the air, and making out.

Terra clung to her Tupperware and tried to cover her nerves by telling the others fascinating historical facts.

"This is the East Wing of Alfea. It was used for war preparations. But since there hasn't been conflict in a while, nobody comes down here." Terra paused. "Except for tonight."

Terra could see Bloom looking a little overwhelmed. That was nice, that Bloom felt overcome as well. It was totally fine: They were the Winx Club, and they were gonna stick together.

Aisha noticed Bloom's expression, too. "You need a beer."

"I need a beer," Bloom confirmed.

119

Bloom and Aisha split off and headed toward the keg. That was totally fine, also! Terra was sure they'd be back soon, and Musa was still here, and perhaps they could find Dane, and with any luck Dane wouldn't be with Beatrix. Or Riven. Terra craned her neck, looking around.

"Looking for somebody specific?" Musa asked, her voice wry.

"What? No. Just wondering where I can put these down."

Terra was aware fibbing to someone who read emotions was futile, but Musa let her get away with it. Musa led Terra over to a shield case that was serving as a makeshift bar.

Musa started to pour herself a drink while Terra put down her Tupperware. She opened it to reveal brownies. Musa glanced at the brownies casually, but then cocked her head.

"Are those . . .? *Terra!*"

"What?" Terra asked defensively. "I can be a cool nerd." Just like Beatrix.

An annoying voice broke in on them. "Look who made an appearance."

Musa turned swiftly to see Terra's brother approaching. *Poor Musa*, Terra thought. She would feel she had to make nice with her roommate's brother.

"With Mom's Tupperware, no less," Sam drawled.

"What do you want, Sam?" Terra snapped.

Musa looked startled by Terra's tone. Musa was an only

child; Terra was pretty sure. She must not realize how irritating brothers could be.

"Just getting a drink. Relax," Sam told Terra. Then he turned to Musa with an interested air. "Musa, right?"

Musa twinkled. "That's me."

Sam twinkled back, a gleam passing between them. "Hi."

Wow, was Terra's brother trying to flirt with her roommate? Gosh, how embarrassing for him! Terra would have to explain to Sam that Musa was only being polite.

Just then, Sam's attention was diverted. "What reeks?"

Sam looked down at the Tupperware, then at Terra.

"They're for the party, not me," Terra said stiffly. Sam shouldn't judge.

Just then, she spotted Dane coming toward them. Okay, it was game time! Party time! Party game time.

"Didn't think you'd make it," Dane said. He looked so cute. That was a great shirt on him.

"Yeah," Terra said, desperately casual. "Decided to come last minute. Anyway. Brownie?"

Dane reached in to grab one. He was so polite. He was eating her food! Terra had a sudden misgiving about her food. She'd seen Dane throw up after one drink. Her delinquent brownies might be too much for sweet Dane.

"I'd take a half," Terra warned. "Even a quarter just to be safe. Like, a bite."

Dane took several brownies. It was so nice of him to be enthusiastic about her baking! Terra was chill.

Terra gave a chill laugh. "Or, you know, whatever."

"I'm gonna take a few to Riven and Sky," said Dane, with his charming smile. "See if they want some. Cool?"

Terra continued her mission to be chill. "Totally cool. Cool cool cool."

Silva might be dying, so Sky could have as many brownies as he liked, but Terra had a dark suspicion about who those brownies were actually for.

Just what she'd always wanted—to feed Riven and his apparently smart bimbo.

FIRE

On a bench to the side of the revelries, I saw Sky nursing a water with his eyes glued to his phone. I approached, beer in hand.

"Haven't seen you all day."

"Have you been looking?"

I smiled. Busted. Sky cracked a smile, too. The smile looked rusty, almost painful, as though it was the first time he'd smiled the whole day.

I sat down next to him. "How's Silva doing?" I asked.

Sky sighed. "Rough. But they're closing in on the Burned One. It's just a matter of time before he gets better."

I pushed, gently. "How are you doing?"

It was a simple question. An obvious one. But he looked

at me like it was a bizarre query, as though nobody else had asked. I wondered if I shouldn't have.

Then Sky confessed, "I feel like garbage, Bloom. I know I'm supposed to be strong, but . . ."

He looked at me with beseeching eyes. I held his gaze, trying to show him that I was listening, that he didn't have to be strong for me. Nobody could be strong all the time.

"Silva basically raised me after my dad died. They were best friends. I know we train to fight. To risk our lives. But I never let myself think that Silva . . ."

This must be so rough for him.

I murmured, "I'm so sorry."

It wasn't much, but I could be sorry and sit with him. Next to me, almost imperceptibly, I felt Sky relax.

"Are you close with your parents?" Sky asked at last.

"That's . . . a tricky question," I told him.

"They live in the First World, right? Not many fairies live out there. That why it's tricky?"

I went quiet, stricken by uncertainty. Would Sky think differently about me if he knew I was a changeling? Besides, he was another girl's boyfriend: I shouldn't pour out all my troubles to him.

Sky, too charming for his own or my good, said: "It's okay. I like a good mystery."

I played it off, waving my beer around. "Don't worry, a few more of these and I'll be an open book."

Sky suggested, "Maybe I'll have one, too. I could use a little distraction."

I offered, "I did hear mention of beer pong, if you want a *big* distraction."

Sky hesitated, then smiled, shimmering as bright as the party bonfires around us.

"You've just made a huge mistake."

SPECIALIST

It was girls against guys in a match to the pain. Sky and Riven, the ultimate beer pong bros. Up against Bloom, the ginger from the human world, and her roommate Aisha, the sporty chick.

When Sky went up to drink, the redhead's eyes glowed red. He nearly spat the beer out.

"Did you . . .? Is this beer *hot*?"

"Drink up. Them's the rules."

Bloom and Aisha erupted into laughter as Sky downed the drink. On the whole, Riven thought Bloom and Aisha seemed like cool girls.

Riven was up next.

"Get cocky," Riven advised the ladies, "get schooled."

Bloom leaned over to Aisha, whispering. Aisha nodded. Riven shot the ball, but before it landed in a cup, Aisha's eyes glowed blue, and beer sloshed right out.

Then every drop of beer from every cup foamed and spilled out like a tidal wave and onto Riven.

Not cool. Riven swore.

"Oh my God," said Bloom.

Bloom and Sky both stifled a laugh, but Aisha wasn't laughing. She looked mortified at the mess she'd made. As well she should. She'd made Riven look ridiculous in public!

Aisha mumbled, "Sorry. Honestly. Sorry. I'm gonna get some paper towels."

As Aisha headed off, Bloom moved to help Sky pick up the cups on the ground. Riven's mood wasn't improved as he noticed both of them were trying not to laugh at him.

"Feel a little better?" whispered cute redheaded Bloom conspiratorially.

"Certainly drunker," Sky conceded.

Riven clocked the sparks flying, and recalled the first day of school. How Sky had got hold of the redhead's number and talked about what he should text her. Until he hooked up with Stella again.

"So much for not drinking tonight," said Riven, and then hesitated. "But this one is a bit more fun than Stella. Reminds me of Ricki."

"Who's Ricki?" asked cute redhead Bloom.

Well might she ask.

Sky shifted, suddenly uncomfortable. "Riv," he said warningly.

Riven didn't plan to listen to any warnings. He was soaking wet and looked stupid and felt cranky.

"You live with Stella and don't know what happened to her last roommate?"

"I don't. But I'd sure like to," Bloom said with conviction.

Sky glared at Riven, but it was far too late to go back now.

"Ricki was Stella's best friend. Till she flirted a bit too much with Sky here and Stella showed everyone what a legit psycho she was."

"What does that mean?" Bloom asked tightly.

"Stella used her magic to blind her. On purpose. She blinded her best friend."

The words sounded too real when Riven said them, the weight of them crushing out the happy party sounds. Sky wasn't smiling anymore.

"That can't be true," Bloom breathed.

Sky cleared his throat. "That's—yeah. That's the story."

Having spilled the tea, Riven headed out to dry off. Yeah, Riven was a jerk. You can count on him to be that.

But the redhead had a right to know what she was getting into. And Sky should really think more about what he was climbing *back* into.

Riven tried to wring out his dripping shirt as he stomped off.

This was a terrible party. Where was Beatrix, the sexpot who actually liked him? Failing Beatrix, where was Dane? Probably with Terra, but he shouldn't be with Terra. How was Riven supposed to mentor Dane and teach him to be awesome if Dane was never there?

FIRE

I wandered through a side hallway in the East Wing, trying to avoid fairies making out. This party made me think of lines from a poem, *"the lonely of heart is withered away, / While the fairies dance in a place apart . . ."* This abandoned wing was a place apart all right, and I was feeling pretty lonely.

And I was desperately attempting not to think about Sky, and what Riven had said about Stella. I searched the corridor for Aisha, for company and help, but instead I saw piles of framed photos leaning discarded against the wall.

There was one in particular that stopped me. Because standing in the middle of the students was a woman wearing a military-trimmed coat with sunken eyes and an intense expression, her thin mouth set in a grim line and her shining blonde hair pinned back.

She was the mystery woman from my vision.

I pulled out my phone to record the evidence when a girl's voice startled me.

Beatrix's words were very slurred. "Are you photo collaging at a party? How are we not friends?"

I turned to see Beatrix. Remembering Terra talking about Beatrix's interest in history and realizing in a flash of inspiration that Beatrix might know something, I picked up one of the pictures. I pointed to my mystery woman.

"Do you know who this is?"

Beatrix's face shifted. It was almost imperceptible. *Almost*.

"Why?" she asked in an odd voice.

"I just know you're all about history—I thought you might know."

"Still curious about the *why*," Beatrix said archly.

I shifted, uncomfortable. The why was tough to explain.

"I'm not trying to sound mysterious or anything, but . . . I just . . . I can't tell you."

"You might not be *trying* to sound mysterious, but you are *succeeding*."

Beatrix eyed me, eyed the picture, and then her shadowy expression suddenly flipped to a bright smile.

"Doesn't matter, anyway," she told me in a chipper voice. "I have no idea who that is. Enjoy your arts and crafts."

Beatrix exited the room, moving urgently as though she had a specific purpose. Maybe she wanted some of Terra's brownies.

I looked back at the picture. A little more carefully this time, and I recognized yet another face.

I murmured aloud, "She's standing next to Ms. Dowling."

MIND

Musa and Sam had found a quiet hallway, filled with moonlight. Even in the midst of a party, Sam could find stillness.

"Lotta people," Sam said now. "Doing your head in?"

He was so chill about her power, but still considerate of her. Most boys would be horrified by her magic. Most people were horrified by her.

"Never underestimate the power of cheap beer to dull sharp emotions," Musa said lightly, then, more seriously, "It's a party. People are happy."

She looked at Sam in the moonlight. Just doing that made her happy.

"I am, too," she added softly.

Sam's gaze went especially warm, even as he continued to banter with her.

Musa worked up her nerve to ask: "You and Terra? Are you close?"

There was a little line between Sam's eyebrows. "We weren't around a lot of kids our age growing up, so yeah . . ."

They hadn't seemed that close, but Musa wasn't an expert on families. Was it good or bad if they were close?

Sam smiled, already wise to her. "Is that why you and I are sneaking around? Terra?"

"She has a lot of feelings about a lot of things. As her roommate, I get to experience all of them."

Right now, Musa was experiencing many feelings of her own. She leaned in a little closer.

Musa whispered, "How do you think she'd react to . . . this?"

"Oh, we're a *this*, are we?" Sam asked lightly.

Musa was instantly mortified. "Not anymore. It's all over. Who are you again?"

Sam smiled. They both laughed, and the laughter turned into a sweet silence, then into a kiss that was even sweeter.

Until Musa felt an unwelcome ripple of emotion, and pulled reluctantly away.

"Sorry, just . . . getting a very strong and sudden read of social—"

She gazed at Sam in sudden panic. Terra rounded the corner to face Musa. Who was frozen in terror for a moment, before she saw Sam had disappeared from her side. He waved at Musa from the opposite alcove before he melted through the wall.

"There you are!" announced Terra happily, and then with a rapid onset of nerves, "Why are you alone; are you okay?"

Terra, who was clearly a little drunk, didn't wait for Musa to respond. She was onto the next topic, and by the feel of her, this one was going to be a doozy.

"So I haven't wanted to ask, but . . . like, what's the point of having a roommate who can tell how people feel, if you don't . . . not that that's all I think of you, but . . . Dane. Me. Could it be a thing?"

Musa was stunned for a second. She'd been expecting something else.

Clearly fearing the worst, Terra said: "Oh God."

Musa rushed to reassure her. "No, it's just . . . When you and Dane are together, he feels comfortable. I don't know what that means specifically, but he does like you."

With painful, transparent hope, Terra asked: "So it could be? A *thing*?"

Musa gave a measured smile as Terra beamed all over her face.

Here it was. A way to make Terra like Musa, and all it took was Musa, the girl who made it a policy to hide nothing. Hiding way more than a kiss with her roommate's brother.

FIRE

I was justifiably filled with outrage. I was angry in a reasonable manner and I had to express it!

I was maybe a little drunk, but that didn't matter. The alcohol was actually helping me to think. I poured myself another as Aisha watched me with worried eyes.

"And you're absolutely sure this is the woman from your memory?" Aisha asked. "Not another, maybe?"

"One hundred percent. Which means Dowling knows something. And she's keeping it from me. *Again*."

I didn't know why I kept trusting Ms. Dowling. I didn't know why I wanted to trust her. I was a fool.

Aisha said in a pacifying manner, "Okay. We'll talk to her tomorrow."

"Tomorrow?" I repeated.

"Let's go home. You're pissed off and a little pissed. And I can do some more homework—"

Aisha clearly didn't understand the gravity of the situation. "She *lied* to me. I'm not waiting until tomorrow to get answers."

Aisha gave me a long, considering look.

Finally, she said, "Okay then. Have fun."

She turned to walk away. I reached out my hand to stop her.

"You're not coming?" I asked in a small voice.

"You wanna see the headmistress at midnight, *wasted*? Go for it. While you're at it, why don't you hit the stone circle and nuke your magic? Maybe you'll get another signal from your long-lost fairy guide. 'Cause that makes sense."

Aisha, who was always understanding, Aisha who was my one real ally at Alfea, looked utterly exasperated with me.

"I'm done pulling you back from the edge, Bloom," she announced. "You wanna jump? Jump."

SPECIALIST

Sky was in the middle of a fight with Stella when it happened. He was demanding she tell the truth about what had happened with Ricki.

"Staying with you after you purposefully blinded your best friend makes me look at best like an insensitive jerk, and at worst, like an absolute psycho," Sky said, realizing how true it was even as he spoke.

Seeing Bloom's beautiful, shocked-still face when Riven spilled the story had made that crystal clear. Sky didn't want her to think badly of him. Bloom was the one person who cared what he was going through.

Why was he carrying on this charade, why was he trying to be with Stella again despite everything, when Stella wouldn't tell the truth? Far more importantly, when Stella didn't even care about Sky's fear for Silva? When Bloom seemed to care more about Sky than his longtime girlfriend cared?

It made a guy wonder what he was doing, being with Stella at all.

And then the text came, saying Marco and his team had killed the Burned One, and all thoughts of Stella and Bloom faded.

Silva was going to be okay.

Sky was so happy. He had to see Silva right away.

He turned and left Stella without another word, running

133

for the Bastion training area. He walked in to find a single light shining by the benches. Silva was sitting there alone. Sky went over to him, feeling his face flush and a smile start on his lips. It had been so difficult to smile, for days, but now it was easy.

"How do you feel?" Sky asked, joy singing in his heart like birds. "The wounds should be healing already, right?"

Silva shifted toward Sky. With an effort. He was clearly still in pain, but he shouldn't have been in pain at all. When Sky looked down, he saw fresh blood on Silva's side.

The scars were *not* healed.

Voice distant in his own ears, Sky said: "You said they killed it."

Silva said, "They did."

Sky's voice faltered. "But then why—"

Silva's hard gaze didn't even flicker. Silva carried an aura of steeliness around with him that was almost impenetrable. Sky had always thought Silva made an exception for him.

But maybe not.

"The one they killed must not have been the one that attacked me. Clearly . . . there's more than one of these creatures out there."

Tensely, desperately, Sky said, "So the battalion will keep looking. It'll find the other one, and—"

With his first sign of real pain, Silva responded, "It's too late, Sky. It's over."

Sky stared down at his own hands. Trained to grasp

weapons, to fight, to protect. But when the one person he cared about more than anything was in trouble, Sky had done nothing to help.

"You told me . . . to wait."

"It was all there was to do."

Sky stood up, fast. Furious. *No.*

"The one thing you always told me about my dad was that he died fighting. And now you're just gonna lie down and take it?"

They stood staring at each other. Sky was sure neither of them knew what to say. He'd never spoken to Silva like that in his life before. He'd always trained to be the best, to make Silva proud. He was forgetting all his discipline.

Sky whirled away so Silva wouldn't see his face. He was supposed to be Silva's perfect soldier. He wasn't meant to cry.

FIRE

Ms. Dowling's expression went dark as I burst into her office, interrupting her in the middle of a meeting. Too bad for her. Too bad for Aisha. I knew what I was doing.

"You should be in bed," said Ms. Dowling.

I fired back, "And you should tell the truth."

Dowling threw a look at Professor Harvey, Terra's dad. He nodded and exited.

Triumphantly, I produced my evidence and showed Dowling the picture on my phone.

"What is this?" asked Dowling distantly.

"This woman! The one standing right next to you in this picture is the woman who left me in the First World."

Dowling looked to the photo and back to me. With a curt nod.

"Rosalind," she said briefly. "How do you know this?"

Rosalind. I savored the first scrap of information that I had.

"Who is she?"

Dowling closed her eyes for a moment. She looked so tired, I almost felt sorry for her. But I needed answers too badly to have time for regrets.

"She preceded me as headmistress. I was her student. Then her protégé."

"So you were here sixteen years ago when she did it."

An edge appeared in Dowling's voice. "I told you. The circumstances surrounding your birth are as much a mystery to me as they are to you."

I couldn't keep the note of accusation out of my voice. "You can see how that's getting harder and harder for me to believe, right?"

Ms. Dowling eyed me with sudden coldness.

"You're drunk. Perhaps we can have this discussion when you're not."

"Every picture of her was shoved into the abandoned East Wing. Tell me that's not suspicious."

Dowling said crisply, "Rosalind was headmistress during a difficult period in Alfea's history. It's not a time we're keen to celebrate."

"I want to talk to her."

"That's impossible."

"Really? Because a week ago, I had a vision. A memory of the day she left me in the First World."

A glint of curiosity appeared in Ms. Dowling's eye. Finally, she was interested in something besides shutting me up and shutting me down.

I continued eagerly, "She said, '*Find me.*' I want to talk to her."

It was all so clear to me now. Ms. Dowling wasn't the one who would give me the answers I craved. She was just the path to finding this other woman. Rosalind would help me.

Dowling said simply, "She's dead, Bloom."

I was so dazed, I couldn't process it.

"What?"

Dowling said, "She's been dead for years."

I stood in the headmistress's office, swaying slightly. I was so desperate for answers, yet I could see my last hope fading away.

Dowling continued, not unsympathetic, but terribly final: "So. I don't know what you saw, or why you saw it, but that is where this ends."

SPECIALIST

Riven, shirtless, his hair still wet with beer, smoked a joint as he flipped through the armor next to him. Dane perused the armor as well, and asked Riven what he was looking for.

"Something cool," said Riven.

He found an awesome helmet, handed Dane the joint, and started to put it on. Beatrix rounded the corner, shook her head, and grabbed the helmet off him.

"Never cover the face," advised Beatrix. "It's one of your few good qualities."

"She's not wrong," Dane contributed.

Inwardly, Riven preened.

Beatrix gave a meaningful glance to the joint in Dane's hand. "Oh. Shotgun?"

Dane appeared confused. Riven shook his head.

"You're hopeless. Inhale."

Dane obeyed Riven. Then, Beatrix moved to Dane, and with a smile that said she knew exactly what she was doing, Beatrix urged: "Now exhale."

Riven saw the exact moment when Dane finally clued in, then Dane blew the smoke into her mouth. She held it in for a beat. Riven moved to her. She returned the favor.

Dane was leaning against a table when Riven and Beatrix came up for air. He looked very pleased with himself, as if this was exactly what he wanted from a party. He also looked a little dizzy.

"Don't know how you can smoke so much after Terra's brownies," he commented.

Riven's mood darkened. He'd known as soon as he saw Dane bring over the brownies. Oh, Terra had it bad. Riven had eaten all four brownies and refused to let Dane have any more.

Dane looked unhappy. What did he think he was, Terra's knight and protector?

"Don't be an idiot. She made them for everybody."

"No, she didn't," Riven snapped. "She made them for *you.*"

Dane looked totally puzzled. So, since Riven had appointed himself teller of unwelcome truths at this party, he felt it was his duty to break it to Dane that Terra was totally thirsty for him. He felt it was best for Dane to know. And best for Terra to get her heart broken sooner rather than later.

Terra liked Dane. But Dane didn't like Terra. Dane liked *him.*

FIRE

I had only one more plan to get answers. So despite Aisha's warning, I stormed through the night and entered the ancient stone circle on the outskirts of Alfea. I was too furious to care about the consequences.

As I entered the circle, I felt my power surge. Flames ignited in the torches around me. Fire formed above my palms. I kept pulling more magic to me. It felt like tendrils of fire were escaping from my spine.

I was ready to set the sky ablaze, and the thought scared me enough to stop.

"Bloom?" Sky's voice said behind me.

I turned to see Sky approaching. Decked out in lightweight Specialist armor, a sheathed sword on his back. Looking more like a knight than ever before.

"What are you doing out here?" Sky asked.

I hesitated. I could be cagey or coy, or I could just spill it.

"I'm a changeling, Sky. That's my tricky family story. I don't know who the hell they are."

There was no judgment on Sky's face. Just an acknowledgment that this was a huge deal.

He swore.

"Yeah," I said. "And I'm out here . . . like a crazy person . . . because I'm apparently willing to do *anything* for the *possibility* of an answer."

There was a pause as Sky took this new information in.

"I have no idea how being out here gives you answers, but . . . I get it."

I appreciated that. Nobody had ever got me before, but I could believe Sky might.

"Uh," I said. "Why are you wearing armor?"

Sky's face was grim. "Silva is dying. The Burned One they killed wasn't the right one. It's still out there."

I paused, putting it all together. "And you're planning to go find it yourself?"

Sky's mouth twisted. "You're not the only crazy person. I can't sit around and do nothing."

I get it, Sky had told me. Looking at the pain in his face, I could've told him the same thing.

My eyes were drawn away from his face, toward the forest. A sound echoed in my ears. Strange whispers, becoming familiar to me.

Slowly, I told Sky, "You might not have to."

SPECIALIST

Terra kept trying to drag Dane off and have a special party moment with him. Riven, in his capacity as Dane's hot mentor, couldn't allow that to happen. So he challenged Terra and Dane to a beer-pong match.

"Nah, I'm good," said Dane.

Riven waited. He knew Terra had a little problem with challenges. Her problem was that she loved them.

"Fine! Don't think I haven't noticed you're wearing Dane's shirt," Terra snapped at Riven. "You made poor Dane give you his shirt just because Aisha got yours wet! Why are you such a bully?"

Riven shrugged. "It amuses me."

Beating them at beer pong would amuse him, too, he figured. Only then his so-called friend Kat let him down, and Terra and Dane won.

Terra and Dane had a victory hug. Terra was clearly loving the shirtless victory hug. Seemed like Riven had, in fact, done Terra a huge favor by taking Dane's shirt.

Dane was clearly thrown by the lingering hug. Riven shot him a *told-ya* look. Terra didn't see it.

Just then, Stella approached Riven and pulled him away from the others when Riven didn't wish to be taken away. How like Stella.

Riven quickly shook her hand off his arm. He wasn't ready for physical intimacy of any sort with the princess, and he wanted to make that clear.

"Have you seen Sky?" Stella asked impatiently. "He's not answering my texts."

"Have you looked for Bloom?" Riven inquired innocently.

Stella blinked. "What?"

"Whoops," said Riven, then cackled. "They are totally just friends. One hundred percent. Nothing going on. No need to blind her."

Stella's carefully made-up face became a frozen landscape.

"I wouldn't waste my magic on a changeling, anyway," she spat.

Riven's spine felt electrified. Oh, here it was. Sky was attracted to Bloom. So, of course, the girl was a disaster.

"Wait. Bloom is a *changeling*?"

"Whoops," purred Stella.

Before Riven could respond, Stella's phone buzzed. Across the way, so did Terra's. From the look on both girls' faces, the texts were important.

Terra snapped into take-charge mode. "Come on, Stella! We have to go."

She abandoned Dane and ran at Stella, seizing her wrist.

"Wait, wait," said Riven. "Where are you going?"

"I don't have time for you right now, Riven," snapped Terra. "Something important is happening. Gotta go, enjoy the party, leave poor Dane alone."

She rushed off, leaving Riven and Dane behind. Riven found that to be unwise.

Leave Dane alone, she said? Oh, Terra, Terra, Terra. Didn't she know how Riven felt about a challenge?

FIRE

The whispers rose in my ears as Sky and I hunted through the woods. They were louder than before, terrifying. I could almost make out words. Sky unsheathed his sword.

"It's close," I warned.

I turned around. We stood back to back.

"Do I want to know why you can track these things?" Sky asked.

Hunt Burned Ones now, Sky, I thought. *Talk later.*

"One of the many mysteries of my life we could be solving in the protective embrace of the Barrier."

Suddenly, Sky spun to see a Burned One bearing down on him. He was clearly thrown, but he got a strike in. Everyone said Sky was the best warrior training at Alfea. Maybe he could just kill the monster and we could go home.

The monster shrieked, then tossed Sky aside and turned. It leaped at me, knocking me down. The Burned One reared back to strike, and I knew in a moment of moonlight-cold certainty that I'd been as foolish as Aisha had warned me, that I was doomed, that I didn't stand a chance.

Stella's voice called out, "Close your eyes."

I shut my eyes, trusting, as the Burned One raised its arm to deliver a killing blow.

The blow never landed. Instead, I saw the pale impression of a blinding light behind my eyelids. When I opened my eyes, the forest was still illuminated. The Burned One was staggering back, stunned.

My suitemates were all around me. I'd texted them, and they had come running.

Aisha raced forward, helping me to my feet. The monster was back on its feet and heading straight for her . . . until a chain of ivy wrapped around its legs, pulling it to the ground. Terra caught my eye and grinned.

The Burned One broke through the clinging ivy without trouble. But Terra had slowed it enough for me to summon my magic again. Flames moved in straight, sharp lines toward the creature. But they didn't reach it.

I yelled, "Aisha!"

Aisha summoned a massive wall of water in front of the flame, and when our fire and water met, the forest erupted in steam.

We saw the dim shape of the Burned One staggering toward us, disoriented, lost in the whiteness. Until out of the fog, a blade gleamed true. Sky's sword pierced the monster to the heart, and the Burned One fell to the ground.

As the steam cleared, we moved toward the Burned One's corpse.

"Wait," Musa said behind me. "Stop, I don't think it's—"

I was within reach as the monster reared up suddenly to strike, but then it was paralyzed by a light emanating from within its own blackened body. Before our eyes, the Burned One incinerated from the inside out.

"No," came Ms. Dowling's cool voice. "It wasn't dead."

SPECIALIST

Sky watched from across the room as Professor Harvey treated Silva. It felt just like the last time he'd had to watch this, helpless to aid Silva, hope and fear seeming to tear his heart in half with every beat. If he'd killed the wrong

Burned One, this had all been for nothing. He didn't know, he couldn't be sure, but Silva seemed to have more energy.

Silva told Sky, in a strong, furious voice, "You're an idiot."

"I know," said Sky, hardly daring to hope. "But is it better?"

Silva continued ranting, "You're a stupid, reckless, impulsive . . ."

"Professor Harvey?" Sky begged.

Sky turned to the professor, desperate for any sign. Harvey looked up with a smile that gave Sky the answer he wanted to hear.

"Don't smile at him!" Silva ordered.

Silva turned, and Sky saw what he'd been desperate to see. The wounds were healing.

Silva was scowling. Sky had spent his whole life trying to please Silva, fearing to inspire that look on his face. Yet in this moment, Sky didn't care one bit. He rushed to Silva, pulling him into a hug, and held on tight. He hadn't failed, after all. He wasn't letting go. He wasn't losing someone else that he loved.

Gruffly, into Sky's hair, Silva muttered: "Your dad would be proud."

LIGHT

"So Dowling can do more than one kind of magic?" Bloom asked. "That's a thing?"

Poor, foolish Bloom. What did they teach kids in California? It seemed a lawless place.

Stella was feeling benevolent about everything. She'd used her magic to save the day! Sky and her Winx suitemates were no doubt extremely impressed. Her mother might be proud when she heard.

A party was only as good as the clothes you wore to it. A battle was only won by the power you brought to it.

"If you're strong enough," Terra told Bloom.

"Which she is. Obviously," Stella chipped in helpfully. Ms. Dowling was strong, and she was teaching Stella to be strong, too.

"So of course we pissed her off," said Musa.

Musa was not a very positive person.

Stella began to feel slightly negative herself as the sound of heels approached. They all stood as Dowling turned a corner to face them, putting her phone away.

"That the lot of you and Headmaster Silva are alive doesn't change how thoughtless you were," Dowling said crisply.

Stella was relieved at this piece of good news. Silva was alive. They had succeeded, and Sky would be fine now, back to his usual self.

But Dowling remained harsh. "We'll discuss consequences in the morning."

As Dowling walked away, Musa's eyes glowed purple. Aisha leaned into her, whispering.

"Is she, like, detention pissed off or expulsion pissed off?"

Musa said, "I'm going with the first one. But only because of the very tiny bit of pride I also felt in there."

More good news.

Just then, Sky entered. He looked steadier than he'd looked since Silva was hurt, and Stella relaxed at the very sight of him. Sometimes she felt as though she was a bit of Terra's beloved ivy and could only flourish with his support.

Then Sky glanced between Bloom and Stella, and for a moment Stella felt a weird tension in the air, as if he was trying to weigh something heavy. Make a decision. Stella felt like Aisha, trying not to let water slip through her fingers.

Bloom took action, making the decision for him. "We should get upstairs."

Stella was annoyed by how grateful she felt to Bloom for that, but this was no time to dwell on it. Not now, when she felt as though everything might finally go smoothly.

Stella was truly thrilled for Sky, and surely Sky would forgive her for being a little weird before. They had all saved Silva together. She remembered seeing him in the woods, wielding his sword like a knight. He was so brave. And it made sense, that a knight was destined for a princess.

As she looked up at Sky, though, she saw an unfamiliar look on his dear, familiar face, and felt panic clutch at her heart. Was it really that he was mad at her, or was it that he wanted Bloom?

Maybe Sky wasn't brave about everything.

Don't go, Stella thought. *Don't leave me alone in the dark.*

SPECIALIST

Now that Sky was feeling better, apparently Stella liked him more. She drifted toward him, clearly wishing to catch his hand and cling.

"I was awful today. I'm sorry. Seeing you scared and vulnerable? I couldn't handle it."

"I know," said Sky. "I felt it."

It had been pretty obvious.

"You're the only one who knows the real me, Sky," Stella whispered.

"That's your choice, Stella."

"It's not, though. I am the heir to the Solarian throne. If you knew the kind of pressure I'm under . . ."

"I do. You know I do."

If he didn't, nobody did. He and Stella had known each other so long, he knew her pain as well as he knew his own. He saw her pain now, written all across her beautiful face as she struggled to speak.

"Your strength is my safety net. I have to know it's there if I fall."

Their patterns together were so set, he could fall into them without thinking. Every cell in his body was telling him to put his arms around her and comfort her, the same way he did every time she revealed her vulnerable side.

Only every time before, he hadn't known she would never reciprocate.

"And what if I fall?" Sky asked. "Who's there to catch me?" He turned and walked away from her.

He kept remembering the warm feeling he'd had, just from having Bloom sit down next to him at a stupid party. He'd made the wrong choice on the first day of school. He wished, so much, that he'd sent Stella away from his room, and that he'd sent that text to Bloom instead.

EARTH

In bed, Terra scrolled through her Instagram stories, and found *Beatrix*. No doubt being cool. Sharing a single piece of fruit. Terra didn't want to see it.

She clicked on the video, anyway.

It was a shaky video of Riven, and a shirtless Dane. Riven winked at the camera. Dane put his arm around him.

"Hey, Riv," he slurred. "Shotgun me."

"What about your girlfriend?" Riven asked.

Dane said: "Who?"

And then they were mocking her, Dane suggesting Terra should get with a flower, Riven snickering. Having fun at her expense. Riven, the meanest guy in Alfea, and Dane, the boy of Terra's dreams.

Riven took another hit, and Beatrix moved into the frame.

"My turn," she said, motioning to Dane, and then added

with all the easy, sexy confidence Terra would never have, "Come on, third degree."

Riven exhaled into both Dane's and Beatrix's mouths. This time, all three of their mouths touched. It looked messy and out of control, and Terra felt messy and out of control.

Dane, who she'd thought was so sweet, who she'd thought really liked her. But no, of course he liked Beatrix, who was everything Terra could never be. And somehow, for some reason, Riven was involved.

Overwhelmed by shock and pain, Terra's hand trembled as she slowly put her phone down on the nightstand. She couldn't process this. Not tonight.

FIRE

Aisha and I got ready for bed, still humming from the near miss, and I filled her in on what I'd done. And more importantly, what I hadn't done. I hadn't summoned all my magic in the stone circle and burned down the forest. I thought she'd be proud of me.

Aisha seemed more worried than proud. She turned to look at me, where I sat on my bed, and I could feel something big coming.

"Bloom, I know you want to find your birth parents,

but . . . What if there's no big conspiracy? You said Rosalind was *headmistress*." Aisha selected her words with obvious care. "Isn't it possible you're just the daughter of a student? A scared teenager who got pregnant and didn't know what to do?"

Put that way, it sounded plausible, but I shook my head. "There are just too many things I can't explain."

A steely note entered Aisha's voice. "You know, some people would kill to be a natural with magic like you. Even if it meant they were just a *regular* fairy."

Aisha glanced over at the bowl of water she couldn't master, and plunged ahead.

"Magic is . . . not easy for me. I had to work really hard to get into this school. And I'm gonna have to work really hard to stay in it. But you . . ."

"What? Are you saying I should be grateful?"

I never wanted to come here. I wanted to go home.

"I'm saying you should be realistic," Aisha told me.

I knew Aisha was only trying to help, trying to be sensible.

"Do you even know what that means for me, Aisha? Being realistic?"

I stared up at Aisha, totally vulnerable, begging her to understand me.

"It means my real mom *didn't want me*. That she looked at me when I was just a baby and *gave me up*. And if you don't think I've thought about that every day since I found out I was a changeling . . ." I struggled to speak. "I have to believe that there's something more. I have to."

And with that, I collapsed on my bed. I couldn't push away tears anymore. Aisha ran to me and threw her warm arms around me, and I relaxed against her, leaning into her strength.

I loved Aisha. I loved my new friend. I really did. But she was wrong. She had to be wrong.

There must be more to the story of me and Rosalind.

FAIRY TALE #4

Come, faeries, take me out of this dull house!
Let me have all the freedom I have lost.
—W. B. Yeats

THE HEART
GROWS OLD

Farah Dowling, Saúl Silva, and Ben Harvey were on
a mission. Just like the old days. Farah's secretary
Callum had gone missing. That would be disquieting at the best of times. At a time like this, with Burned
Ones stalking the woods and Bloom asking questions about
Rosalind, it was actively alarming. They had to find out
what had happened to him.

Someone had tried to access the secret door in her bookcase, but nobody had reached what lay at the end of the
secret passage.

Farah reset the spell, a trap laid for anyone who found
the door, but they needed to know who it had been. Her
missing secretary Callum was the prime suspect, but if it
had been him, how had he evaded the trap, and where was
he now?

Had he had help getting in through the door? Had he
had help getting away?

Time to find out. Ben was at her bookcase, preparing a solution of nettle amalgam in a beaker. He poured the solution into an earthenware censer, sealed the censer, and then lit the flame beneath it. After a moment, mist seeped out of the censer, and near the bookcase, something began to take shape. A huddled, incomplete form that had once been a body.

Callum's face re-formed. His expression was a rictus of pain, his eyes filled with the terror experienced in the moment of his death.

Ah. So Callum hadn't gotten away, after all.

"Callum," Farah said heavily. "Yes."

She hadn't loved Callum, but she'd felt responsible for him. As she did for everyone at Alfea.

"He was killed. With magic," said Ben.

Every inch Professor Harvey right now, Ben pulled out a specimen jar half filled with Vessel Stones. He scooped the jar through the image of Callum's dead face, collecting a sample. Then he closed the lid as the remnant of Farah's secretary vanished.

"At least now we know where he went," said Farah.

She and Saúl exchanged a look of grim understanding.

"And that there's a murderer in our school," Saúl said.

Someone in this school had tried to break in, through all Farah's defenses, to the worst secret she'd ever kept. Someone lethal. And not long ago, she'd told Bloom that Rosalind was dead.

They had to find Callum's killer.

SPECIALIST

Riven was pretty sure Beatrix was actually his girlfriend. He'd never had a proper one before, and it was nice. She was in Riven's dorm, wearing one of his T-shirts. They were just hanging out, enjoying each other's company.

While she stared at a picture of the weird changeling Bloom on her phone, but okay! Riven had heard women were mysterious.

"It's your fault for spreading it around that she's a changeling," Beatrix informed him. "She's now the most interesting person at school."

Riven shifted, uncomfortable with guilt. "People will forget in a few more days. They'll move on."

"I won't," said Beatrix.

There was an intensity to her comment that wasn't lost on Riven. He just didn't know what it meant.

"Is this like one of those obsession movies where you dye your hair red and take over her life and then, like, wear her skin or something?"

"Don't be disgusting," said Beatrix. "I have much better skin."

Beatrix's hair was currently dark auburn. Riven liked it the way it was. He grinned and decided he didn't care what her hang-up was. She was funny, in exactly the petty and mean but whip-smart way he enjoyed. She was a challenge. He liked her, and he hoped she liked him.

"I guess I'll just have to fight for your attention, then . . ."

Riven kissed the back of her neck. She let him, closing her eyes. When he stopped, she sighed.

"No, no. Keep fighting. A little to the left."

Riven kissed her, and wondered why he always had to battle so hard for everything he wanted.

Then again, if he didn't have to fight, would he want it?

FIRE

I crossed the courtyard under a cloud. Literally, in that a cloud hung over the castle, but also figuratively, in that I was under a smoke-dark cloud of suspicion. I was carrying much-needed coffee and breakfast in takeout containers. As I went past knots of chatting students, I heard two fairies gossiping. And I knew the burning-hot topic of gossip was me.

One fairy said, "I'm telling you, she lit her nursery school on fire."

The other claimed, "Nope. Softball team. Torched 'em at an away game. Her human parents never stood a chance. Did she kill them both, or just one of them?"

"Neither," I said loudly.

When they turned, cringing, I smiled. They cringed more.

I told them, "So I'm due for a murder or two."

Then I spun on my heel, and took the coffees up to Ms. Dowling's office. Actually, just outside Ms. Dowling's office. Aisha was filling in for Ms. Dowling's secretary, Callum, while he was away.

While she was there, I'd asked her to do one little thing for me.

I sat down across the desk from her, laying down coffee and breakfast offerings. "You haven't found anything?"

Aisha was almost hidden by stacks of paper files as we drank coffee and ate breakfast from the containers.

"I've only been at Callum's desk for two days, Bloom. Also, kinda doing you a favor, so maybe try being grateful?"

"Come on, you didn't take Callum's job for my sake."

"Weird, 'cause I remember you—"

"Making a helpful suggestion—"

"Begging me to volunteer so I could snoop for info on your past," Aisha said.

"That seems like something I *might* do. But it also seems like you *might* jump at the chance to earn brownie points with Ms. Dowling." I coughed. *"Suck up."*

"Suck up? Really? Suddenly, I've lost the ability to read the files."

"Wait. Did you think I said *suck up*? Weird. I actually said . . ." I coughed again. *"Suc-h a good friend?* Who is smart and beautiful? Also kind and—"

Aisha's smile as she watched me flounder faded a little.

"Isn't sure she can help," she finished softly. "These records here only seem to go back to Ms. Dowling's start as headmistress. Everything else must be archived somewhere."

"Or shredded because Dowling loves withholding information."

Aisha shot me a look. Perhaps I hadn't done a good job hiding my bitterness on the Dowling front.

"Even if I knew just a little more about Alfea back then, I could piece together why Rosalind put me in the First World—"

Aisha sighed. "I'll keep looking, promise. I have to read every file in this place, anyway. Don't know who taught Callum how to run an office, but he was terrible at it. And I can't even call him to ask questions."

"Why not?" I demanded.

Aisha sounded doubtful. "He apparently left for a family emergency. Dowling doesn't want to bother him with 'trivial nonsense.'" She turned to her breakfast. "Thank you for this, by the way. I mean, since you're using me as an excuse not to eat in the canteen, it's the least you could do."

"I'm not avoiding the canteen," I claimed. Aisha just looked at me, and I doubled down. "So everyone's talking about me being a changeling? So what? That's literally the least weird thing about me."

"True. They don't know how bad you snore." Aisha threw me a grin. I tossed a piece of granola at her grinning face just as Musa entered, food in hand. She plopped down immediately on the floor.

"'Sup?" Her eyes glowed briefly. "Is Bloom still pretending she's not upset about the gossip?"

"Are you still pretending you're not dating your room-mate's brother?" I shot back.

Aisha stifled a laugh as Terra walked in with her breakfast.

Terra blinked. "Who's pretending what?" She continued, smiling, "I mean, other than Stella pretending she's not dreading being outshined by her mom all day."

"You could enjoy that a little less," Musa pointed out.

"Could I, though? I guess we'll see at the assembly."

As Terra dug into her food, I looked around at my Winx suitemates, who had turned this little office into a cafeteria. For me. It was so kind, but it was going overboard. They'd already done far too much for me.

"I don't need this." I spoke so loudly everybody looked at me. "I don't need you all to change your breakfast plans to eat with me like I'm some weird loser mess. I'm fine."

No one seemed convinced. I scrambled to my feet and walked away, mumbling excuses about potions and papers.

I knew, and they knew, that I was anything but fine.

LIGHT

"It's one day, Stella," said Stella's maybe-still-boyfriend. "Half a day."

Stella sighed. "Half a day of everyone adoring her like she is literally the sun."

"She is the Queen of Light," Sky reminded her, a little wry. A lot charming.

She knew she hadn't been great to Sky lately, but she was sure she could do better and fix what was wrong between them. Stella repaid his effort with a small smile.

"This whole Burned One assembly she's doing . . . I know she's really here to check on my progress."

"Did you tell your suitemates you need a buffer? I bet Bloom could use a distraction about now—"

She was tired of hearing Sky talk about Bloom, or wondering if he was thinking about Bloom. Stella knew she'd done Bloom wrong. She was the one who'd spilled that Bloom was a changeling, and she hadn't owned up to it. Guilt wouldn't let her ask if Bloom was all right.

Instead, she blurted out, "I don't need them. I have you."

Then she caught herself, realizing she was doing it again. Leaning on him too much, when she hadn't let him lean on her. But despite the recent past, Sky stepped up to her side, laying a hand on her arm in a comforting gesture. Maybe he didn't know how to stop letting her lean, just like she didn't know how to stop leaning. This was how they'd always been.

"I'm a text away. But you can handle this. You can handle her."

Stella wasn't so sure, but now it was time to find out. Two black SUVs pulled up to the curb. Between them was a pristine black Rolls-Royce.

Sky gave her a reassuring look and walked away.

Alone, Stella took a deep breath and drew herself up so her posture was perfect, just like her mother had taught her. A Solarian royal guard, a bow sheathed on his back, exited one of the SUVs and opened the Rolls's back door.

A five-inch-heeled, red-soled Louboutin emerged from the SUV. Then the body it was attached to.

Queen Luna of Solaria stepped into the sunshine. Stella used to ask, as a child, if she'd be as poised and powerful as her mother when she grew up. Nobody ever answered her. They just seemed embarrassed that Stella didn't realize it would never be possible.

"Stella," said her mother. "You look stunning."

Stella stepped forward, trying to smile bright enough to outshine the sun.

SPECIALIST

Not only did Riven have a girlfriend, he had a gang. He and Beatrix and Dane were hanging out a lot, the three of them.

While Beatrix spun tales about dangerous changelings to an overly credulous Dane.

"Changelings were a way for pissed-off fairies to get revenge on the First World. Swap a fairy for a First World baby. Wait for it to wreak havoc."

"What does wreak havoc even mean?" Dane asked innocently.

Beatrix glanced at Riven. He rolled his eyes at her, but Beatrix smiled and went for it.

"Heard of the Great Fire of London?"

As Beatrix elaborated, sweet gullible Dane was wide-eyed and buying every word of it. He was clearly about to ask for more info when he spotted Terra walking in the direction of the greenhouse. Riven noticed how Dane suddenly went on the alert.

"Changelings are bad news. That's why we stay on their good side," Beatrix finished.

"Or try to, at least . . ." said Riven.

Were he and Beatrix trying that hard, though? If Bloom heard how they were discussing her, she'd be within her rights to set their hair on fire. That would be so bad. Beatrix had really pretty hair. And Riven's was even prettier.

Eyes on the greenhouse, Dane mumbled, "I'll see you two at the assembly."

Whatever, Dane. Terra wasn't going to let this go. She hadn't liked Dane that much. And the girl was proud. Dane could just get used to not having Terra in his life and stick with Riven and Beatrix.

Dane rushed off on his hopeless mission.

Riven glanced over at his girlfriend so they could share the joke. "I'm not sure what's more tragic. That he thinks Terra will forgive him for the video or that he believes all that changeling garbage you spoon-fed him."

"It's not all garbage. Changelings can be dangerous. You did everyone a favor—"

164

He wished Beatrix would quit acting as though it'd been Riven who did all the talking. Yeah, Riven had spread it around, and he was a jerk. But he hadn't been the one pouring poison into Dane's ears about changelings.

But no, it was fine. They were in this together. That was what Beatrix meant.

"Technically, Stella let the cat out of the bag. But the fact that nobody can trace it to either of us is probably a good thing," Riven remarked.

He hadn't known how intense and nasty the gossip would get. The whole castle was buzzing with rumors. Every time Riven glimpsed Bloom, she seemed braced for more bad news.

Sucked to be poor little redheaded Bloom. If she burned down Alfea, Riven wouldn't blame her.

EARTH

Ah, family time. Terra's dad was looking worried about a project, while Sam harassed Terra about whether she was done with her homework or not. *None of your business, Sam!*

Terra was still trying to squint at what her father was working on. He had a specimen jar, and inside it were Vessel Stones. He was tipping them surreptitiously into a glass cylinder. If Terra recalled correctly, Vessel Stones were used to trace magic, so—

Her train of thought was derailed by a knock. The Harveys turned as one to face the door, and beheld Dane. He stood nervously on the greenhouse threshold.

"Hey, Terra," began Dane. "Can we—"

Just then, both her dad and her brother stood up. The ultimate mild-mannered professor and Terra's almost terminally laid-back brother, both suddenly looming with their faces turned furiously cold.

Everyone in Alfea had seen Beatrix's story, or heard about it. Everyone knew what Dane had said about Terra.

"While I appreciate that the historical perspective of the patriarchy is that women need to be saved from upsetting situations . . ." Terra told them, *"I got this."*

She gave them the *Stand-down-boys* stare, and they sat back down. Still, she was fighting off a smile as she met Dane at the door. Dane didn't matter, not really. Her family did.

Dane looked lost, in the same puppy-dog way that had appealed to her so much at first. "You didn't answer my texts."

"I've been busy."

Dane could barely meet her eyes. "I just wanted to say I'm sorry. You've been great to me, and—"

Past the hurt, Terra mostly felt amazement. He thought they could be friends again, after his little mockery and make-out session with Riven and Beatrix? He couldn't possibly think she was this much of a pushover. If he did . . .

Boy, had he got her wrong.

"I know I have," she told him. "Because I'm a good person, Dane. I *think* you are, too. Not sure I care to find out anymore. But a word of advice. Be careful who you trust."

She shut the door in Dane's face.

From behind her, Sam said, "Still kinda want to punch him."

She and her annoying brother didn't often share a smile, but they shared one now. Terra kinda wanted to punch Dane herself.

WATER

What had Aisha got herself into? She couldn't make heads or tails of Callum's paperwork. Callum didn't seem to have been a team player.

She was doing this for Bloom, but she wanted to do a good job for Headmistress Dowling as well. Maybe then she'd feel less sneaky, less like she was doing something wrong.

The door opened and the queen walked in. Professor Harvey and Specialist Headmaster Silva were with her, but Queen Luna was the type of person you couldn't look away from. She had far more presence than any picture could convey. She was the most magnetic person Aisha had ever seen.

"Queen Luna, if there's anything you need during your visit—" Aisha offered.

"So sweet, Aisha. But I'm far more low maintenance than you'd imagine."

Wow, the queen knew Aisha's name.

Ms. Dowling entered just then, walking with purpose as she always did. Aisha admired that, though she wasn't sure she admired Ms. Dowling's attitude to administration.

"Ms. Dowling, I have a few questions about this filing when you have—"

"If you can't figure it out, then create a new system."

Ms. Dowling's tone was sharp. Aisha winced, feeling as though she must have deserved the reprimand, though she didn't know how. She nodded, and the door closed behind Dowling and Queen Luna.

Aisha took a deep breath, and decided to devote herself to her task. As she turned, she knocked over a stack of files, undoing hours of work. Hours of work she'd undertaken for her roommate, and was Bloom even grateful?

Aisha wanted to scream, so instead she shut the drawer of the filing cabinet too hard. A piece of trim came off.

"Perfect," Aisha muttered, and bent to remedy the situation.

Only the piece of trim hadn't fallen off. It had been cut away to create a secret compartment. There was a metal ring inside the compartment, no bigger than a quarter, and as soon as Aisha reached out and touched it, the ring filled with crackling static.

She held it up to the light. Nothing.

Then Aisha held it up to her ear.

Instantly Queen Luna's voice, sounding totally different and far less warm, snapped out: "Your assistant died here. In your office. You *must* have a theory about what happened."

FIRE

I was walking through the courtyard, trying to keep my head down while other people failed to keep their voices down, when Aisha ran over to me.

Aisha, not usually excitable, was having a hard time keeping her own voice down.

"Bloom!" she said. "You will not believe what I found in my desk!"

I tensed. "Files?"

"A ring that acts as an eavesdropping device!" Aisha almost yelled. "It must have been Callum's. Queen Luna came into the office—she looks just like Stella, except even more intimidating—and I knocked over some papers. I only meant to put things away. Then I found a metal ring in a desk and I just picked it up and I heard a little static. So I put the ring to my ear. And, I swear this is true, Queen Luna's voice in my ear said, 'Your assistant died here. In your office. You *must* have a theory about what happened.'"

"Wait," I said. "Callum's not visiting family? Callum is *dead*?"

Aisha and I kept walking, with Aisha in full voluble storytelling mode.

"And *Dowling* told me he left for a family emergency. So they're—"

Oh, Ms. Dowling was the worst. I couldn't believe I'd ever trusted her. I couldn't believe I'd wanted to.

"Lying. Shocker. So something happened to Callum. What did you do with the listening thing?"

Aisha said, "I put it back."

I stared at my poor, sweet, innocent roommate.

"Don't tell me you're going to just put it away and forget about it."

"That's exactly what I'm going to do. It felt . . . wrong."

"Callum clearly didn't agree. What do you think he was after?"

Aisha gave me a meaningful look. "Maybe he had a friend who needed him to spy on Dowling, too?"

I ignored the snark.

"Or he was on to one of Dowling's secrets and wanted to know more."

Callum had always been quiet and unobtrusive. If only I'd caught on to something about him before it was too late. Maybe he could've helped me.

He'd been killed in Dowling's office. Who could have done it? The only student I was aware of who kept slipping into Dowling's office was me, and I wasn't the murderer. Though no doubt everyone at Alfea would be ready to believe I was.

As Aisha and I walked, the stares increased in intensity and the buzz of conversation rose. I lowered my voice so other people wouldn't hear Aisha and me talking about murder and sneaking around.

"You're sure she didn't shred those old records . . ."

Aisha looked confused by this hard left turn in conversation.

"What?"

"The Alfea records that predate her," I reminded Aisha. "You don't think she destroyed them?"

"Are you kidding? That woman loves paper. I offered to start scanning the files into the computer system, and she looked at me like I had two heads. The records are somewhere."

I stopped walking. That was the moment Aisha visibly registered that a disaster was about to happen.

"Bloom," said Aisha. "The assembly is mandatory."

"Which means everyone is distracted."

"Bloom—"

"I'm not asking you to come," I assured her.

"It's a bad idea!"

"A bad idea is going to that assembly where everyone will stare at me like I'm a freak." I paused, trying to marshal my arguments. "I can't sit around and listen to people make stuff up about me. Especially when I don't know what the truth is myself."

Aisha opened her mouth to object further, and then saw my face. Perhaps she saw how serious I was.

She sighed. "Fine. You had a terrible migraine. Could barely stand up. Good?"

I smiled.

FIRE

I had an idea about where to search for the lost records. Where better than the place where they'd stored Rosalind's picture, where they had all the old artifacts of war hidden away?

I made my way back to the abandoned East Wing.

I hadn't expected the East Wing to be eerie, but it was a million times creepier when it was empty of party people and music. Without the blazing bonfires, it was dark in here, and the hallways seemed narrower and more winding. Mazelike. I negotiated cautiously around corners.

I moved toward a door and tried the knob, only to find it unlocked. As good a place to start as any.

I smiled, and pulled the door open.

Then a hand slammed the door shut.

I jolted back, scared out of my mind, and looked up to face someone who didn't seem happy to see me.

"What are you doing in here?" demanded Sky.

SPECIALIST

Riven was making his way to Queen Lunatic's assembly when he saw Beatrix slipping from one shadow to the next with the air of a woman on a mission.

Riven slid up alongside her with a devilish grin. "Where are we going?"

"Look at you, clinger. Mandatory assembly is a mandatory ditch."

For a moment, Riven's good mood faltered. There was a strangely hostile expression on his girlfriend's face, as though she didn't want him around, or was planning to do something nasty to him if he stayed.

She gave him a sexy smile. "So . . . you coming or what?"

She pivoted and made for the East Wing, walking fast. That was good thinking. They could have some privacy there.

What a woman! Riven quickly followed.

MIND

Stella sat in the front row, far apart from her Winx suitemates. Two Solarian guards were on either side of her. To look at her, anyone would think Stella was glorying in finally being in her rightful place as princess, but Musa was getting a faint hint of something else. She tried not to pursue it. An assembly was a crowded place. Let someone in, and she'd be overwhelmed.

Dowling, Silva, and Harvey were walking among the students, monitoring their behavior.

Just then, everybody hushed as from the side of the assembly hall, Queen Luna approached. Her eyes glowed, and the lighting shifted into a moody, underwater light tone. A hush immediately came over the room. Luna looked around.

"That's a bit dramatic, isn't it?" the queen asked, sounding amused.

Her eyes glowed again, and a warm, soft light illuminated her. She took a beat, commanding the stage with ease, grace, and a disarming *I'm-just-like-you* smile.

Politicians, Musa thought. Luna was clearly good at what she did, but Musa didn't have to use her powers to know not to totally buy the act.

"There we are," Queen Luna declared with satisfaction, and then her melodious voice slipped into storytelling mode. "I always had a love/hate relationship with assemblies when I was at Alfea. *Loved* getting out of class. *Hated* getting lectured . . ."

Her tone shifted, more serious.

"But I'm not here to lecture. I'm here to treat you like the adults you are. To talk about the Burned Ones."

Musa was sitting with Aisha, Terra, and Sam. Terra and

Sam seemed to be getting on pretty well today, which Musa found encouraging.

Less encouraging was the royal fever all around.

"Still can't believe she's Stella's mom," Aisha gushed.

"I know, right?" Terra gushed back. "Massively powerful fairy. Zero ego. Boss goals. I bet it drives Stella crazy."

Next to them, Musa was only half paying attention to the fangirling. She was reading a text from Sam that said: *I'm starting to think you're actually into all this sneaking around stuff.*

Queen Luna continued her lecture of doom and gloom. "It had been years since the last one was sighted, but recently, as you all know, two have been killed."

Sam leaned his leg into Musa's. She fought a smile, and let her arm brush against his. She caught him smiling, too.

"Musa," said Terra.

Musa snapped out of her hormonal daze and realized that Terra was staring at her.

"What?" Musa's heart raced. Had Terra seen what was happening? Then—

"What is Stella going through right now? She's miserable, right?"

Musa breathed a sigh of relief. She'd do whatever Terra wanted as long as Terra didn't suspect. She called on her power, chasing the hint of strangeness in Stella's mood . . .

"Please wait," she murmured to Terra.

"Every sovereign of this realm has carried the

responsibility of defending our land from these creatures. That duty is now mine," intoned Queen Luna.

But as Musa's magic worked, Dowling passed near Stella's seat and pulled Musa's attention to her.

The words popped out of Musa's mouth. "What the hell?"

She watched carefully as Dowling walked around the room. It looked like Dowling was making sure her students were paying attention. But there was an object cupped in her hand, a glass cylinder of some kind. Musa got a read on what Dowling was feeling. Suspicion? But of whom?

Suddenly tense, Musa murmured to the others, "This assembly isn't just about the Burned Ones. Something else is up."

FIRE

Sky quietly went through the treasure trove of Rosalind-related pictures with me. He hadn't said much since I'd explained what I was up to.

"If you're gonna judge," I told him, "kindly join the rest of the student body and do so behind my back."

Sky spoke gently, "No one is judging you."

I scoffed. "I didn't know you were blind. And deaf. You should get that checked."

Sky smiled, in what seemed to be a reflex. Like he was helplessly charmed by me. Charmed by the changeling. And that won him an admission. If there was anyone I could trust with the truth, it was Sky.

"I've tried really hard to play it cool. Let people whisper when I walk by and not constantly scream that they're jerks." I paused. "But the truth? It sucks. A lot."

"People *are* jerks, Bloom. So maybe you *should* scream."

His sincerity made my heart almost hurt, as though there was a magnet in my chest wanting to draw me to him. I took a step forward, getting closer. Until Sky stepped away. I felt the loss of his closeness in my chest, too.

"I didn't know this existed," said Sky.

I looked at the photo. Rosalind stood in the center, a majestic general in total command. She was flanked by a younger Dowling, Silva, Terra's dad Professor Harvey, and a handsome man with eyes that reminded me of Sky's.

"Is that your dad?" When Sky nodded, I asked eagerly, "He knew Rosalind?"

"I knew his commander was a woman, but I'm not honestly sure I ever heard her name."

Because Dowling had suppressed any talk about Rosalind at all. I nodded and stared at the image a beat longer. Rosalind and Sky's dad had the most intense gazes of anyone in that picture. They seemed like a powerful team all by themselves.

"You look like him."

Sky imitated Silva's voice, "'And act like him and maybe one day if I work hard enough I can be half as good a warrior as he was.'" He dropped the act. "Sorry. Reflex."

"Is it weird feeling like everyone knows your dad more than you do?"

"Probably not as weird as not knowing who he is at all." Sky's voice was soft. "This place. Alfea has been my home my entire life. I can't imagine what you're going through, Bloom. How impossible it must all feel."

I could sense his understanding, and I needed it. So much. More than I should.

Once again I felt that pull in my chest, wanting to be close to him. Not to do anything wrong, but to lean against him. Share strength, share understanding. Share warmth.

"Looks like we aren't the only ones up to no good," murmured Beatrix.

Sky and I both looked up hastily. Beatrix and Riven were standing there, smug as cats who'd just found a whole coal mine full of canaries.

WATER

"Dowling is anxious," Musa murmured to the group.

"I mean," said Aisha. "Her assistant did die."

Aisha was worried, too. This was no time to be irresponsible, yet she'd let Bloom run off again. Dowling was trusting Aisha, by letting her act as her secretary. And Aisha wasn't worthy of that trust.

"But Silva's on high alert, too. Like there could be a threat anywhere. And . . ."

Musa trailed off. And Terra glanced at her, picking up why.

"And my dad?"

"He's scared. Like, über-scared."

Terra looked at her dad measuredly. Then her eyes flicked to Dowling, and the glass cylinder in Dowling's hand. Terra was no fool. She was clearly putting some clues together.

"He was making something earlier," she said slowly. "With the stones they use for the Vessel. It tracks magic. And now Ms. Dowling has . . ."

Queen Luna's voice cut across all other voices, the announcement ringing through the room like a bell.

"We're tracking at least five Burned Ones throughout Solaria. The threat is serious. And growing."

A rumble moved through the crowd. The students were suddenly dealing with the gravity of this situation. Aisha wondered if any of them felt like she did. Some part of her had been thinking of Alfea as a game she could excel at, but this wasn't a game at all.

Queen Luna continued, "There is conflict on the horizon. In the past, Alfea was the primary training ground for the fairies and Specialists who fought the Burned Ones. It appears as though it will be again. It's time for all of you to pay attention."

SPECIALIST

This was pretty great, Riven thought. Him and his best girl, his best friend and his best friend's . . . it's-complicated changeling pal. They were prowling around the East Wing in search of adventure. They were doing crime, though Riven hadn't actually worked out which crime they were doing yet. It was nice to see Sky skipping assembly and getting a little wild. Riven and Beatrix were teasing Bloom and Sky about their illicit-yet-pure relationship. Riven was happy.

"Oh. An emotional affair," Beatrix mocked the definitely not-yet lovers about their relationship. "That's actually much worse."

Sky's face darkened. That clearly touched a nerve. Riven didn't want their good time ruined, so before Sky could react, Riven pulled at a door across the room. A heavy padlock rattled. The sound caught Beatrix's attention.

"Ooh, love a locked door."

Riven lived to entertain.

"What's back here?" Riven inquired. Since they were trespassing, they should make a proper job of it.

"I don't know," Sky said stiffly. "Silva's the only one who has the key."

Bloom slowly walked over to the door, looking intrigued. See, no hard feelings about the changeling gossip. Riven was helping her with her crime.

"So how do we get in?" asked Bloom.

"We don't," said Sky. *Buzzkill.*

Bloom thought so, too. "What if there is more stuff in there? That's kinda the whole reason I came down here, and—"

"I'll ask Silva next time I see him."

Sky was trying to end the conversation, but Bloom stubbornly eyed the door. It was becoming a battle of wills. Sky, Riven reflected, really didn't know about redheads.

"Sky!" said Bloom.

"The more you say no, the more she wants it. Give in," purred Riven.

"Do we need to have a talk about consent?" Beatrix teased.

Did they need to have a talk about double entendres? Because Riven refused to give them up.

Bloom spun to face Beatrix and Riven.

"What are you two doing here again?" she demanded.

Wow. They were helping! Sky was the one getting in the way.

"Being on your side," responded Beatrix. Which was true: Riven's girlfriend was entirely correct!

"I don't need help from people who post videos mocking my friend!"

Riven winced internally, but refused to do so externally.

"Look, I know the video was extra, but *I* didn't say anything about Terra. I was a bystander." Beatrix paused, a long, considering pause. "If you're gonna be mad at one

of us, think about the douche bag who's been telling everyone you're a changeling."

Sky and Bloom both froze in their tracks. They both
looked to Riven.

And suddenly, Riven didn't feel warm, or included, or
happy at all.

"Not exactly the way I thought you'd screw me today,
Bea," he said, his voice icy. He stormed off, declining to hear
what Saint Sky had to say about the situation.

He couldn't bear to hear another word out of Beatrix. He
couldn't bear the disappointment on Sky's face. He hadn't
known Sky had any expectations of him at all. He strode
out onto the grounds, racing under the open sky, wanting
nothing but to get away.

"Seriously, you're running from me?" Sky demanded.

Riven responded to the goad. He wheeled around. "Fine.
I stand ready to hear what a jerk I am."

"You are," Sky said bluntly, and Riven restrained his
instinctive flinch. "I mean, you have always been one. But
ever since . . ."

Sky hesitated. Clearly, Saint Sky was worried about
hurting Riven's little fee-fees, even though Riven was awful
and Sky had apparently always thought so.

"Ever since, what?" Riven encouraged. "Exactly. I can't
wait to hear."

"Okay, fine. You have upped your game to new levels
since you started shagging Beatrix!"

Riven teased, "You have no idea."

Sky didn't look amused by the joke. And what did they have, if Riven wasn't making Sky laugh? Riven knew that was the only reason Sky kept him around.

"Take something seriously," said Sky.

Riven met his eyes.

"I am," he said furiously. "I like Beatrix. And she's the first person at this damn school who likes me as is."

To Beatrix, he wasn't a project, like he was for Saint Sky. Not . . . whatever he'd been to Terra. Not just a crush on a hottie, like he was for Dane. Beatrix had chosen *Riven*. She went too far sometimes. So did he. It was okay. She hadn't meant it. Riven understood. They got each other.

"And what does that make me?" Sky said quietly.

"The guy who always thinks he's better than me!" Riven waited for Sky to deny it, and knew he wouldn't. "And why are you all up in my face about this? You have a girlfriend. Maybe stop creeping on the first year while you've got the princess dangling."

"That is not what's going on!" Sky snapped.

Riven didn't want to hurt Sky. But he would, because he was awful. Because he was tired of everything being awful when he did it, and perfect when it was Sky.

"Are you sure?" Riven asked. "Because maybe that's what everyone else sees. Stella included. Which, honestly, is probably why she told me Bloom was a changeling in the first place."

MIND

Musa knew Terra was worried about her dad, and Dowling, and whatever was going on with them. She was worried, too, but it all faded away when Sam was kissing her.

"I wanna do this in public," Sam said softly, kissing her again. She loved it, but she pushed him away.

"And I like that we have a thing that's just ours. It's not just Terra. If the school knows we're a thing, I have to feel everyone's reaction to that. Good or bad, positive or negative."

Sam sighed. "I know you have to feel them, but do you have to care?"

"I wish it were that simple."

Musa wished she could explain how it was for her, how every thought about her was like a wave that could carry her away or drag her under. She didn't know how.

From the way Sam was looking at her, it seemed as though he understood how difficult it was for her to get the words out.

"No offense, but it seems like being an empath . . . kinda sucks."

"Dating an empath doesn't seem like a walk in the park, either."

Musa meant it to be a joke, but it came out sounding too real.

Sam said softly, "Worth it."

He said that now, but Musa knew someday he'd be mad at her. Terra would be mad at her. When people believed you were the girl who knew everything, they expected you to give them everything. But right now, she wanted this for herself.

FIRE

I tried the locked door again while Beatrix idly perused the pictures of Rosalind I'd pulled out.

"So," Beatrix said. "Rosalind. Let me guess. You think she was the one who swapped you out in the First World."

I didn't answer. Beatrix continued to study the pictures.

"She was fierce," commented Beatrix.

That gave me pause.

I said warily, "At the party you told me you didn't know who that was."

Beatrix gave a shrug. "You were cagey about the why, so I was cagey about the who."

"It doesn't matter, anyway. All I've found are dead ends. Except this."

I stopped, frustrated, in front of the locked door.

"So let's go in," suggested Beatrix.

"It's locked," I pointed out.

"And you're a Fire Fairy. I've seen you in class, Bloom. I know you're powerful. I guess my question is, how powerful?"

As powerful as I needed to be. I met Beatrix's dark eyes.

"If I wanted to, I could get through this door. Might light the whole school on fire in the process, but *power* isn't my problem."

Beatrix purred, "Good to know."

My phone buzzed with a text from Sky reading: *You still down there?* I considered the door, and then considered the text.

"I just don't want to put Sky in a bad spot."

"But you do want answers . . ."

What Beatrix's tone insinuated was, *Which do you want more, Sky or answers?* But of course, I wanted answers. And I couldn't want Sky.

I made a decision. I texted back: *Nah. Suite drama. Chat later.* When I was done, I looked up.

"I guess I can just fry the hinges?"

Beatrix's face said she was a little impressed by the suggestion. But then, she held up the lock. It was no longer on the door. "Or I could just pick the lock."

That hadn't occurred to me. I guessed I didn't operate on the same bad girl plane as Beatrix, but I thought I could bad girl hang.

"That's much cleaner," I admitted.

We headed through the door together.

LIGHT

A beam of white light was streaming from Stella's hands as she stood in the headmistress's office. She'd practiced this with Dowling a hundred times, but now she had her mother watching. Queen Luna's face was inscrutable.

Dowling asked, "What do you want the light to do?"

Stella gathered all her determination and her magic. Then that single beam separated into seven identical strands of white light.

"Remember your intent," Dowling said. "You have control of the light. It does not control you."

Stella moved her hand, bending the seven strands. The result was the same as putting the light through a prism. The beams formed a perfectly colored rainbow.

"Beautifully done," said Dowling in her grave voice.

Stella felt like she was glowing, even as the light disappeared.

Until her mother said, "Please tell me that was a joke." Queen Luna regarded Dowling coolly. "You instructed her to make a rainbow. To display her power."

This was her mother's private voice and face, very different from the display she'd been putting on all day. Stella wanted to shrink in on herself and disappear.

Dowling said steadily, "We discussed this at the end of last term. Rehabilitating magic is a process."

The queen snapped, "I didn't send my daughter back to

Alfea for a *process*. I sent her back because you promised to fix her after the incident with Ricki."

The mention of Ricki's name. The way her mother was talking about Stella like she was a broken toy. Both were body blows to Stella, but she tried hard not to act as though she felt the pain.

Dowling said, a thread of steel in her voice, "An incident that occurred because her previous training focused solely on results."

Stella's mother regarded Dowling with icy royal hauteur.

Dowling glanced at Stella, and her tone shifted back to entirely neutral. "When she's ready, we'll move on to stronger magic. It will take time."

"Shall I recite the list of threats we're facing while you take *time*?" Queen Luna demanded.

"Mom . . ." Stella whispered.

Queen Luna's eyes darted to Stella. Her voice didn't rise as she said to Stella, "Do not speak while I am speaking." She shifted her attention back to Dowling. "Solaria is the strongest realm in the Otherworld. She is its heir, an extension of that strength."

Stella didn't want to argue, but she was fighting for her life. "But what she's doing is working. My power's increased so much—"

Queen Luna said, in harsher tones, "Do not speak while I am speaking!"

Stella remembered what she'd done in the clearing, to

protect Bloom. She was proud of that. She could take courage from that.

"I blinded a Burned One," she announced.

Dowling said, "And did it with precision and skill, I might add."

Stella's mother asked, "And you think that is power?"

The queen's eyes flared a sudden scorching yellow. The light seemed to capture the room, and her mother vanished away. Stella turned to see Dowling had vanished as well.

Stella's breath tightened. She closed her eyes. When she opened them, she was no longer in the office, she was now in the dark. All alone. Feeling as small and scared as she had as a child. She knew it wasn't real, but she was still terrified.

She spoke, very quietly. Begging. "Please stop."

She squeezed her eyes shut. Suddenly, thankfully, she was back in the headmistress's office where she felt safe.

Her mother stepped directly in front of Stella. She wasn't a creature made of sunshine any longer. She was a being of ice and fire, dazzling and terribly cold.

"When you control light," said Queen Luna, "you control what people see. And despite what anyone says matters in this life, appearances are everything."

Stella couldn't stop trembling. Her mother whipped around and switched her focus to Dowling.

"You know that better than anyone, Farah. Especially given my efforts to help you maintain appearances."

"Yes, we've both done a great deal to preserve Solaria's reputation," Dowling admitted.

Stella had no idea what that meant, but she could tell there was more between her mother and the headmistress than she had ever realized. Maybe Dowling wasn't on her side. Maybe they were both against her.

"Stella," Dowling said crisply, "you did excellent work. You're dismissed."

Stella stumbled past Aisha as she went out. Aisha was fumbling in her desk for something. Stella could only hope Aisha wouldn't notice how shaken Stella was.

EARTH

Terra caught her dad swearing at the glass cylinder full of Vessel Stones in the greenhouse.

"Did something go wrong with your project? I can help," she offered instantly. "Just—"

"This is not a good time," her father snapped.

Terra recoiled. Her father never spoke to her like that, and she saw the regret on his face at once.

"I'm sorry, love," her dad said, using his *you're-my-little-girl* voice. "But I'm okay. Thank you, though."

She didn't feel reassured at all.

"If there was something going on, you'd tell me, right?" Terra asked desperately.

"Of course I would," her father told her.

She stared at him, trying to hide her heartbreak. Then she ran back as fast as she could to the Winx suite, where she found Aisha and Musa.

She told them, "He lied to my face. Why are they all lying to us?"

"Maybe they had to. Queen Luna's . . ." Aisha looked troubled, as if she knew something they didn't know. "She seems kinda big on secrets."

Musa gave Aisha a particularly sharp glance.

Aisha continued, "Whatever's going on, I'm sure they think what they're doing is right."

Musa said grimly, "They always do."

"Then say 'I can't tell you, Terra.' Don't lie to me!"

Terra was on the point of wringing her hands. Musa looked away, as though feeling bad for some reason. Aisha, as usual, tried to problem solve.

"He made Ms. Dowling a concoction with Vessel Stones, right? And the point of Vessel Stones is to read magic, which is what they were doing at the assembly."

They all looked at one another. Doing the math.

Aisha continued, "So, dead body. Worried adults . . ."

"What if they think a fairy killed Callum?" Musa asked.

Aisha said, "A fairy in that assembly."

The teachers were searching the student body for a murder suspect.

"They were still on edge after," said Musa, and Terra nodded, thinking of her dad fiddling with the cylinder in the greenhouse. "So they clearly didn't find them."

The door banged open and Sky blew into the room, totally interrupting their detective work.

"Is Bloom here?"

Aisha ignored his question and lobbed one of her own. "Did Silva tell you? What was happening today? He must have."

Sky frowned. "Is this the suite drama Bloom was talking about?"

"Uh," said Musa. "There's no suite drama."

Sky frowned. "Okay, I'm so lost right now."

Terra knew how it felt to be lost. Besides, she was done with secrets, and she trusted Sky. He was good to Riven. He'd be good to anyone.

So she spoke up. "Dowling's assistant died, and the faculty thinks a fairy did it, and they were using the assembly to find that fairy, but they didn't because he or she clearly wasn't there, and now we don't believe in or trust literally anyone—"

Sky swore. "Beatrix."

For a moment Terra was simply puzzled. Sky had come here looking for Bloom. What did Riven's cool-nerd girlfriend have to do with Bloom?

FIRE

Inside the no-longer-locked room, there were maps strewn all around. Military relics rested in corners. There were boxes of files. And settled over everything was the dust of a room that hadn't been opened in years.

In the center on the floor was a circle covered with sand, which was just weird.

"I knew Alfea had a military past, but it's still a school. This place? It's like a . . . war room," I said, disturbed.

Beatrix did something, I wasn't sure what. Suddenly, the texture of the sand seemed to change, flowing into lines and circles. I looked down to see a map of the Otherworld forming in the center of the room.

"It's not like a war room. It *is* a war room. A place where powerful, shady people decide who lives and who dies."

I didn't know what to do with that, so I headed for the files. What I needed was solid evidence.

Beatrix just watched as I sifted through boxes. Soon enough I had papers laid out on top of the cabinets. I was putting together a timeline.

"It looks like Rosalind was barely at the school in 2004."

"No duh," said Beatrix. "She was leading the crusade against the Burned Ones."

"I need to find out where she was in December. That's when I was born."

That seemed to interest Beatrix, though I had no idea why the date of my birth was of any concern to her. I was more occupied by a discovery I'd just made among the boxes.

"I think this might be Rosalind's diary from that year."

My phone buzzed again. Then again. And again.

"That's mildly annoying," remarked Beatrix.

I pulled out my phone, half glancing at the messages. Not really seeing them.

"The endless suite group text. I'll deal with it later."

I put my phone on the table and brought the diary to one of the shelves. Trying to piece things together.

Beatrix's gaze didn't leave my phone as it buzzed again. It must be annoying her.

I tried to get her to focus on the important stuff. "It looks like Rosalind was in a place called Aster Dell."

Beatrix sidled closer to my phone. Just then, it stopped buzzing entirely. That was great.

I continued, excited, "What if my birth parents weren't students? What if they're from this Aster Dell place?"

Beatrix looked at me, her tone pleasant. "Did you say Aster Dell?"

"Yeah. Can you make that map thing work again? Maybe I can find it."

A smile crept over Beatrix's face. "No need. I actually know where that is. Wanna go?"

I'd wanted answers, but suddenly being offered them made me feel dizzy. "What? Now?"

"It's a few hours from here," tempted Beatrix.

I hesitated, not sure how to respond.

Beatrix pursued, "You ditched the assembly, lied to Sky, and broke into a secret war room. Now you're gonna give up?"

She had a point. But I couldn't help but imagine how appalled Aisha would be if she knew what I was doing. So maybe I shouldn't do it.

"I'm saying it's getting late, and maybe I don't want to ditch school with somebody I barely know."

"You know that I helped you get further than anyone else has. And that I'm also ditching school with somebody I barely know."

Another fine point well made. But still, I trusted Aisha more than Beatrix, and Aisha's voice in my head said no.

Beatrix's voice, out loud, went soft and insinuating. "But maybe Ms. Dowling will spill her guts now that you found the room she keeps under lock and key. To keep people from knowing things."

I knew Ms. Dowling too well by now. She would keep her secrets. She'd never tell me anything.

I took a deep breath and a leap of faith. "How do we get there?"

SPECIALIST

Riven was lying on his bed, scrolling through his phone, when Sky barged in demanding to know where Beatrix was. Riven couldn't believe Sky's attitude. What, Sky needed three women now?

"Beatrix is not surgically attached to me. So the answer is, I don't know. Why do you need her?"

"I'm looking for Bloom!" Sky said. Much too loudly.

Oh my God. C'mon, Sky, Riven wanted to live.

Riven tried to signal Sky to shut up with his eyebrows and also all the force of his mind, but Sky missed it completely and continued his suicidal ranting.

"No one's heard from her, and Beatrix was the last person I know who was with her—"

The bathroom door opened, and Stella stepped out. Riven had tried to signal Sky she was listening!

Stella was a tower of blonde fury. "Seriously? I've sent you, like, twenty texts, and you're running around looking for Bloom?"

Looked like it was blinding o'clock!

"Yeah, have fun with this," Riven announced.

Riven tossed Sky an *I-told-you-so* look as he scrambled up and walked out of the room, closing the door on their drama. He had his own girlfriend to find.

EARTH

Terra marched with Aisha and Musa to the headmistress's office, where they faced down Dowling. And Terra's father.

Aisha, the levelheaded one, explained their suspicions of Beatrix, and how she'd been alone with Bloom in the East Wing.

Terra couldn't believe Dowling was actually trying to maintain her high ground. "And why was Bloom down there?"

"That's what's important to you?" Musa demanded.

"What matters is that Beatrix wasn't at the assembly," Aisha said with quiet force.

Dowling and Harvey shared a look, still keeping tight-lipped. Terra couldn't control herself for a moment longer. Everybody had to stop with the secrets, or someone was going to get hurt.

"Oh my God. We know! That somebody killed Callum. That it was a fairy. And we know you were using the assembly to find out who. So can you just drop this crap?"

Her dad began, "Terra—"

"No! You don't get to shush me. And if something happens to Bloom because you kept this from us . . ."

Musa put her hand out and laid it gently on Terra's arm. Aw, that was so nice. Right, they were the Winx Club, and they were going to stick together and solve this. Terra nodded at her sweet roommate and reined it in.

"We haven't heard from Bloom in hours. And nobody's seen Beatrix," Aisha said urgently.

They were interrupted by Mr. Silva bursting through the door, almost vibrating with what was obviously vital news. He checked himself, giving the Winx Club a doubtful look. Terra felt ready to explode with indignation again. No more keeping stuff from them!

But Dowling nodded. "They know."

Silva said crisply, "One of the Queen's guards was knocked out. His SUV is gone."

Terra exchanged glances with the others, suddenly terrified. Beatrix was knocking out guards and stealing SUVs? Where was she going? Where was she taking Bloom?

Suddenly, Terra didn't feel so sure she and her suitemates could handle this. She felt like a scared kid, wanting to be told everything would be all right.

But not if it was a lie.

"We'll find her," Dowling said, and Terra clung to the authoritative sound of her voice. "I promise."

LIGHT

Stella moved across the room toward Sky. "I need you."

For the first time, the words didn't seem to have any effect on Sky. He looked at her as if he didn't know her and her problems were no concern of his.

"Bloom is missing," he said, as if that was the most important thing in his world. "I don't know if she's in danger or just hiding, but whichever it is, it can probably be traced back to everyone knowing she's a changeling. Thanks to you."

Guilt slashed through her, and Stella was struck speechless. She had no idea what to say, because there was no good excuse for what she'd done, and Sky clearly wouldn't accept a bad one.

He was always the protector, but now he wasn't protecting her. He saw her as someone others needed to be defended from. If everyone thought about her that way, even Sky, maybe they were right.

Finally, Stella faltered. "I didn't mean to hurt her—"

Sky cut her off. "You tell me you don't want to be like your mother. But all I see is someone who treats other people exactly the way Luna treats you."

It was like a slap in the face. But Sky wasn't finished.

"I'm done with this, Stel," he announced. "Full done. Goodbye."

Sky moved to the door. She kept thinking he would turn around, see how upset she was, relent and put his arms around her, as he always had before. But he walked out, leaving Stella utterly alone.

FIRE

As we pulled up on the bluff, I was still wondering where Beatrix had gotten the SUV. Maybe she'd sweet-talked someone into letting her borrow it.

My wondering was interrupted as I got out of the car and stared around at the wide-open space.

"Aster Dell is a town, right? Are you sure this is the right place?"

Beatrix said, "I'm positive."

We walked a few steps, which was when the entire land-scape came into view. We were on top of a steep mountain, with gorse yellow on the granite and the fields so far below they looked fuzzy, like green mist. I was momentarily stunned, but I knew I had to keep investigating. I needed to get a sense of where I was. Had I been born here?

Beatrix headed up the peak, taking a position above me.

"How could a town be marked on a map on the side of a mountain?" I asked.

As I continued my wandering, I stepped on something and it cracked. I looked down at it. Then I knelt to get a better look at what.

It was part of a skull. My stomach hollowed out, sick, as I suddenly realized something else was happening here.

"What the hell is this place?"

Above me, Beatrix's eyes glowed gray. And Beatrix tightened her hands into fists at her sides. Calling on her magic.

I saw the electricity crackling around Beatrix's hands. Beatrix's eyes were glowing ever brighter. And slowly, Beatrix lifted her hands from her sides. Calling up a storm.

"What are you *doing*?"

"You're not the only powerful fairy at Alfea."

Alarmed, I summoned wisps of flame from my hands. But it was too late. Beatrix raised both hands, and from the clouds, lightning struck.

Directly at me.

The world went brilliant white. I thought that white would be the last thing I ever saw, but then the brilliance dissipated like mist.

Beatrix said, "Welcome to Aster Dell."

I turned, stunned. Where there had been empty mountainside, there was now a settlement in ruins. Everywhere I looked were crumbled walls or sunken roofs, destroyed by some unforgiving force.

Beatrix continued, "It was a beautiful place. Full of people trying to live their lives. Until one winter, when Burned Ones surrounded the settlement. And a military unit from Alfea decided that destroying the creatures was more important than the lives of the innocent people here."

I tottered a few steps toward the ruins. "This isn't real. You're making this happen somehow."

"I'm simply piercing the magic veil that Queen Luna placed to hide the atrocity that happened here. Think about that: The leader of our realm tried to erase a war crime."

Beatrix gazed at me, and I saw more sincerity than I

could have ever imagined was possible on that face. Beatrix walked over to me and stared at Aster Dell.

"I was born here. And my family died here. On December 10, 2004. Two days before your First World birthday."

I realized now why she'd cared about my birth date. "You . . . you think my family was killed here."

"Not think," said Beatrix. "Know. Because everyone here died. Except me. And you."

"I don't understand. How could you know that?"

"Because I saw it. Saw the death. The bodies. But someone scooped me up. Carried me away. But I saw them as we ran. Walking through the carnage like conquering heroes."

I wasn't sure I wanted to know the answer, but I asked. "Who did you see?"

Beatrix pronounced the names as if passing judgment. "Dowling. Silva. Harvey."

No. That didn't make sense.

"That's . . . you were a baby. How do you know what you saw was real? That you remember the truth?"

Beatrix said intensely, "Because the woman who saved me used her magic to burn the memory into my mind."

I knew now who Beatrix was talking about. Because the same thing had happened to me.

"Rosalind . . ." I whispered. "She rescued you."

"She rescued *us*," Beatrix corrected. "She had a crisis of conscience. Couldn't bring herself to destroy a village, no matter how many Burned Ones they could kill in the process. But her most trusted allies turned on her. They staged a coup and carried out the mission."

My head was reeling. I couldn't help but think of the first time I ever saw Dowling, surrounded by light. How much hope I had, how much I wanted to trust her.

"I know they've lied to me. But they're not . . . monsters."

Beatrix turned to me. I could hear the hatred behind every word she hissed. "Then why are they covering it up?"

I had no answers for that. The magic veil the lightning had struck away slowly began to return, obscuring the settlement, leaving only the mountainside, and the emptiness of devastation and confusion.

I shook my head, and made for the SUV. I wanted to go back to Alfea. I wanted to ask Dowling about all this myself. I still didn't know what to believe, and Beatrix kept pushing me.

"Why would I make up a story about our teachers being murderers?" Beatrix demanded as we drove. "Where's the gain in that?"

"I don't know. I don't know what to make of any of this. I'm supposed to just trust you? Trust a memory of some dead fairy . . ."

I trailed off. If I doubted Beatrix's memory of Rosalind, I had to doubt my own. Then I had no answers at all.

"You shouldn't trust me until I've proven myself trustworthy. That's what the faculty expects. And I'm nothing like them. What you need are answers."

I wanted answers so desperately. Beatrix was saying all the right things, but that was why I didn't trust her offer. She was promising too much.

"From a woman who died and left nothing but cryptic messages and half-truths. We need more," I told her.

Beatrix began to smile, slowly. "And we'll get it. Because Rosalind's alive."

It felt like being struck by lightning all over again.

"Dowling told me she was dead!"

"Dowling imprisoned her." Beatrix looked very pleased with herself. "I'm at Alfea to break her out."

But before she could tell me anything else, a loud pop interrupted our conversation. The car swerved, startling both of us. Then Beatrix steadied it.

"Do we have a flat?" I asked.

There were three quick, soft sounds outside. One by one, I felt the other three tires go.

"Nope," said Beatrix.

She slammed on the brakes. Both of us looked around, wondering what the hell happened. We both jumped as our eyes found Specialist Headmaster Silva.

He was armed with a bow, standing in the middle of the road. I couldn't help but think of Beatrix's story of him raining down destruction on Aster Dell.

Clearly, Beatrix was thinking the same thing I was. She swore, leaped out of the car, and made a break for it. But Beatrix hardly got more than a few steps before the asphalt road turned to black liquid beneath her, and her legs became tangled in the tar. She was trapped.

Desperate, I looked to her right and found Professor Harvey, his eyes a vivid green. Terra's gentle dad was doing this to a student.

In his hand there was a glass cylinder full of stones. As he drew nearer to Beatrix, the stones inside lit up.

Dowling walked toward Beatrix, face set as though the brilliantly lit stones had confirmed something for her. Beatrix's hands were still free, and I could see her frantically trying to call up her magic.

"Not today," Dowling snapped.

Dowling slapped strangely carved metal bracelets on Beatrix's wrists. Beatrix's lightning crackled for a second, and then disappeared as the metal edges of the bracelets cut into Beatrix's skin like teeth.

Bleeding, struggling, Beatrix called out to Dowling, "What are these things? Why can't I . . .? It *hurts*."

I overcame my frozen horror and scrambled out of the truck, horrified by the pain Beatrix was in.

"Stop it!" I screamed.

I tried to run to Beatrix, but Silva grabbed me from behind. I struggled, but I couldn't break free from his unyielding grip.

Silva, the man Sky loved like a father, panted harshly in my ear, "This doesn't concern you."

EARTH

Terra was standing with Aisha and Musa at the entrance of Alfea with the rest of the students, in an anxious crowd whispering about murder and secrets.

Then the SUV pulled up, and Terra's dad and Bloom climbed out. Bloom, pale and shaken, but safe and well. Terra, Aisha, and Musa dashed forward as one.

Bloom moved sharply away from Terra's dad and into their arms. Terra ignored her father as she hugged Bloom tight, even though she saw the flash of pain on his face as he moved away. He shouldn't have lied to her if he wanted a hug.

Bloom was trembling in Terra's arms.

"We were so worried about you," murmured Aisha.

Musa confirmed, "Legit freaking out."

"What did Beatrix do to you?" Terra demanded.

In a strange tight voice Bloom replied, "She didn't do anything. She's not some *monster.*"

That was surprising for everyone, given the facts. Bloom must not know.

"Bloom," said Terra. "She *killed* Callum."

"Who told you that?"

Musa blinked. "Dowling. Silva. Harvey."

If the Vessel Stones had lit for Beatrix, it proved she'd killed Callum. Terra expected Bloom to be instantly horrified, but Bloom's face only went more strained.

"They have proof?" she asked.

Aisha's face grew even more worried. "Bloom, why would they say it if it wasn't true?"

"You never know why people really do things," Bloom said distantly.

That made everyone feel lousy, Terra included. All this time, worried sick about Bloom, and she was acting as though Beatrix was her only friend, cruelly ripped away from her.

"Maybe we should just get some rest," Aisha suggested.

Yes! Aisha was so right. Bloom must be in shock. She needed a blanket. Terra would find a blanket.

Only Bloom's gaze had left them, and was locked on Sky as he approached.

"You guys go," she murmured, and she moved toward Sky, as though they were two magnets snapping together.

Terra cut her eyes politely away from whatever was going on there. She hoped Stella was nowhere nearby to see this. Bloom had enough going on without getting blinded tonight.

Whispers rose from the crowd about murder, and Callum, and Beatrix, and a spy in their midst.

Riven was standing off to the side in the dark, alone and looking utterly gutted. As Beatrix was led away, Terra saw Dane walk up to him.

"What the hell happened?" Dane demanded in a voice gone thin with anguish.

Dane must have really liked Beatrix, Terra thought with a

distant pang. But she was already looking away from Dane, back toward Riven.

Riven's response to Dane's plea was to push Dane away in an explosive fit of anger. She didn't know what he was angry at, but she suspected it was at himself as much as at Beatrix. At everything.

Dane stumbled back, staring at Riven in shock, but Terra thought she understood.

She knew what it was like to be betrayed. By Dane, and by her dad. Terra could almost feel sorry. Even for Riven.

FIRE

I moved toward Sky, whose handsome face was twisted in distress.

"I'm sorry," he said as soon as I was near. "I left you alone with her. I shouldn't have. She—"

I knew his concern was genuine, but I couldn't bear another round of hearing Beatrix was a monster.

"She didn't kidnap me, Sky. I'm okay. I promise."

I avoided his eyes, but he ducked his head and made me meet his gaze. Once I did, I felt the first relief I'd experienced since seeing Aster Dell.

"Whatever happened out there . . . you can tell me," he said gently.

There was a moment of silence and connection between us. I wanted to open up to him. Maybe I could.

Then out of the corner of my eye I saw Dowling and Silva, leading Beatrix away. I went stiff, and he saw it.

"When you're ready," he assured me. "I'm just happy you're back."

Sky pulled me into a hug, seemingly careless of who saw us. I could feel his relief, like his strong arms, engulfing me. I felt the same. I wanted to cling to him and whisper everything I'd learned in his ear.

Then Silva's voice commanded, "Sky."

And Sky let me go. He headed off toward Silva, the man who commanded his loyalty, and Beatrix, the prisoner who might have the answers I sought. The answers that would lead me home.

MIND

As Musa walked back to the Winx suite with Terra and Aisha, Terra's mood was darkening with every step until Musa felt as though they were under a black cloud indoors. It took Musa about twenty paces to snap.

"Terra," Musa asked desperately, "can you please just let it out? You're killing me right now."

Terra took a deep breath. "My dad lied to me today.

Legit lied, and when I called him on it, he tried to act like it was for my own good. They all did."

Aisha, looking troubled, said, "They had good intentions."

Terra's voice was steely. "They can justify it all they want, but you don't lie to people you care about. Not if they matter."

Musa's magic flared with guilt as Terra unintentionally called her out. And in the moment, it felt like there was only one thing to do.

Musa gulped. "I have to tell you something."

Aisha and Terra halted. Musa didn't dare glance up and see Terra's face. She only let the words spill out.

"A while ago I met this guy and I like him, like, a lot, but I didn't know how you'd react if I told you, so I didn't tell you, and now it's been weeks and . . . I'm dating your brother."

From Aisha, there was only surprise that Musa had fessed up. Musa finally looked at Terra, dreading the onslaught of feelings she was about to experience.

But then Terra laughed out loud. At length.

"Thank you for telling me the truth," Terra said eventually, voice weak from giggling. "I really needed that. Even if you do have horrible taste. Sam is . . ."

Musa was starting to feel insulted on her man's behalf.

"Objectively attractive!"

Terra's eyes danced. "The spitting image of my dad at his age. And I think his hair went at eighteen? Maybe nineteen? Bald teenagers. Very cool. Have fun with that."

All three of them laughed, and for a moment, all their

stress was released. Even though, deep down, Musa thought they all sensed that today was only the beginning of something bigger than they could imagine.

Then Musa's eye caught movement, headed away from their suite. She tapped the other girls on their arms as they all turned to look at the guards carrying fancy suitcases.

They ran up to the Winx suite, but Stella's stuff was already gone.

LIGHT

Stella sat quietly in the Rolls-Royce, waiting to leave.

"This school has taken a turn since I attended," her mother observed. "Back home, I can teach you everything you need to know."

It was more threat than promise. Stella suppressed a shudder. Her whole body yearned back toward the warm familiarity of the Winx suite and the girls she'd been annoyed to be stuck with. She didn't let herself move a muscle.

In a low resentful voice, Stella muttered, "You could've let me say goodbye to my friends."

Her mother sounded calm and amused. The queen, always in control.

"They're not your friends, Stella. If they were, they'd be here."

FIRE

I found Dowling at her desk, signing forms. Without looking up, she said, "Don't lurk."

I hesitated, and then stepped through the doorway of the office. Dowling stopped her work and looked up.

"May I help you?" she asked politely, as though it was just another ordinary day.

A military team, Beatrix had called Silva and Dowling and Professor Harvey. A strike force that had destroyed Aster Dell. That was what they'd looked like when they'd brought her down.

I asked a question of my own. "What were those . . . bracelets?"

"Runic limiters. They prevent a fairy from using her magic."

"They're barbaric," I said flatly. "They tore her skin open."

Dowling was, obviously, not surprised by this information. Her stoicism was chilling. She didn't betray the slightest sense of guilt. She wasn't backing down, but I wouldn't, either.

"You're certain you're uninjured?" Dowling inquired.

"I'm fine. She didn't hurt me."

"Still, you were with Beatrix for quite a while. What did you two talk about all that time?"

I thought about it a long, hard moment, and then I shrugged.

"Boys. Clothes. Who could drive faster. It was a joyride, Ms. Dowling. That's all."

Dowling studied me. I couldn't tell if she bought it or not.

At last, she said, "Well, perhaps next time you'll choose your company more wisely."

I held Dowling's gaze and told her, "You can count on it."

SPECIALIST

Sky watched Silva close the cell door on a girl in obvious pain. Who was also a murderer, and might have intended harm to Bloom. He wished he knew what to do. He feared he'd already done wrong.

As he and Silva walked away from Beatrix's jail and down a hallway toward the castle courtyard, Sky said, "After the Specialist party, you told me, 'Stick close to Bloom. We'd like to know more about her.' That's not the same as, 'Bloom may be in danger from a killer.'"

Silva was tight-lipped. Sky tried not to let himself be overcome by frustration, but Silva knew him too well.

"What you're doing is important, Sky. You have to trust me."

"I do," said Sky. "You know I do."

He trusted Silva with his life. That was different from trusting Silva with Bloom's life.

Sky lifted his chin. "But I need to know the whole truth."

"One of the lessons you're at this school to learn is that sometimes a soldier just has to take orders."

Silva's tone lost even the barest hint of softness as he switched to a voice of command.

"So I will reiterate them to you. You are to gain Bloom's trust. Learn everything you can, including what happened on that road trip. And then you are to tell me. That is where your loyalty lies, Sky. To me. To Alfea. And no one else."

FAIRY TALE #5

Through all the lying days of my youth
I swayed my leaves and flowers in the sun;
Now may I wither into the truth.
—*W. B. Yeats*

FIRE

The towers of the East Wing were like twin blades waiting for me in the dark. There were two Specialists guarding Beatrix's prison, the faces of teenage boys I knew turned suddenly grim, soldiers who would cut down anyone who dared to enter. Soldiers who seemed ever so slightly panicked by the situation they found themselves in. I knew how that felt.

I watched from the shadows. Dowling and Silva were in there, interrogating Beatrix. The other students whispered that they tortured her every night. That our headmistress was obsessed by the wish for revenge.

Dowling and Silva left the East Wing as I kept watch. Dowling's face was cool. She didn't look like a woman obsessed by revenge. But she didn't look like a woman satisfied by the answers she'd received, either.

I bet Beatrix was being stubborn.

Beatrix had offered *me* answers. And I wanted them badly.

I jotted notes in my phone: *12:15. Dowling and Silva.* Then, surveillance completed for the night, I put my phone away and turned to head off when a silhouette loomed out of the darkness and came at me.

Caught.

But then the figure emerged from the shadows, and I saw Dane in his Specialist uniform, clearly on guard duty. Just like the other guards, he looked suddenly older.

"Late-night stroll?" Dane asked.

"Needed some air," I claimed.

"This particular air? The air outside the place they've been holding Beatrix? I know what you're doing."

I gave a sharp, unconvincing laugh and started to walk away.

"You don't know anything."

"You want to talk to her, don't you?" Dane asked.

Just walk, Bloom, I told myself.

Then he called after me, "I can help you."

That stopped me in my tracks. I turned back to face him.

216

"My guard shift is tomorrow night. Maybe you'll need air then, too."

Dane walked away, leaving me to look back at the East Wing. Answers were waiting there, with Beatrix.

But to get to tomorrow night, I had to get through tomorrow.

FIRE

The walls of the hedge maze were tall and green around me and Sky, walls so high there was nothing but green around me and blue above.

Until a Burned One burst into view, and began a deadly charge to where we stood, together at the end of a long arm of the maze. Side by side. Sky wielded his sword, and I focused my magic, as the Burned One drew near.

I felt my magic rise. The Burned One burst into flame.

It didn't stop. It didn't falter, but came at us like a fireball on legs. Sky tried to parry the blows its fiery fists rained down.

Just as the Burned One was about to score a hit, a whistle blew, and the creature vanished into dust. A crystal, every facet glittering with magic, fell onto the ground where the monster once was.

I tried to regroup, and helped a frustrated Sky to his feet. As he rose, I noticed a cut on his face.

"You're bleeding," I murmured.

"Bad?"

"Nah. Want me to . . .?"

I waved my fingers with a smile. He nodded, so I laid my fingertips gently against his cheek. My magic flared inside me as I touched him, like a tiny spark coming alight, and the wound closed as I used my magic to cauterize it into a scar that vanished like a whisper.

I breathed, "Good as new."

We stood looking at each other for a moment that went on for a little too long. It seemed like Stella and Sky had broken up, but maybe that was just because her mom had taken her away. I still didn't want to get in the middle of a complicated situation. I dropped my hand and turned to where the Burned One used to be. I picked up the crystal.

"I wish they would just tell us how to fight these things."

I wished they'd tell us a lot of things.

"I think that's part of the fun," remarked Sky. "Us not knowing."

"Very on brand for Alfea faculty," I said bitterly.

Sky was a soldier on task, looking around, and didn't seem to register my bitterness.

"Professor Harvey?" he asked. "Can we go again?"

Now we were moving toward the exit of the maze, and Terra's dad moved across the field toward us. "Every failure brings you one step closer to success."

He should make fortune cookies.

I gave him a chipper smile. "A good lesson, Professor. As usual."

Sky gave me a sidelong glance, but I firmly ignored him. Professor Harvey picked up the crystal, looking excited to share the wonder of knowledge.

"Fire magic is effective, if wielded properly. Inside each Burned One is a magical core called a Cinder. With time and finesse, your magic can extinguish it and destroy it."

"Got it," I said.

I could do this on my own. All I needed was to learn more.

As though he could hear my thoughts, Professor Harvey said, "The key is mutual trust. You must trust your Specialist to hold the Burned One off while you channel controlled magic. And you must trust your fairy to get the job done."

When Harvey walked away, I joked: "I guess that's the question, then . . . Can I trust you?"

I meant to be playful, but Sky stared across the field at the distant figure of Silva. Sometimes I got the sense Sky was keeping secrets from me.

Sky said, "Kinda want to ask you the same thing."

He might be deflecting, but he was right. I was keeping things from him, too.

Mutual trust? Not so much.

"*A good lesson, Professor, as usual,*" Sky said in a squeaky voice that definitely didn't sound like me. "Who was that girl?"

"After my trip with Beatrix, they're all still watching me like a hawk."

That was the truth, as far as it went.

When we left the maze completely behind us, the massive training day was spread out like a feast in front of the castle. I could see Dowling and Silva walking by pairings of fairies and Specialists, sparring with assistants provided for the day. Water Fairies drew water from the lake. Earth Fairies snagged them with vines. Fire Fairies blasted them with flames.

I glanced covertly at Dowling. She already had her eyes fixed on me. Aisha and Musa were walking with Dowling, industriously taking notes like good little helpers. Musa had definitely never struck me as the helper type. Aisha made an *I-hate-this* face at me, and I smiled back at her.

The same bright, false smile I'd given Professor Harvey. Only Sky had seen through the smile. Sky knew me well enough for that. It seemed like I could always find comfort with Sky.

"I have to show them I'm not one of her . . . evil . . . hench-women," I explained to him.

Sky cracked a smile. "Because Beatrix is a Bond villain?"

I had regrets. "A bad choice of words."

"Are you gonna help her carve her name on the moon with a laser?" Sky asked.

"Shut up," I told him. He was too cute.

Sky grinned like he knew it. "Steal the Eiffel Tower?"

"Can we go again, please?" I yelled.

Grinning together, Sky and I headed back toward the training maze.

Mutual trust? Maybe someday.

MIND

Musa trudged through the field of combat, alongside Aisha and Headmistress Dowling. Aisha eyed her clipboard in a highly professional manner.

"That'll be attempt five for Sky and Bloom," Aisha reported.

Dowling addressed Musa. "And?"

Musa said wearily, "He's slightly winded. She's . . . frustrated? But neither of them are fatigued."

"Good," said Dowling.

The headmistress looked to Aisha, who quickly made a note. Musa was fatigued herself. And conflicted. And jealous of the others, whose task was so comparatively simple.

"I know they know that I'm reading them, but it still feels invasive. Can't I use my magic against an actual enemy?"

"Not all fairy magic is suited to combat roles," Dowling said repressively. "Support is equally, if not more, important. Your magic can help us assess fragile mental states or uncover hidden enemies."

Her voice was pointed. Musa exchanged a quick look of alarm with Aisha. Was Dowling talking about Bloom?

Swiftly, Aisha put in, "Like Beatrix?"

Dowling hesitated. "Exactly."

Musa chanced directing a little of her magic at Ms. Dowling. "How is she, by the way? Have you found out why she . . . killed Callum?"

Dowling's walls were higher than the hedge walls in the maze.

"Let's keep focused," their headmistress said crisply. "Who is next?"

EARTH

Terra staggered toward the Bastion benches, barely able to walk after her training session. Her path to rest was cut off by her own father.

"You doing all right there, love?"

Terra didn't dignify that with a response.

"I made Popsicles earlier, if you—"

Terra nodded curtly. She wasn't taking Popsicle bribes to forgive him for lying to her.

"I'm fine . . . but thank you."

Her dad nodded, message received, and left her alone.

At last, Terra reached the benches and grabbed her water bottle. She was so hot and thirsty, and she felt super gross. She was sure her face was the color of an overripe tomato, the kind of tomato that made everyone wonder how a tomato got in such an awful state.

Lean, muscular, and barely looking phased, a Specialist named Kat grabbed up her bag from next to Terra. Terra hated her deeply.

"That vine restraint move's not half bad, Ter."

Actually, maybe Kat was okay. Maybe she was awesome, and they would be friends.

"Yeah," Terra said eagerly, even as she gulped water. "It's all about . . . tensile strength . . . of the cellulose . . ."

Kat gave her a blank stare and veered away from the benches.

Clearly, Kat did not care about tensile strength. Nobody did. Terra was so dumb. She should know better than to talk like this by now.

Terra closed her eyes, willing herself to cool down.

When she opened them, Riven was sitting next to her. Terra almost jumped out of her skin. Had Riven not seen her there? Terra had been told she wasn't difficult to spot.

Riven looked absolutely wrecked, his usual swagger nowhere to be found. His eyes were all hollowed out from lack of sleep. He seemed to have lost his hairbrush, and his hair resembled a gorse thicket run entirely wild and in need of urgent pruning.

As Terra studied Riven's tired, sad face, she accidentally made eye contact. Terra swiftly looked away and sprang up to gather her stuff. Riven stared straight ahead.

"Tensile strength?" said Riven quietly. "Hot."

He offered her a tiny smile, gone as soon as seen.

"She's right, you know. You're a force out there."

Terra was astonished. Were these compliments? Was Riven feeling well?

But one look at him would tell anyone he wasn't.

"You, too," she told him softly.

Riven dismissed that with a swear. "I was crap. After two attempts with me, Aisha quit combat and switched to support."

It was totally natural Riven wasn't at his best after all the traumatic events. He was good normally, Terra considered. Maybe not as good as Sky *yet*, but he had potential.

Riven must be lonely. Terra was a little lonely with Stella gone, their Winx Club missing a key member, and Stella had just gone away with her mom. Stella wasn't a murderer.

"It's been a weird week," she reassured him. "You . . . I'm sorry. I know you and Beatrix were close. This must be really hard."

Riven swallowed and glanced up at her. This time Terra didn't look away. His eyes held hers and a true smile began to curve his mouth, brightening his face immeasurably. She thought he might be about to say something important, then Dane walked over and interrupted them. God, if only Terra could hit Dane's beautiful face with a melon.

"Sweet moves, Riv," Dane sneered. "I've never seen somebody die so many different ways so quickly. You should go out for *Alfea's Got Talent*."

Riven shook his head, trying to ignore Dane. Terra thought that was the right attitude to take!

Dane scoffed and walked off, but the damage was done. Riven's shoulders had slumped. He wasn't smiling anymore.

"Um . . ." Terra said to Riven. "What was that?"

She'd thought Dane and Riven were friends. Of course, she'd once thought Dane was sweet.

Riven said tiredly, "*That* was a sick burn from the first-year monster I created. Or Beatrix created. He's still got a thing for her. Like a weird gay thing?"

Wait, gay? thought Terra. She'd thought the Instagram story was just cool-fairy debauchery. Oh no, Riven had thought Dane liked *him?* No wonder Riven had taken to Dane. Riven liked it when people liked him. And it hardly ever happened, because Riven was the worst.

He'd thought Dane liked him, and of course he'd believed his girlfriend liked him. And he'd been wrong on both counts. *Oh, Riven.*

"Is he even gay? I don't know anything anymore."

Riven gave a defeated sigh, and then looked wearily around as though wondering where he was. Slowly he got up and trudged away.

It would have been the action of a maniac to rush after the worst person in Alfea and get him a blanket and that deeply needed hairbrush.

So Terra just watched Riven go. For no good reason at all, she felt her heart break a little.

MIND

All was peaceful in Musa and Terra's room. Well, as peaceful as it ever got.

"In your mind, I just sit on my bed listening to nineties

225

grunge, half doing runes homework, and sexting your brother, don't I?" Musa asked, hiding her phone.

Terra considered the matter, then visibly decided she didn't want to consider the matter, and then grabbed another plant pot.

"Just a few more plants and it won't feel so . . . ghostly in there," she announced, determinedly chipper.

"A Stella Plant Exorcism?"

"An empty room just *creeps* me out! It's been a week. We need to accept she's not coming back. No matter how much we wonder how she's doing or text or call or check her Insta. Snap. Tumblr. Pinterest."

Well, that wasn't an unexpected feeling, but it was coming off Terra in waves. No wonder Dane had turned out to be a weasel. Terra actually liked awful people.

"Wait. Do you . . . miss Stella?"

"No!" said Terra. "She was mean and insulting and left without saying goodbye, which is actually the meanest . . ."

"Do you want me to insult you?" Musa asked. "Will that make you feel better?"

"What? No!" Terra paused. "Maybe just . . . my outfit?"

Just then, a crash sounded from Stella's room, and Terra rushed out to remedy the situation. Terra must have placed the eighteenth plant in a precarious position.

With their door open, Musa could hear Aisha, trying hard to have a heart-to-heart with Bloom. So much suitemate drama. Musa had never thought she'd feel this way, but she was actually happy she had Terra as a roommate. Terra was the best one.

Plus, Terra had that hot brother.

"Bloom," said Aisha. "You know I'm here if you want to talk, right? I know after everything . . . you feel like you can't trust Dowling, but I would never . . . You can talk to me about anything. It's between us."

Yeah, or not, Musa thought. She wished Terra had closed the door.

"I know. I don't have anything to talk about. I want to focus on training this week. I've spent too much time focusing on everything other than school, and—" The sound of a phone ringing cut off Bloom's feeble excuses. "I should grab this."

Bloom walked out of the suite.

As soon as the door shut behind Bloom, Aisha bolted out of her room and into Musa and Terra's.

"We need to talk about Bloom!" she announced. "She's been single-minded about her birth parents and Rosalind for weeks. Are we actually meant to believe she's just . . . over it?"

Terra nodded, acknowledging how unlikely this scenario was, and put down her plants in surrender.

"Has she said anything about what happened that day with Beatrix?"

"Nothing," Aisha answered.

Then both Aisha and Terra turned to look at Musa with dawning suspicion.

"All the wisecracks about me broadcasting feelings, and you think I was going to volunteer that Bloom's a mess?"

It was Bloom's business. Aisha and Terra shared a look, as if to say: fair point.

"I know she's keeping something from us. I just don't know what it is. Like why would she be texting Dane?" asked Aisha.

"She was texting Dane?" Terra demanded.

Musa got hit by a wave of emotion from Terra. Fear. Betrayal. Longing. Something about melons.

"That was laced with more alarm than seems appropriate," she remarked.

Terra and Aisha both turned to Musa, startled. She stared back, giving a mental shrug. People. Can't escape from reading their emotions, can't stop them getting upset about it. *Can't win.*

Terra came to a decision. "Yeah . . . I saw him today. Riven said he's still Team Beatrix."

Musa didn't need to read emotions to know they were all alarmed by this information.

FIRE

My heart beat fast as I refused the call from my parents and made my way to the East Wing that was Beatrix's jail. I couldn't face them, knowing so little, with the awareness

I knew even less. I could only talk to my mom again when I knew who I truly was.

Dane was standing guard as he'd promised. Next to him, apparently asleep in a chair, was another Specialist.

"It's okay," Dane said. "He's out."

Dane held out a baggie of powder. I was alarmed by the possibility it was poison or hard drugs.

Dane sighed. "Relax. It's a minor sedative. He'll be awake in an hour. She's waiting."

I ventured near the cell bars to find Beatrix curled in the corner. She looked up when she saw me. I thought it was a genuine smile, but there was a touch of the tigress about this lady.

"Somebody took her sweet time," Beatrix purred, rising to her feet as I got closer. But I didn't have the energy for any of Beatrix's usual garbage.

"Did you kill Callum?" I demanded.

"Right at it, then. Good girl," said Beatrix.

"Did you?" I pressed.

"Short answer. Yes."

That was honest enough. So honest I was stunned. "Do I want to know the long answer?"

"How about the medium one?" Beatrix suggested. "Callum wasn't some suck-up assistant. He wanted the same thing I want."

Realization descended on me. "He was here to break Rosalind out?"

"A bit more complicated than 'evil Beatrix kills hapless

assistant.' That's the story the faculty is going with, right? I mean, I get it. Who wants to deal with nuance?"

It took a moment to absorb. Then I said the names of those Beatrix was dismissing as "the faculty." "Dowling, Harvey, Silva . . . They didn't tell me the truth about a lot of things. But just because they haven't doesn't mean you have."

Beatrix's voice went taut. "You still don't believe me that they torched Aster Dell?"

"If they did . . . if they *killed my birth parents* . . ." I didn't know what I would do. "I have to know what actually happened that day."

In almost a singsong, Beatrix said, "I know somebody who can tell you."

She didn't have to say the name. *Rosalind.*

"Where are they keeping her?"

"I can show you," Beatrix promised. "Where Rosalind is, how to get to her. All this and more can be yours."

"What do you want?"

Beatrix indicated the magical manacles that I'd been informed were called runic limiters.

"These lovely accessories Dowling gave me hurt like hell. On your way out, Dane will give you a trinket that can help get rid of them. Think of it like a fairy battery. If you use your magic to charge it in the stone circle . . ."

"You want me to free you?" I demanded.

I was speechless at her audacity. She'd just admitted to killing someone!

But Beatrix didn't push too hard. She just dangled the carrot.

"You don't trust me. You *shouldn't*. You shouldn't trust the faculty. You shouldn't trust your friends. The only person you should trust is Rosalind. And if you want to see her, this is your only option."

I left the cell without another word, wrestling with the decision. I was still wrestling when Dane approached and handed me a textbook. I glanced at Dane. He was a piece of work, but he wasn't a killer. As far as I knew.

Doubtfully, I began, "I know you and Beatrix were friends, but . . ."

"Why am I helping her? Easy. She's the only person here who ever let me feel like being different was a good thing. The odds are stacked against the outsiders at Alfea." Dane paused significantly. "Isn't that why you're here?"

MIND

Musa stood in the Bastion training area and tested the balance on a staff. She wondered if wielding a weapon for a while would get her mind off things.

"You like holding that big stick?" asked Sky's annoying friend, Riven.

Musa spun the staff around, stopping with her weapon

poised inches from his head. She stayed there a beat as a flirty smile crept up on Riven's face.

"Guess that's a yes," murmured Riven, in a low rumble.

Oh, this guy. He looked a mess. And his head was an even worse mess.

"I think I just threw up," scoffed Musa.

That was the right attitude to take with Riven. There was a gleam in his eye suddenly. Well, maybe not a full gleam. Maybe a spark. It lit something within Musa, too.

"Saw you on support rounds with the headmistress at training. Wouldn't expect a Mind Fairy to have such good moves."

Blood still racing, Musa admitted, "I used to be a dancer. Kinda miss being physical. Using my body."

Musa cursed herself for handing Riven that line. Riven only looked morose. Apparently, he only wanted to be flirty if he might get beaten up.

"Too bad. You're a fairy. They don't care what you want to be in this place. Only what they want you to be."

Musa's eyes narrowed as her magic surged. She got desperation, longing, wanting to be—somewhere not here. With someone else.

"You really hate it here, don't you?"

Riven's face twisted in horror and self-disgust. Cursing, he stormed off, and warned Sam off Musa as he went.

Sam came closer. And suddenly Musa could think of another way to deal with all her pent-up feelings.

"You wanna go back to the suite?" Musa suggested.

She practically tackled Sam when they got there.

"This is hot," Sam panted against her mouth. "You're hot."

"Hotter without commentary," Musa breathed.

She kissed him harder, trying to stop the words and the feelings, but felt Sam's mouth form a protesting shape.

"Right. Okay. It's just . . . I don't want to say aggressive, but . . ."

"Sam," Musa murmured. "I promised I'd meet Terra and Aisha, so let's just—"

Have a moment. For ourselves. She wanted to lose herself in kisses, but Sam pulled away.

"I can't believe I'm being this guy, but just because I'm not an empath doesn't mean I don't have empathy. What's going on?"

She considered his sweet, concerned face. She didn't have much practice at opening up.

"I'm just annoyed with training. With sitting on the sidelines and not being able to *do* anything."

Sam said in a pacifying tone, "Musa, Mind Fairies are some of the most powerful fairies—"

"Bull. We are powerless when things actually go wrong."

She remembered, from the time when things went worse than wrong.

Her response was too sharp. Sam's glance at her was pretty sharp as well. "Yeah, this is about way more than training. Did something happen?"

"No. I mean, yeah, but it was a long time ago. Family stuff. And all this training is just . . ." She gave up. "It's not a big deal. I'm just frustrated. And if I were you, I'd take advantage of that frustration while you still can."

Kind Sam obviously wanted to push it, but he let her have her way for the moment. "Fair enough. Be frustrated."

Wise decision, Sam. He smiled, and she shoved him down on the bed. She tugged her shirt off, and saw his expression turn awed.

As Musa crawled on top of him, a pot fell off the dresser and shattered. Sam let out a little shout, startled. At the noise of distress, Musa's magic instinctively flared, and then she felt a wave of self-consciousness from Sam.

"Please do not judge me based on my legitimate and completely masculine fear of ghosts, which are objectively creepy and—"

Musa smiled at him, and gave him a quick kiss.

"Moment's passed. I should probably get changed and catch up with them."

He gave her another kiss, and she walked him out of the room.

After Musa heard the door to the suite close behind Sam, she turned and faced the empty room. She surveyed the space carefully, then reached out with her magic, and sank back down on the bed. She knew what she'd felt.

Who she'd felt.

"Wanna come out now?" Musa inquired softly.

There was silence for a long moment. And then the empty space in front of Musa shimmered, revealing Stella.

"New magic? Not bad," Musa said as calmly as she could.

"Thanks." Stella was doing her best to sound indifferent. "I've had some practice."

"How long have you been hiding here?"

"A few days?" Stella sounded like she wasn't sure. She was bare-faced, wearing baggy clothes, with her hair in a bun. Musa had never seen Stella appear actually vulnerable before.

"Wanna talk about it?" asked Musa.

Stella didn't answer. *She looked almost afraid*, Musa thought.

When Musa reached out with her power, she realized what Stella was feeling was terror.

FIRE

Rays of light pierced the mist of morning, making the stone circle seem an even more magical space than usual. I stood looking around uneasily, holding the textbook Dane had given me.

When I was sure the coast was clear, I opened the book and took out a metal disc. It was intricately wrought with runes I couldn't even guess the meanings of.

When I called my magic to me, at the very edges of the disc, the wrought metal glowed red as an ember. My power felt like a spark lighting a fuse. As I let my own magic ebb away, the glow remained. I'd keyed the disc into a source of power, and now it was drawing magic from the stone circle. Fire slowly traced its way through the metal. I watched the delicate tracery, mesmerized, until an unwelcome sound snapped me out of my daze.

Sky's voice rang out in the morning air. "Is this where the overachievers hang out?"

Quickly, I shoved the disc behind my backpack and turned to watch Sky approach.

His gaze went to the textbook.

"Gets kinda loud in the suite," I said, as casually as I could.

I couldn't tell if he bought the act.

Sky asked, "What is that thing?"

I widened my eyes. "It's called a book? Bit concerned you've never seen one, but—"

Sky's face twisted as if he'd reached a breaking point. "I don't want to do this, Bloom," he burst out. "I don't want to lie to each other. I don't want to play some game."

I kept playing. "There's no game."

Sky was clearly struggling, trying to force words out. As if each word was forbidden, was breaking a direct order.

"Silva wanted me . . . to watch you. I told him he was crazy! That there wasn't anything weird going on. That you were frustrated, but . . ."

"You've been *spying* on me?" I demanded.

Even though he'd just confessed to spying on me, apparently hearing me reiterate it stunned him. As though he was so sure he was a good guy, he couldn't possibly have done what he'd done.

I was such a fool. "I should've expected that. And you just blindly did what they said—"

"He gave me an order," Sky told me helplessly.

"Which he could have given to anyone! But he chose you. Used our friendship. But I'm the bad guy, right?"

In answer, Sky grabbed at my bag, revealing the disc and the fact that I hadn't exactly been forthcoming myself.

"What is it, Bloom?" he demanded.

I hesitated for a long guilty moment. Sky took the time to collect himself.

"I want to be on your side here, but you're making it really hard. Tell me," he urged, soft, insistent. "You can trust me."

He'd just proven that I couldn't. Or had he? At least he'd told me. Maybe I should try telling him something.

I took a deep breath, and began to spill the truth about Aster Dell.

LIGHT

Stella hadn't been looking to bond with her suitemates. They were first years, and besides, she'd always known Terra would spill about what had happened with Ricki, and they would all judge her for what they believed she'd done. Judge her and hate her.

So she'd judged and hated them first. She'd hated Terra, for telling what she believed to be the truth, and also for Terra's ghastly taste in blouses. Bloom, for maybe being the girl of Sky's dreams. Aisha, for always trying to do the right thing. And Musa, for her terrible power of seeing into Stella's soul.

She'd feared Musa's magic. Now, though, she found the idea of Musa's power almost liberating. Stella was literally forced to be invisible. She was done keeping up appearances.

Musa knew people's innermost feelings already. Stella could spill it all, pour her whole heart out, and it wouldn't matter.

"I ran away days ago. I'm sure my mom has the entire army looking for me. But you won't hear about it."

"And she won't look for you here?" Musa asked, doubtful.

"Not at first. To do that, she'd have to admit she'd lost control of something. That'll never happen."

Musa's eyes glowed, and Stella knew Musa was sensing Stella's conviction of this. Feeling exactly how inti-midated Stella was by her mother, how the longing for love and the longing to please her mom were overlaid by stark fear.

Stella was glad. Stella wanted Musa to see her. She felt as though she'd been invisible far longer than a few days.

Stella's voice underlined her feelings, saying, "Project strength and power. Never show weakness. It's all she cares about. And I am an extension of her strength. My magic has to be powerful at any cost. That's what she taught me. My mom tutored me growing up. When positive emotions didn't work, she went right to the negative. Hard. My magic is erratic . . . because of her."

Stella swallowed, on the verge of the most important revelation. It was easy saying these things to Musa, because Musa could tell Stella truly meant it. Nobody else would believe how sorry Stella was.

"Ricki was my best friend. I didn't mean to hurt her," Stella whispered, and hoped the truth and regret rang through Musa's bones as pain rang through Stella's own. "But I lost control, and it was better . . . for my mom . . . if people thought I did it on purpose. Because at least if I'm a raging bitch, or a monster, *I'm not weak*."

"That is messed up, Stel," Musa said gently.

Stella was so utterly exhausted, she couldn't even be ashamed. "Tell me about it. And the second I got home it started again. So here I am. Until I figure out what to do next. Please don't tell anyone."

Her mother had raised her to be proud, to be royal, and here she was begging. She waited, every muscle tense, for Musa to mock her for being brought so low. Stella was alone. She'd always been alone, really.

The purple had faded from Musa's gaze. As Musa gazed at Stella, her eyes were soft with sympathy.

"You don't have to hide," Musa promised. "The rest of the girls in the suite will be okay with you being here."

For a moment, Stella felt as though she could almost believe Musa. As though her mother had been wrong, and she did have friends after all.

EARTH

Dane chugged from a big water bottle as he finished lunch, and then glanced around in what Terra found to be a suspicious manner. He headed away from the crowd in the courtyard to a quiet back area where he wouldn't be observed. Terra sneaked after him, just in time to see him pull out a joint and light it up.

Terra felt she had to speak now. "In the middle of the courtyard? 'Cause that's smart."

Terra approached. Dane took another hit.

"Yep. Want some?"

Dane exhaled smoke aggressively into her face. Terra flapped her hand, waving the smoke out of the way. "What is *wrong* with you?"

"Oh, you care about me again?" Dane asked bitterly.

That was the last thing Terra expected to hear. It had never occurred to her that Dane might actually miss her. She faltered, "I've always cared about you."

Dane's tone went savage. "Really, 'cause it seemed like I did one bad thing and you cut me off."

"So you're all about Beatrix now?" Terra demanded.

"She definitely never did anything to make me feel bad."

Terra snapped, "No, she just *murdered someone*, Dane."

And if Dane had mocked Beatrix on the internet like he'd mocked Terra, Beatrix might have murdered *him*. Right now, Terra felt that would have served Dane right. Why did Dane think his wounded fee-fees were more important than someone's life?

Dane rolled his eyes and Terra felt every last drop of sympathy in her evaporate.

"Done with this," Dane announced.

He moved to stand up. But he couldn't. He looked down and saw a vine, wrapping around his legs, fastening him to his chair.

"Except you kinda aren't," Terra pointed out.

Dane laughed, not bothered. He took another defiant hit, but then a tiny jet of water put it out.

Aisha approached. "What's going on with you and Bloom?"

Dane looked back and forth between them with a carefully blank expression on his face.

Terra lost patience and commanded, "Tell us. Or—"

"What? You're not going to hurt me."

Terra said noncommittally, "Depends what your definition of *hurt* is. Might not be physical pain, no. But don't think I'm above leaving you in that chair as long as it takes for you to talk. And that . . ." She gestured meaningfully. "Looks like a pretty big bottle of water. Hope you can hold it. Otherwise, messy."

Dane finally seemed to realize he was trapped. Terra folded her arms and waited.

Dane might be feeling injured she'd stopped being his friend, but that was rich considering he'd bad-mouthed Terra to amuse Riven and Beatrix, and he hadn't tried hard to make up for it. Hadn't tried much at all. Hadn't thought she was worth it.

Terra wanted to help Bloom. But she'd be lying if she said she wasn't enjoying taking a little revenge for herself as well.

FIRE

All was silent in the stone circle, once I'd told my story.

"I've lived at Alfea my entire life. Silva raised me," Sky said numbly at last.

I understood it was hard for him to believe, but he had to know the truth. "I saw Aster Dell with my own eyes."

Sky was clearly still focused on Silva. If it had been my dad, I would've felt the same way.

"He would've never helped massacre an entire village!"

"Not even if he thought he was killing Burned Ones? If he thought he'd save more lives in the future?"

Sky opened his mouth, and then closed it.

Yeah, that was what I thought, too. "I don't think they're *evil*, Sky. I just think they're . . . complicated," I said helplessly. "They think they're protecting this place. But they're also protecting themselves. So whatever the truth is? Whatever happened that day? They're not gonna tell me."

He moved toward me, as he heard the desperation in my voice. Perhaps he could sense where the desperation would lead.

"I know how hard it is to not know your parents, Bloom, but—"

"Do you? At least you were raised by people who knew yours. You heard stories. Saw pictures."

I stared out at the green hills beyond the stone, trying not to cry as the empty landscape blurred in my vision. The wind kicked up, sending chills all through me.

"Are you cold?" Sky asked, instantly concerned. "You need a sweater?"

I pulled out my water bottle, turning back to see that Sky had shrugged his jacket off and was holding it out to me.

"That's sweet, but—Fire Fairy."

Six fires ignited around us. Warming us, like a circle of stars to go with our circle of stones. Sky looked around, and every dancing flame caught the brightness in his eyes.

"Right," Sky scoffed a little. "Because you never need help."

I offered my water to Sky. As he took it, and drank, I tried to shrug his words off. "Part of my charm."

Sky gave me a look that said he couldn't be shrugged off. "Frustrating charm."

"'Cause you're a fixer. And I don't need to be fixed."

Sky turned away from me slightly. I wondered if I'd sounded harsher than I intended, but then he spoke, with difficulty, and I realized he was just trying to get the words out.

"I've heard more stories about Andreas than I can count. Like he's still alive. Except he's not. He's an ideal. A void. An impossible ghost. Do you know how hard that is to live up to? Even Silva . . . it's like he's playing some role out of a sense of duty. All I really want is a dad."

I drew closer to him and laid a hand on his arm. "Sky . . ."

Sky said desperately, "I'm a fixer because I'm supposed to be. Because I have to be. Because when I fix other people, I don't have to think about how broken I am."

He turned to face me. It was like seeing him for the first time, with the careful mask of duty completely gone.

"We're all broken, Bloom. We all need to be fixed. There's charm in that, too."

His face was so close to mine, and once again I felt that yearning pull toward him. This time I didn't resist. This time I couldn't.

Our lips met, and I finally understood why I had always felt so drawn to him. We fit together like two broken pieces that could form a whole.

Then against the darkness behind my eyes, I saw the brilliant glow as magic lit up the disc Dane had given me.

Sky and I broke apart, both of us looking toward the light. I hesitated, and then reached for the disc. Sky reached for me, and put his hand over mine.

"You haven't told me what that's for. You still don't trust me?"

I looked down at his hand over mine. Just the sight of that, us touching so simply, filled me with sorrow.

"I do, actually. But I also know if I tell you, you'll stop me."

Sky looked ready to argue the point, but then what I'd been waiting for happened. Sky staggered, eyes going unfocused, and grabbed at the bench as he tumbled down to the ground. It was heartbreaking to watch Sky, with his soldier's grace lost as his body betrayed him.

Because I'd betrayed him.

"What's happening . . .?" asked Sky, but I could see he already knew. He just didn't want to believe. He'd wanted to trust me.

I slid the disc back into my bag, alongside the bag of powder Dane had given me. Sky's eyes were already sliding closed. He would sleep, for a little while.

"Dane said it wouldn't last long," I told Sky's unconscious body. "I'm sorry."

I put out the dancing flames surrounding us, knowing that the fire between us was already lost.

SPECIALIST

Silva had sent a group text to the Specialists saying to suit up. Riven had no idea what he wanted, but he climbed morosely into his armor. Probably it was another drill. Maybe he'd feel better if he hit someone. Maybe he could cut off Dane's head in an unfortunate training accident. He walked out of his room, buckling on his sword and shaking his head, trying to pull himself together.

Then Terra came charging through the Specialist corridor, headed right for Riven.

She grabbed his arm. "Hey! I need help."

Riven reached for his sword. "What do you need?"

There were bits of vines in Terra's hair and a wild look in her eye. "Bloom's about to do something absolutely insane, so I have to find Sky."

"You have to find Sky," Riven said flatly. "For help."

"Yes, obviously!"

"Have you ever even had a conversation with Sky?"

"We have conversations!" Terra protested. "Multiple ones! Anyway, everybody knows he's a great guy, and I think he really cares about Bloom. Hope Stella doesn't—"

"Blind her," Riven murmured. "I've been concerned about that, too."

"Blinding's very concerning!" said Terra. "But it's not the issue right now. The problem is this. Dane is a weasel. He is a weasel-faced weasel. Had you noticed that?"

"It had come to my attention."

It hadn't bothered him. He'd thought it was something he and Dane had in common.

Terra pointed an accusing finger. "And yet, you kinda made out with him!"

"And you just *wanted* to make out with him," Riven shot back.

"That's not important at this time! Dane was up to no good, so I bound him to a chair with vines and threatened to keep him tied up there forever—"

"I'm sorry, you did what?" Riven gave Terra a scandalized glare. "Terra, has it occurred to you that you have something of a vine management problem?"

Terra waved this off. "I mean, not forever, but I wouldn't let him pee. I had to extract information from him somehow, you must see that!"

Riven swore. "Did you shake your vines at him in a menacing fashion and say, 'We have ways of making you talk'?"

"No, Riven. Be reasonable. Why would I do that?" Terra shook her head and waved an object at him.

Riven squinted at it. "Is that Dane's cell phone?"

"Yeah. Will you please focus!"

"I wanted to be clear," said Riven. "You're mugging people now."

Terra was really blossoming. Into a criminal maniac flower.

"Bloom and Dane are plotting a jailbreak of your deranged, murderous ex," Terra announced. "Dane gave Bloom some sort of magic key."

They were what? Dane had done what?

"We didn't technically break up," Riven pointed out.

"Murder means breaking up," said Terra.

Riven nodded. "Yeah, that's fair."

"So I desperately need help and I must find Sky! Who else could possibly help?"

Riven gave her a wry smile. "Certainly not me."

"Nobody would ever ask you for help," Terra agreed absentmindedly. "Sky can talk sense into Bloom! Do you have any idea where he is?"

"I thought he went off to find Bloom, to be honest."

"Oh no." Terra's eyes were saucers. "What if Bloom's already eliminated him?"

What, did Terra suspect another murder? Blindings. Murder. Kidnapping and bondage with vines. Why was nobody content with being a low-key delinquent like Riven himself?

"I don't *think* Bloom would murder Sky," Riven decided. "She's too warm for his form to put him on ice permanently."

Terra punched Riven in the arm. She punched pretty hard. "Bloom is my friend! She would never murder anyone."

"You just said she was gonna jailbreak a murderer!"

"That's not the same thing at all," Terra told him severely. "I'm sure she just tied up Sky and stashed him somewhere safe. All right, I'll deal with Bloom. You should probably go find Sky."

"That's all you want me to do?"

"Uh," said Terra. "I guess you could also untie Dane?"

Riven felt his eyebrows hit his hairline. "Did you not already untie Dane?"

"No, Riven," Terra said. "Dane might have got in my way."

She whirled around and hurtled off. Well, that had been an unhinged interaction. Apparently, Terra was a spy of the realm now.

Riven looked after Terra and murmured, "I genuinely don't think Dane would dare."

He shook his head and set off toward the courtyard when Silva marched past him. Silva's always-set jaw currently looked like granite that was disappointed in the world.

"Good that you suited up. Where's Sky?" snapped Silva.

"I'm glad nobody's even bothering with 'hey, Riven' anymore," grumbled Riven. "Just cut right to the chase, guys."

Something deeply military was about to happen to Riven; he could feel it. Why did he have to be tormented like this?

Silva snapped out the words. "There's at least six Burned Ones massacring people on the other side of the Barrier. Marco's team is already down. It's our job to stop them."

Riven stared at Silva with his mouth falling open. He hated to point out the wildly obvious, but if a whole team of trained adult Specialists had been taken down, the trainees at Alfea were just gonna get slaughtered. He tried to find some non-insubordinate way to ask, "What's my motivation to get slaughtered?"

"Don't ask questions," Silva growled. "Find Sky."

Okay, Riven got it. Everybody wanted Sky. It was Riven's job to fetch him.

Since the Burned Ones were gonna kill them all, he'd better hurry and untie Dane, too.

FIRE

I headed for the gate, and then stopped dead when I saw a strange guard.

Swiftly, I shot Dane a text saying *I have the key. Where are you?*

Terra's voice behind me said simply, "He's not coming."

I turned to behold Terra and Aisha. Terra held up Dane's cell. Aisha was almost vibrating with disappointment and anger.

"What the hell are you doing, Bloom? Breaking Beatrix out?"

Every justification I could think of to offer sounded feeble under their furious gazes. But my friends weren't soldiers. They'd helped me before. Maybe if they knew the truth about Aster Dell, they would help me again.

"Dowling is lying to me. Everyone here is lying. You don't know what I know."

"We do," Aisha said flatly. "Dane told us about Aster Dell."

Terra's voice rang with righteous fury. "My dad would never do that, Bloom. Beatrix is a liar. And a murderer."

I glanced back and forth.

"Of course. You're his daughter, and you're Dowling's little helper. I'm never gonna convince either of you. Just like Sky."

I tried to walk past them. But Aisha stepped in front of me, blocking the way.

"I'm not Dowling's little helper," she said. "I've been spying on the woman. For days. For you."

Terra sounded disconcerted. "You what?"

Aisha waved this off. "The point is, all I've seen is how hard she's trying—they're all trying—to keep us safe."

Dowling was trying really hard to conceal the truth. I knew that much. I could never forgive her for that.

"They've lied about a woman being dead for sixteen years. About a war crime. I know you want to believe in them, but they're destructive. Maybe dangerous—"

"Listen to yourself!" Terra snapped. "You literally sound like a crazy person."

Fury spurred me to try getting past Aisha. She blocked me again, as though I was on an enemy team and she would never let me score.

The movements of Aisha's body were sure, but her voice was faltering and desperate. "We haven't told anyone what you're doing. If you just give us the key, we won't. But if you don't . . . I don't want to see you in the cell next to her."

I stood there, furious, feeling like an animal at bay. Only I had a better weapon than teeth. I could feel my magic curling hot within me, wanting to spring. The temptation to use magic on my friends was very real.

Aisha took a step back, and there was no fear on her face. Only concern. And hurt.

"*Bloom*," Aisha said.

Only that.

The look on Aisha's face snapped me out of it. I lost my grip on my magic, and sick regret made my stomach lurch. What had I almost done?

It killed me, but I reached into my bag and pulled out the disc. My last chance at answers. I handed it over. Aisha took it away.

"I know how hard this must be," Aisha whispered.

"No," I told Aisha. Loving her, hating her, hoping I wouldn't always resent her for this. "You don't."

MIND

Stella leaned over Musa's phone, reading a barrage of texts from Aisha about Dane.

Stella's tone got snippy. "I just can't believe everyone is listening to Aisha like she knows everything. You have no idea how hard it's been to keep my mouth shut while the suite goes haywire. I can only bear so much."

Musa's eyebrows rose. "So you're the reason stuff keeps falling and breaking and—"

"I have opinions," Stella said with dignity. "And if I can't express them verbally, I'm not above poltergeisting."

Just then, the door swung open, and Aisha and Terra entered. As soon as the door moved, Stella vanished.

Terra was in full swing already. "I just wonder what else we can do . . ."

"We can put this all behind us, and—" Aisha stopped, seeing Musa. "Where have you been? Didn't you get my texts?"

Musa didn't know if she could bring herself to spill Stella's secrets. "I did. Sorry. I was . . . busy. Sam was here and—"

Terra made a face. "Wait, not in our room, right?"

Aisha ignored her, holding up a runic disc. "It's okay. We stopped Bloom. I think she's losing it. I know I said we wouldn't, but I wonder if we have to tell Dowling."

A flash of irritation made Musa jump. It wasn't her own irritation. She looked at the shelf, where a flowerpot trembled. It started to move on its own toward the edge. Musa pointed at the empty space.

"Don't you dare."

Aisha, naturally assuming Musa was talking about her, said, "No. I think we should tell her."

The vase moved another inch. Actually, Musa was over it. She felt totally ready to spill Stella's secrets.

"Stella has an opinion about that," she declared.

"What?" said Terra.

"Huh?" asked Aisha.

"I refuse to keep cleaning them up," Musa informed Stella. "Just tell them."

Her suitemates stared at Musa as though she had lost

it . . . until Stella appeared next to the vase. She gave Musa an annoyed glance, and then turned to Terra and Aisha.

"I have an opinion," announced Stella.

The girls were stunned. Terra started to speak, but Stella's tone didn't welcome comments.

"Everyone in this damn suite is so black or white. Did it ever occur to you, like, ever, that there's somewhere in the middle to land?"

Stella looked at Musa. New understanding passed between them. It was kinda beautiful.

"Bloom's a pain in the ass," said Stella, which was less beautiful. "But she deserves to know who she is. Really. Not the stories the faculty is telling her. So we can worry about being right, or we can help our friend. Which is it?"

FIRE

I found Dowling in front of an open dresser, staring at an outfit that looked almost like Specialist clothing. The outfit Dowling had worn in the old pictures. She turned at the sound of the door, slamming in my wake.

"Excuse me?" Dowling said thinly.

"I want to see her," I stated. "Rosalind."

"I told you, she's—"

My voice was another slammed door. "I know she's alive! So don't lie to me again."

There had been too many lies. I wasn't sure I could bear hearing another.

"I don't have time for this right now, Bloom." Dowling started to walk past me.

"I'm from Aster Dell."

I threw the words at her, and they stopped her cold.

"Yep. That's where I was born. And that's where my birth parents lived. That is until you, Mr. Silva, and Professor Harvey destroyed it."

For a moment, Dowling didn't speak. She didn't even need to answer. I could see the guilt on her face.

In a shaking voice, I whispered, "So it's true."

I hadn't realized I hoped it wasn't. She was the woman who'd come from another world to rescue me, surrounded by light. The woman who'd lied to me over and over again.

I clung to rage, because it felt safest. "How could you do that? How could killing Burned Ones be more important to you than people's lives? Than my . . . *parents*?"

Dowling's expression altered. "You think we did it on purpose?"

"That's what Beatrix said." I faltered. "That Rosalind had a crisis of conscience but you did it, anyway."

Tell me it isn't true. No, I thought. I didn't want her to tell me what I wanted to hear. I wanted the truth.

Dowling shook her head. "Rosalind. She's still manipulating people after all these years."

"What does that *mean*?" I demanded. "Tell me what happened that day."

There was a long, awful silence. I saw Dowling take a deep breath and prayed she wouldn't lie to me again.

"That day . . ." said Dowling, "I made a mistake."

And the pain and resolve on Dowling's face let me, at last, believe.

"Rosalind was my mentor. The most powerful fairy at Alfea. Feared, but respected. I never doubted her. Never questioned her. So when we heard about the Burned Ones at Aster Dell, we followed."

As Dowling talked, I could almost see the picture of Rosalind's team, come to life and walking through the green forest. Before the devastation of Aster Dell. Dowling, Silva, Terra's dad, Sky's dad, and Rosalind the trusted leader. Being a team, trying to do good work. How had it all gone so wrong?

"The magic we unleashed that day was immensely powerful. Until then, we didn't know fairies could combine their magic. It was a secret Rosalind kept. Not the first. Still, we never questioned her. She told us she had taken pains to evacuate the village. She told us that only Burned Ones would be killed in the blast."

I remembered the vision Beatrix had showed me. So much devastation. So many people had died in that wrecked village. My parents hadn't been Burned Ones.

Dowling's face was filled with regret. All she had to say was, "We should have questioned her."

So it had been Rosalind's fault? Did Beatrix know? Who was lying?

Maybe all of them were lying.

"When we realized what she had done? What we had done? That day has lived in my mind for sixteen years." Dowling's voice was harsh. "If Aster Dell is where you're from, there are no words I could say that would make right the damage I have caused you."

"Why would Rosalind do that? Lie?" I whispered.

Why did everybody lie? I was so tired of it.

"She was a zealot. She wanted every Burned One dead, no matter the cost. I'm sure she thought if she told us she couldn't evacuate, we'd say no. She would've been right."

I tried to puzzle it out, unravel the whole sorry mess. "But what about me? Why did she rescue me? Why did she put me in the human world? Why did she tell me to find her?"

Weariness seemed to overcome Dowling, there in her shadowy office, with the doors of her past open before us.

"That much I do not know, Bloom. Rosalind kept many things from me."

Hope flared in me. "Which is why I want to see her. I know you're holding her. Beatrix told me she's under the school."

Dowling shifted uncomfortably. I suspected she hadn't expected me to know that. But she didn't deny it.

"Whatever she has to give you is not worth unleashing her back into the world, Bloom."

Dowling approached me. More open than I'd ever seen her, as though she might reach out and take my hands. Pour out the truth into my cupped hands, the truth I needed. About my birth parents.

"I will help you get any answers you need," Dowling told me. "I give you my word."

I wanted to believe her, so badly, but I didn't want to be a fool. And just then, Silva arrived. He demanded Dowling's presence. There was something more important than finding me my answers.

There always seemed to be something more important. For everyone, except for me.

SPECIALIST

When Sky came to in the stone circle, it was dark and cold, and Bloom was long gone. He ignored all the texts on his phone, staggered to his feet, and headed back for the castle. Before he got there, Riven found him.

"You look like garbage," said Sky's always-sympathetic best friend.

"I feel like it. So that makes sense."

Riven seemed to feel he should explain his presence outside the gates. "Terra the superspy got Dane to spill. He said Bloom came out here to do something with a magic key, and no one could reach you, so . . ."

Sky's friend was wearing full armor, and he was holding a gear bag.

Sky tensed. "Where is Dane?" That traitor. Sky would make him pay.

"Gearing up."

"*What?*" exclaimed Sky. "Please tell me Beatrix is—"

"Still locked up," Riven said briefly. "We have bigger problems."

He tossed Sky the gear bag. Riven always threw too hard, but Sky could always catch whatever he threw. Sky unzipped the bag to reveal his own armor, and his sword.

"The hell is going on?" asked Sky slowly.

"Silva needs us at the Barrier," said Riven.

At once, Sky's hand closed around the hilt of his sword. He knew what that must mean. The Burned Ones were attacking. Sky's duty was clear.

As they headed for the Barrier, Riven explained to him that the Burned Ones were coming at them in force. There was a video circulating of them decimating a Specialist team. Sky's mind sheered away from the idea of so many Burned Ones, of how much destruction they could cause.

As soon as Sky's mind went wandering, it went to Bloom.

"When we see Silva . . ." said Sky. "Do you think we could not mention . . ."

Riven sighed. "One crazy girlfriend is an accident that could happen to anyone. Two is a pattern. You want me to not mention you getting drugged by a ginger maniac hellbent on freeing murderers from prison?"

"Uh," said Sky. "Yeah."

Riven shrugged. "Whatever, man, I don't judge your kinks. Ugh, what a day. Hope Terra smashes Dane's phone." He brightened, as if that was a pleasant thought.

Sky frowned. "Why did Terra steal Dane's phone?"

Riven shook his head. "Too much crime to explain. C'mon, bro. We've gotta go get murdered."

FIRE

I sat on the ground and stared out through the Barrier. The Otherworld beyond was beautiful, and strange, and nothing like home. I couldn't see even a gleam of hope in this whole landscape.

Then, with a soft sound, something small and bright dropped into the grass beside me.

"You need answers," said Musa.

"People have kept them from you," chimed in Terra, to whom truth was so important. "We don't want to be those people, too."

I felt so impossibly touched, felt as though finally someone had seen me for the first time in a long time. And it was these someones, my friends. Then I realized who was missing.

"Where's Aisha?"

Terra grimaced. "You know she has some strong feelings and she didn't totally exactly agree with what we were thinking about—"

Musa said simply, "She's in the suite."

"I guess . . . that's as good as I could ask for." I nodded to the disc. "So you're going to let me break Beatrix out?"

"Yeah, so that's kind of the part Aisha couldn't get on board with . . ."

And at that moment, Stella emerged from the gloom. I stared. Where the hell had Stella come from?

Stella said archly, "She never likes my ideas, anyway."

WATER

The rasp of the Burned Ones filled the nighttime forest like the sound of rustling leaves with teeth. Headmistress Dowling, Professor Harvey, and Specialist Headmaster Silva, with the Specialists arrayed around them, were standing before the Barrier ready to fight.

The rest of their suitemates had thrown in with Bloom. It was time for Aisha to pick a team.

"How many of them are there?" she asked.

The others turned to look at her. Sky's weird friend Riven gave Aisha some serious side-eye, but Headmistress Dowling looked at Aisha with simple concern.

"Get back to school. You shouldn't be out this close to the Barrier."

"I came because . . ." Aisha could only offer the device she'd found in Callum's desk.

"A listening device!" said Professor Harvey.

Dowling's face was stern, but it almost always was. Still, she'd chosen Aisha and trusted Aisha with responsibilities, and Aisha had repaid her by deceiving her in order to help Bloom. Now lives were in danger, Dowling would soon face nightmare creatures to save her students, and Bloom was still bent on her personal mission.

It was horrible, to think she was betraying her roommate. But if Aisha didn't speak now, she was betraying Dowling and Alfea.

"It was Callum's. I found it after he was . . . killed," Aisha confessed. "I've been using it. It felt like there were all these secrets, and I didn't know if I trusted you. But now I know. You're protecting us."

Silva snapped, "You need to get back to the school now. This is not the time for extra credit or—"

Aisha agreed. This wasn't a time to think about doing well, or wanting friends. This wasn't a game. It was time to do what she believed was right.

Desperately resolute, Aisha interrupted to say, "I'm not looking for extra credit. I'm here because you need to know what's happening. What Bloom is going to do."

Riven was now giving Aisha so much side-eye there was side-eyebrow involved. Sky shot Aisha a look that pleaded with her not to tell.

Aisha told, anyway.

FIRE

I marched into the East Wing to free the prisoner. This time, with the support of my friends.

"And here I was, doubting you," Beatrix said as she placed the runic disc over her bracelet.

The disc worked fast. Beatrix's magic returned even faster. Beatrix's eyes glowed gray, and it was scary to see how quickly she accessed her power. She put her finger on the locked door. At once a tiny spark arced through the metal and the door popped open.

"Here we go," announced Beatrix, as though we were embarking on a great adventure.

As Beatrix strolled out of her cell and led the way toward Dowling's office, there was a spring in her step.

Once we got there, she showed me how to move aside the stone bookcase to expose a hidden door. I stood at Dowling's desk as Beatrix cautiously peered through the doorway.

"Once Dane gets here, we can chuck him through," Beatrix told me brightly.

Apparently, that was how it worked.

"Seems kind of harsh, using him to spring the trap," I said casually.

"He'll be game." Beatrix pondered this. "Or he won't, and we'll do it, anyway!"

"What about you?" I asked. "Are you game?"

Beatrix tilted her head in a puzzled, birdlike gesture. She was studying me. She didn't even have time to react when Stella popped into sight right next to her and shoved her hard through the doorway. As soon as Beatrix hit the ground, her eyes clouded with magic, and she lay paralyzed.

I guessed she'd gotten the drop on Callum just like this. Turnabout was fair play.

"That was much more satisfying than a flowerpot," Stella remarked mysteriously, dusting off her hands.

Terra and Musa walked through the door of Dowling's office, less chipper than Stella, but looking determined. Loyal Terra eyed Beatrix with resentment.

"By the way," she said. "Dane would not be game."

Stella clearly wished to be admired at once. "See? Break out the villain to get what Bloom needs, and then trap her again. Simple. My ideas rock."

Musa glanced down at Beatrix, her own eyes glowing.

"In case anyone was wondering?" Musa asked dryly. "She's not happy."

I wasn't wondering. I was staring at the secret doorway, and thinking of the answers that lay beyond.

EARTH

The tunnels beyond the secret doorway were dark and creepy. Terra supposed that made sense.

Stella was using her magic to light her way with one of those pretty bright wisps she used to make all her photos so gorgeous. Terra stuck close by Stella, even though Stella was scary and nasty, because of that light.

Also because it was nice to see Stella again. The suite was complete!

"I feel like I'm going to regret this, but . . . are you okay?" Stella inquired.

There was so much on Terra's mind, she hardly knew what to say first. She was so relieved Stella had asked.

Stella's expression didn't look relieved, but too late! Terra was already talking.

"I just freed a prisoner. Broke into the headmistress's office."

Stella nodded. Yeah, Terra supposed Stella had been there the whole time.

Terra heard her own voice pick up speed, feelings tumbling out. "Since I can remember, when I've been scared or unsure, I've always turned to one person for answers. My dad. I've always been able to close my eyes in the dark and know he'd lead me the right way. But I don't think he'd lead me down here."

Stella seemed to consider her answer carefully before she replied.

"Even the best parents are doing what *they* think is best for us. At some point, we have to take over for ourselves."

She paused, and concentrated. Stella's eyes glowed topaz, and another bright wisp of light appeared. Next to Terra. Just for her, lighting her way.

Terra gazed at her magic light. She felt so touched, she might cry. She wondered if Stella would be receptive to a hug.

"Oh, and by the way, your outfit?"

Stella gave her an up-and-down look. Withering without saying a word. Terra felt a pang of totally normal humiliation, there in the creepy tunnel. And she beamed.

I love my dumb mean friends, thought Terra. *I love the Winx Club.*

FIRE

At the end of the tunnel, there was a door. I stopped in front of it, knowing it was where I needed to be. But I held still, too frantic with fear and excitement to move. I felt as if I might stay here, waiting for answers, my whole life.

Until Musa approached. Her eyes didn't glow, but I felt as though she could see into my heart, anyway.

"Everything I've been looking for is right through that door," I whispered.

We stood together for a moment, on the threshold.

"We'll be here when you come out," Musa said steadily.

My friends. I knew they would.

I walked through the door and saw a barrier. Almost like the Barrier to the forest, but this was a latticework of bright magic.

I took another step forward into the light.

FAIRY TALE #6

The blood-dimmed tide is loosed, and everywhere
The ceremony of innocence is drowned;
The best lack all conviction, while the worst
Are full of passionate intensity.
—*W. B. Yeats*

FIRE

I entered a strange, bright room. The walls were undulating like beams of light on water. Held in a translucent prison, Rosalind hung suspended. She looked just like my vision of her, like her photographs: a woman with such force of personality she could've set the air around her burning.

I touched the undulating light between us, and a forbidding jolt of magic made me spring back.

"Sorry. Should've warned you."

A voice echoed, but only in my mind. I could see Rosalind's lips, and they weren't moving.

"Rosalind?" I whispered, just the same.

She replied, "I can only imagine how many questions you have for me."

Rosalind's voice in my mind was warm, but confident. It had been so long since I felt comforted. Hearing her almost brought a tear to my eyes.

"Just a few," I admitted.

"Well, I've only got one for you. Do you have any idea how special you are?"

I hadn't expected anything like that. Her question was rough, but sweet. Honest. The best part was, she seemed so utterly different from Ms. Dowling.

I couldn't help a startled smile.

Playfully, Rosalind asked, "Wanna learn a new trick?"

"Right now?"

Was now the time for tricks?

"Access that flame inside you. Use the joy you're feeling, because you're about to get answers. Or how pissed off you are at me for leaving you in the First World without them. I won't be offended."

I closed my eyes, and felt all the tangled emotions in me spark and then catch fire.

Maybe now was *exactly* the right time for tricks.

Rosalind encouraged, "Here comes the fun part. That flame? Your instincts are telling you that it'll burn you. Your instincts are wrong. Grab on to it."

It felt as though the fire was enveloping me, but not consuming me. I gasped, feeling myself come alight with power.

"Now. Touch the barrier again."

I hesitated.

"Don't be a wuss," Rosalind told me. "You've got this. Do it."

Rosalind directed me with such easy authority, and it felt so natural to obey. I reached out and touched the barrier. This time, my hand wasn't blown back.

When my vision cleared, the barrier was gone. Standing in the center of the room was Rosalind.

She spoke out loud now. Her voice scratchy, but filled with personality.

"Sixteen years. No mirror. No makeup. How great do I look right now? Don't lie. Okay, lie a little."

She cracked an intensely disarming smile. Then, she took a step, and her legs gave out. I rushed to her.

"You need food. Water. Rest."

"No," said Rosalind. "I need magic."

EARTH

"Bloom has been in there a while," Terra fretted. "What could they be talking about?"

Stella gave her a disdainful look. "Once I heard you talk about dirt for two hours. *Dirt*. Two hours."

"*Soil*," Terra corrected sternly. Get it right, Stella! It was an important distinction. "And we left Beatrix lying there. I wanna make sure she's not awake, fashioning three shivs."

"Don't be ridiculous. She'd use one shiv three times. Stab stab stab," Musa said.

Oh, Terra loved Musa, but her roommate was not a reassuring person.

"Can we just go check?"

"Fine, but you're overreacting," said Stella with a lofty air.

Stella kept up the attitude all the way through the tunnels, right up until they reached the doorway and were confronted with the space in the floor where Beatrix used to be. Terra stared accusingly at Stella. Musa eyed the door.

Right! They had to regroup. Terra was making a plan. "I'd like my apology via scented handwritten note after we find her."

Musa murmured, "It gets worse . . ."

At the door, Dowling stood with Aisha. And, far worse, with Terra's dad.

"You have no idea the trouble you've caused. You especially, Stella," said Dowling.

Oh no. Stella must be protected.

"We were just—" Terra began valiantly.

Her father interrupted. He'd never addressed Terra with his pure *Professor-Harvey* voice, but he was using it now. "Not another word. Come with me."

As Terra's dad led them out, Stella paused by Aisha.

"I hope the brownie points you're getting from this will keep you company when you have no friends," she said sweetly.

Once again, Terra found herself a little grateful for Stella's meanness.

MIND

Everyone was having too many loud, intense, awful feelings, and Musa hated them all.

She sat quietly beside Stella as Professor Harvey read them the riot act, and tried to sink through the floor. Terra was standing near the door, her every nerve jangling like wind chimes in Musa's head. Aisha sat across the room. Just watching.

Professor Harvey said, "Insubordination. Breaking and entering. Endangering the lives of your classmates. And releasing Rosalind? Do you have any idea what you've done?"

None of them said a word. Professor Harvey turned to address Terra specifically.

"I'd say I'm disappointed in you, but this goes far beyond that."

Harvey moved to leave, shaking his head. Terra's face was a mix of frustration and devastation. But then she glanced over at Stella. Stella nodded, encouraging the fury building in Terra like an avalanche, and Terra found her voice.

"You *lied* again!"

Musa wondered when people would stop underestimating Terra. She responded to every challenge like a bull yearning for a red flag.

"Excuse me?" said Professor Harvey.

"About Rosalind. About Aster Dell. About all of it. And now you're mad? At me?" Terra fixed her father with a stern and disappointed look. "You can't punish me for not knowing what you didn't tell me. That doesn't make any logical sense."

Professor Harvey clearly didn't have a comeback, so he pulled the parent-slash-professor card. "I think you all need to cool off."

He straight up left, closing the door firmly behind him. And when Terra grabbed the doorknob and tried to open it, the door wouldn't budge.

"He used his magic to seal the door!" She rattled the doorknob furiously. "I caught him in a logic trap, and he used his magic to ground us!"

"That means you won," said Stella.

Terra didn't seem comforted by this information. Musa tried to soothe the frustration coming off Terra in waves.

"He's just overwhelmed."

But Terra wasn't listening. Aisha used this opportunity to try and slink to her room, which Musa thought was wise, but Stella intercepted her.

"And where are you going?" Stella demanded. "I knew you were a teacher's pet. I just didn't know the pet was a rat."

"I was planning on de-escalating the situation by removing myself from it, but if you want to escalate—"

Aisha stepped up to Stella, clearly ready for a fight. *Oh no, teeth and feelings were going to fly everywhere!* Musa looked desperately around.

"Can you wait thirty seconds, please? At least let me get my headphones," she begged, leaping to her feet and running into her room.

Musa closed the door behind her and took a breath, and then felt a tug at her magic, sensing something. This time, it made her smile.

She turned to see Sam. His smile was instant relief. She made an eloquently pained face at him, then went to hide her head in his chest. He pulled her in. He was her sanctuary.

"What the hell's going on out there?"

Sam could hear what was going on for himself. Beyond the door, Aisha and Stella were in a full-on fight. At least it seemed to be just yelling. So far.

"No matter what, you don't tattle," Stella raged. "Anybody over the age of five knows that. Even Terra knows that."

Terra's voice, the only one not yelling, said, "*Hey.* I mean, yeah, but . . . *hey.*"

Aisha shouted, her rage filling Musa's head, the door no barrier at all: "There are Burned Ones outside the Barrier. Bloom is being selfish. The last thing Ms. Dowling needs is to be worried about Rosalind!"

FIRE

I watched as Ms. Dowling entered the mystical space of the stone circle. She stood there for a moment, eyes searching the grass and stones, and then she began to walk away.

She couldn't see me or Rosalind standing right there, Rosalind's eyes glowing faintly in the gloom. As I watched Dowling depart, I wheeled on Rosalind.

"I thought you were weak? That you couldn't do magic? But you can make us invisible?"

"In the stone circle, I can draw on the magic of the land," said Rosalind. "That's why I had you bring me here. So I could recharge the ol' batteries."

Rosalind placed her hand near one of the stones. Tendrils of magical light reached out, connecting hand and stone. She took a seat, with a long groan of relief.

"If you're strong enough to do magic, you can answer questions. I have risked so much to find you and get you out. Please, just tell me: What happened at Aster Dell?"

Even I was startled at how forceful my demand was. Rosalind seemed mildly impressed.

"Everything Farah told you is true. I lied to them. Said Aster Dell was evacuated. It wasn't."

Farah, I thought, and then realized she meant Ms. Dowling. It was almost impossible to imagine Ms. Dowling as having a first name. She tried so hard to be an authority figure, an adult for her students to rely on. For a moment,

I wanted to run after Ms. Dowling and tell her everything I'd done.

Instead, I asked slowly, "You killed those innocent people?"

"That," said Rosalind, "is where it gets complicated."

Rosalind's eyes glowed for a passing instant. The moonlight seemed to respond to her, casting strange shadows. Six hooded figures drifted from outside the circle toward us.

"One of the fundamental tenets of the Otherworld is that only fairies can do magic. The settlers of Aster Dell were an exception. They were humans who drew on sacrifice and death the same way we draw on the elements: *Blood Witches*. It is lost magic. Dangerous magic. If anyone knew it was possible, it would shake the foundation of the Otherworld. So I lied to even my most trusted advisers. Those witches lived in the shadows for centuries. But their actions suggested they were getting bolder. It was only a matter of time before they made a move."

The figures stopped moving, and turned toward the center.

"So when the Burned Ones descended on them, I saw my opportunity. A flock of birds, one powerful stone."

The figures vanished in a flash of light, and Rosalind's eyes returned to normal.

I did some mental math. "Wait. If the settlers of Aster Dell were *witches*, and my birth parents were *fairies*..."

"She's quick," Rosalind said with approval. "Good. This will go faster. You're right. Your parents aren't from Aster

Dell. You were kidnapped. Your fairy parents were nowhere to be found."

"So they could still be out there." My fairy parents could still be alive! "Why didn't you try to find them?"

Rosalind's intense blue eyes were fixed on me, wholly absorbed by me, as though I was something wonderful. "You weren't safe in the Otherworld. The power inside you is too great. I knew it the second I laid eyes on you. It's why the witches wanted you. To use your power. And why the Burned Ones outside the Barrier want you, too: to get rid of you before it can be used on them."

This wasn't wonderful at all.

Everyone said the Burned Ones hadn't been seen in sixteen years. Now suddenly they were here, near Alfea, killing people. Hurting Silva, who was like Sky's dad.

Would Sky hate me, if he knew it was all my fault? Would my friends be afraid to be near me? I'd believed that if I came to Alfea, I could keep my parents safe, but perhaps I brought danger everywhere I went. To everyone I loved.

I couldn't repress the chill coursing through me. "They've been after me the whole time?"

"Sucks to be special sometimes." Rosalind grinned. "But now you've got me. And that's gonna suck for the Burned Ones even more. Ready for trick number two?"

Rosalind smiled. It was oddly comforting. At least I wasn't in this alone. She would help me. She'd give me the answer I needed most: how to keep those I loved safe.

SPECIALIST

They were at the edge of the forest, in the dead of night, and Riven was pretty sure they were all going to die.

Sky and Silva were at the head of their little group, being joint fearless leaders. Riven was eavesdropping on them shamelessly.

Unfortunately, they were stoically surveying the pale shimmer of the Barrier, searching the woods beyond for signs of monsters. Still, Riven could tell they both wanted to break their manly reserve and spill secrets. Silva had cleared his throat four times.

Eventually, Silva asked, "Should I be worried I had to learn from Aisha that Bloom drugged you?"

Aisha the sporty babe had turned up, thrown herself at Dowling in a burst of teacher's-pet love, and handed over some kind of super convenient magic listening device she'd been using to spy on Dowling. Then she'd confessed all about Bloom's delinquency, and she, Dowling, and Terra's dad had gone off to possibly arrest Bloom? Riven wasn't sure. He couldn't believe trusty friend Aisha had squealed and he, Riven, hadn't. He should definitely have squealed. He'd tried, but Dowling had already marched off to stop Bloom from freeing Beatrix, and Sky had elbowed him in the ribs when Riven started tattling to Silva.

"I don't know," Sky returned now, very quiet. "Should

I be worried I had to learn from Bloom what happened at Aster Dell?"

Sky's tone was almost menacing. Okay, what *had* happened at Aster Dell? Riven wondered. Was Aster Dell, like, a fairy strip club Silva enjoyed visiting? Hilarious.

He knew it probably wasn't that, but he was thinking about their imminent deaths, and he wanted to cheer himself up.

Silva had braced himself and gone suspiciously still. Seemed like it was time for him to release the intel on the strip club.

"I think it's through here," murmured Kat.

Wow, Kat. Riven was trying to eavesdrop; why did she have to keep being an efficient super-soldier and focus on the getting-killed job?

"We'll discuss this later," Silva decided.

There was no later, they were getting murdered! Riven wanted to hear about the strip club now.

But Silva and Sky were already turning back toward the group, and Kat had focused her steely super-soldier gaze on Riven.

"Pull it up again."

Riven pulled out his phone, and then handed it to Kat.

"You do it."

Kat tossed him a scornful look.

Riven defended himself. It wasn't Riven's fault everybody else was a bloodthirsty lunatic!

"It's *dark* watching somebody die! Don't look at me like I'm a jerk for not wanting to see it."

Kat, a certified bloodthirsty lunatic, rolled her eyes as she took the phone. As she watched the screen, Riven heard screams. Flesh tearing. He repressed a shudder.

Kat reported, "I recognize that hollow. It's near the barn. Not far."

"Let's move!" snapped Silva.

Riven had a better idea. *Let's not!*

"Wait. Without fairies? We counted at least six Burned Ones out there. That's freakin' stupid."

Sky glared at Riven for making insubordinate statements of fact.

"It's an order, Riv," Sky told him without sympathy. "Suck it up."

Riven cringed. There were times in a guy's life when he had to ask himself the real questions. Why did I ever agree to wield a stupid sword, and why did I ever become friends with this censorious idiot?

Right. Because Alfea had left him with no other choice. And now Alfea's rules were telling him to go and die.

Silva addressed the whole team. "I understand this is scary. You've been lucky enough to grow up in an era of peace. But heading into a forest, against all odds, to fight a creature that chills your soul? That's what being a Specialist is. And it's the minimum I expect from each of you."

Great speech, Riven thought, except for the fact it was

dumb. Why not try to even out the odds so that—Riven was just spitballing here—they didn't have to *all die?*

Then there came a loud, terrible rasp, a sound of sandpaper that rang like thunder. They looked toward the forest, where their enemy should be, but there was something wrong here.

Sky was the one who realized first. "That's not coming from the forest. It's coming from the school."

Silva snapped into action. "Split up. Get to the school. Find as many students as you can, and get them to the courtyard. Go. NOW."

There were people in that castle he cared about, thought Riven, then wondered: Who? The answer came to him almost at once. *Beatrix.* If Bloom hadn't gotten her out, Beatrix was bound and helpless in that castle.

He found himself running just as fast as Sky.

EARTH

It was great that Sam and Musa were dating, Terra figured, because now they were her captive audience and she could share many thoughts with them. Outside her room, it was too scary. Everything had gone quiet, which meant Aisha and Stella had either headed for their rooms or killed each other. Terra didn't wish to know. She fussed with her plants and talked to Sam and Musa about Dad, and it made thinking of Dad hurt a little less.

"I used to think he was never wrong," she said sadly.

"Parents are still people, Ter. And people are flawed. The sooner you learn that, the better."

Musa was so wise. When Musa and Sam got married, Terra thought Musa would be a very calming influence on the family.

Sam studied Musa. "You never talk about your parents."

"There's a reason," Musa said briefly.

Her brother was annoying but also right. It was time to share all their horrible family secrets and bond. They could help Musa.

Terra offered, "You can, you know . . . talk about them. Whatever happened. We're your friends. I mean, Sam is more than that, obviously, but for the sake of this discussion—"

"It's not a discussion," Musa said flatly.

Before Terra could push further, the lights flickered. On and off.

"That's weird," murmured Terra, and they moved to the door in a knot.

In the common room, the lights were flickering on and off as well. It felt as if the whole castle was blinking.

Stella and Aisha came out of their rooms, each with the same startled expression on their face. *Yay*, Terra was happy they hadn't killed each other. But this was still very weird.

"Are we having a . . . power outage?" asked Stella.

Aisha frowned. "How does that even happen here?"

Terra leaped to provide this information. "It shouldn't. Alfea is an outpost. The 'electricity' it runs on is magic. Beneath the school are energy wells that were designed by—"

"I'm gonna skip the history lesson and check it out," said Sam, who never appreciated when Terra shared fascinating information.

Her annoying brother moved through the front door of the suite with his magic. It seemed as though he was vanishing away into the gloom.

Brothers were so irritating. Off he went, for what reason? So he could find some other dudes and they could say it was weird the power was out? What they should do was analyze this situation, and take action to remedy it.

Terra continued her lecture. She had a lot to say. "The wells of course were designed in a spirit of cooperation between Water and Air Fairies. And when the wells fill with enough magic, it's like a battery—"

Sam burst back through the wall, and collapsed on the ground of the common room. There was blood all over him. There was so much blood.

The world seemed to spin as they ran to him.

"*Sam,*" said Terra. Suddenly, his name seemed like the only word she knew.

Sam gasped, wetly, "There's a Burned One in the school."

The lights went out completely, leaving them in darkness.

FIRE

I stood in the center of the stone circle, Rosalind at my side. The torches were smoldering all around us, and my magic was a banked fire inside me.

"Dig deeper than you have before," Rosalind urged. "What you did to free me is just a fraction of the magic you need."

The torches flared at her words. Rosalind's guidance grew sharper and sharper. When the torchlight hit her hair, it burned gold.

"More. Let the fire consume you."

I felt the same way I had once before, as though there was too much power inside me and it must spill out.

"Keep going."

The thing was, I wanted to. Power coursed through me, and it felt so sweet. But it had felt good to set my home alight, too. Until it hadn't. Until I hurt someone.

"What if I lose control?" I asked.

"Control limits you!"

"I'm scared," I whispered.

"Good," said Rosalind. "The moment you learn to enjoy that feeling is the moment the world unlocks for you. A wildfire burns within you, Bloom. With the right people around you . . ."

Good that I was scared? Good? Ms. Dowling had never

wanted me to be scared. I let the rising magic drop, and turned to face Rosalind.

"You mean, you? With you around me? You want me to listen to you and trust you and let you guide me, but I just met you. You hid me from Ms. Dowling. You didn't even tell anyone I existed."

I hadn't thought about it this way before, but now I remembered the fire crackling through my parents' bedroom, and my mother on the floor. I was a danger to my parents, and Rosalind had put me there!

"I almost killed my parents because you left me in the First World with no guidance, and . . ."

"*The guidance you needed was love,*" Rosalind said sharply. "Farah could never give that to you. Vanessa and Michael could."

The mention of my parents' names knocked me back. Mom and Dad. I kept thinking of my parents, of my birth parents, of getting home. As though somehow, if I got all the answers, I could transport myself back to the time before I set my house on fire and put my mom in danger.

But *parents* wasn't just a label I could slap on a pair of people. *Home* wasn't just an idea. It was a real place. I knew who my parents were.

And so did Rosalind.

"You know their names," I said quietly.

"I chose them. I knew they were about to lose a daughter. I gave them a second chance. And gave you a hiding place from the monsters that wanted you dead." Rosalind's sharp, command-giving voice softened. "I will always look out for you, Bloom. And when this is over, we'll find your birth parents, *together.*"

I wanted to believe in her promise so much. All the answers I got only served to make me more confused. As I tried to sort out the revelations in my whirling mind, my phone buzzed and I glanced at it absentmindedly, and then went still. It was a text from Stella, saying: *Burned Ones inside school. Stuck in the suite.*

"They're in the school?" I demanded of the night air. "How?"

I tried frantically to text back, but it was no use. My mind filled with visions of what might be happening to my friends at Alfea, I turned desperately to Rosalind.

"I just lost service . . . I have to go. Are you charged? Can you help?"

"I can't," Rosalind answered. "But you don't need it."

There was no more time for questions or answers. No time for anything but action. I bolted toward the castle.

Running flat out, I'd almost reached the castle when I heard familiar whispers. At the far tree line, I saw a glowing light, brimming over as though the horizon was a cup, suffusing the whole skyline. *What the hell?* My mad dash arrested, I moved toward that glow.

A hand landed on my shoulder.

A voice said, "There you are."

I spun around with my heart in my throat.

"Sky," I said. "Hey."

It wasn't a battle to death with a monster. But it was a very awkward moment nonetheless.

"You seem . . . okay?" I offered.

"I am. Whatever you gave me wore off a few hours ago." He proceeded, all business, "Come on, we have to go find everyone else."

As he walked off, I took another look back at the tree line, but whatever had been there was long gone.

SPECIALIST

Kat and Riven entered the castle in darkness. They carried torches, and as they moved cat-soft through the halls, Riven heard the creak of beams overhead. There was a flickering red light in the distance.

"Hello?" called Kat.

It was like Kat had never seen a horror movie in her life.

"The hell are you doing?" Riven hissed. "What if it's one of those things?"

A Fire Fairy Riven didn't know emerged from a corner, and then several fairies came stumbling toward the Specialists, toward rescue. Kat shot Riven a frankly offensive side-eye.

"This way, guys," she told them.

The Fire Fairy said, "I saw more students in the greenhouse."

Kat nodded. "I'm gonna bring them back. You grab the greenhouse stragglers."

"Wait—" Riven began.

He didn't want to split up—that was a one-way ticket to murder city! And he didn't want to be alone. But Kat was already moving down the hallway. Riven was dismissed.

Then he thought . . . students in the greenhouse. Who else could it be?

Terra.

Riven went quietly into the greenhouse, shining his torch around the familiar space, the twining vines and blooming flowers, the carefully separated pots of dirt. No, soil. Terra got very stern about that. Riven liked it here. He felt charmed and comforted.

Until the spotlight of his torch illuminated the "stragglers."

On one of the tables, lying unconscious, was Beatrix. Standing over her like a mad scientist with a sword was Dane. In front of Dane were various herbs and beakers and other laboratory equipment.

With deep feeling, Riven said, "What the hell?"

Riven realized the expression on Dane's face was panic.

The words spilled out of Dane's mouth. "She triggered a trap in Dowling's office. Some kind of paralyzation thing. She gave me instructions for a potion to fix it, but . . ."

Riven considered the situation, and then made an executive decision. "Sucks for her. Come on."

"I'm not leaving her!" said Dane.

Riven could have left Dane with Terra and not inter-
fered. Dane would've been fine. He would've been happy.
He'd be safe right now, and not desperate here in the dark.
What had happened to Dane was Riven's fault. So Riven spoke
with all the fury born from Beatrix's betrayal. He spoke to
him as if Dane was Riven at the start of the year, arrogant
and about to make a terrible mistake.

"Dane. She's *not worth it.*"

"She cares about you, and I know you care about her.
Don't act like you don't. *Please,*" Dane was begging, looking
at Riven as though he trusted Riven could and would save
him. "You have to help."

Riven glanced at the door. He didn't want to go out there
alone and face monsters that ripped people limb from limb.
He didn't want to be alone at all.

Did Beatrix care about him? Could Dane be right?

He looked back at Dane, with his puppy-dog eyes, and
Beatrix lying there helpless. Where else was Riven gonna
go? What else could he do?

Terra had said, *Nobody would ever ask you for help.* Dane
was asking. Dane seemed sure Riven would do it, looking
at Riven as though Riven mattered to him.

Riven wanted to believe Dane. And he didn't want to go
back outside.

Already knowing this was a bad idea, Riven asked,
"What did her instructions say?"

FIRE

Sky and I made our way toward the Winx suite. We had to push through the flood of students headed in the other direction, bent on escape. At first our quiet seemed like only the silence of urgency, but quickly, even in this frantic and terrible time, it was clear it was the silence of deep awkwardness.

I broke first. "Will you please say something?"

"What is there to say?" Sky asked distantly. "You kissed me and then you drugged me."

"Technically, I drugged you first," I joked.

Sky's face stayed stern. Tough crowd. Tough, roofied crowd. That was fair.

I tried being serious. "I didn't know we were gonna kiss when I dosed your drink. Then I got wrapped up in the moment, and—"

"A kiss seemed like a good way to distract me. Thanks for the recap."

No. That wasn't what it was. How could Sky think that? He must know how I felt about him.

"I wasn't trying to distract you!" I halted. "You would've stopped me, Sky."

He stopped walking, too. I would've thought nothing could stop my soldier boy when he was on a mission. There was genuine pain and frustration on his face.

"I opened up to you. I told you stuff I've never told any-one, Bloom. I trusted you, and—"

"And you still would've stopped me," I finished. "So you can say you trust me, but you were still gonna treat me like some damsel who needed to be protected from herself. Sorry. But that's not trust."

Sky said flatly, "You let a murderer out of jail to free a crazy ex-headmistress."

Well, when he put it like that . . . I had to show him a different point of view.

"And what if Rosalind isn't crazy? What if she had a reason to lie? The more I learn, the more I think maybe everyone did what they thought was right."

When Sky answered me, he was using his soldier voice again, seeing things only in black-and-white.

"Just because somebody thinks what they did was right, doesn't mean that it is."

He marched off.

EARTH

Stella was still trying to get a signal, wandering back and forth and past the center of the room where the rest of them huddled. Aisha and Musa were helping Terra hold Sam down as his body spasmed. Her brother's eyes were going black.

"The infection will shift soon. He'll turn erratic if he doesn't get Zanbaq. We have to get *out*."

Terra leaped for the door, but then saw Musa shudder as Sam writhed.

"Musa, you okay?"

Musa whispered, "Somebody do something."

Terra intended to.

Suddenly, there was a banging on the door. Stella and Terra exchanged a wary look, and then backed up. There was more banging. *If it was a Burned One*, Terra thought, *they had to fight it.* She hoped Stella had her light show ready.

Just then, the wood splintered and the remains of the door swung open, revealing Sky, who'd kicked the door down. Bloom stood next to him.

There was a split second of tense silence when Sky and Stella came face-to-face. Bloom's gaze stuttered between them, but their quiet and Bloom's hesitance didn't last long.

Sky said softly, "Hi."

Stella said, "Hey."

Terra said, "We need to get help!"

Terra genuinely could not have cared less about their thing. Her brother was bleeding out, with poison in his veins.

That was when Bloom and Sky looked past Terra and Stella and saw Sam on the floor.

Bloom whispered, "Oh no."

Sky cursed, then said, "Let's get him to the courtyard. Everyone is there."

As they all headed out of the suite, Bloom lingered for a moment.

"What?" said Aisha. "Did you think you weren't going to have to face her?"

Terra didn't stay to hear what Bloom replied. She didn't care about the Aisha, Bloom, and Ms. Dowling teacher love triangle any more than she cared about Sky, Bloom, and Stella's thing. Terra was focused on her brother.

Hold on, Sam, she thought as they made their way down dark corridors with her brother's pained breath ragged in her ears. *Just hold on until we get to Dad. He'll fix this. He'll make everything okay.*

The courtyard was now the scene of a castle under siege. Bright wisps of magic conjured by Light Fairies wreathed the night air, giving them illumination enough to see what was happening, but what was happening was terrifying. Dowling was giving orders to Fire Fairies to weld the doors shut. Silva was issuing commands to Specialists, all arming themselves even more heavily and helping fairies into armor. Terra saw Kat oiling a sword, but she didn't see Riven anywhere. Typical.

Sam moaned. Musa made a little sound, as though his moan was a blow to her.

"Almost there," Terra murmured to Sam, and was glad she didn't have to lie to her brother.

The courtyard canteen where they ate lunch every day was now an assembly line for the dispensation of healing herbs. Fairies were pruning Zanbaq, and distilling oil, preparing bandages, and tending to patients. Her father was in their midst, wrapping a bandage around a Specialist's wound, and then turning and taking a breath before he addressed himself to another task. He looked every inch the professor he was, the soldier he had been. Utterly calm. In control.

Terra said, "Dad?"

Her father looked up to see Terra and Musa, with their arms around a barely conscious Sam. The color drained from his face. His mouth opened, and for a second no words came out. Terra's desperate confidence in him went shaky.

Her father turned to a fairy. "I need Zanbaq," her dad said. *"Now."*

As Terra and Musa gently laid Sam down on an empty table, her dad did a preliminary inspection. Sam was so pale. There was blood everywhere. Her dad flinched away from the sight of his son's wounds, and then turned to Terra. His snarl echoed against the stones of the courtyard, his familiar, trusted face as strange to her as her embattled school.

"He's lost so much blood! Why didn't you get him here sooner?"

Terra had still hoped they would be saved by the adults, that, despite all the evidence, her father was ultimately capable and invincible. Now the last of her hope drained away.

She met her father's accusing gaze without flinching.

"We were grounded, Dad. Remember?"

FIRE

All the fairies in the courtyard applauded when Ms. Dowling made a speech announcing that Queen Luna was on her way with reinforcements. But I couldn't stand in the crowd. I had to find an opportunity to talk to her alone.

I seized my chance once the Water Fairy she was instructing departed. Ms. Dowling gave me a look that heralded the next ice age.

"I know you're mad," I said.

"An understatement," Ms. Dowling responded.

Once I explained, she'd understand. Then we could all work together.

"Rosalind isn't the monster you think she is. She lied for a reason. The villagers at Aster Dell weren't innocent. They were *Blood Witches*. And my birth parents weren't even there."

My birth parents might be alive, and Ms. Dowling could have her mentor back! Surely Ms. Dowling would be glad.

Ms. Dowling gave me an assessing look. "She certainly has a way of winning people over, doesn't she?"

Her tone was a smidge condescending. Or more than a smidge.

"Is your ego so fragile that you can't even consider that you might be wrong about her?" I fired back.

She was silent for a moment, as though I'd struck a nerve. Still, when she answered me, her voice was measured.

"Rosalind gave you just enough information to string you along. She's manipulating you, Bloom. That's what she does."

"Then what the hell have *you* been doing?" I demanded. "You were the one who kept things from me. Not her."

"And why isn't she telling me this herself? Why isn't she by our side helping fight?" Ms. Dowling's demand cut through the air like a whip. *"Where is she?"*

Ms. Dowling still didn't understand. I had to defend Rosalind. "She's still weak. Not charged up enough. But she said when she was—"

"So you *were* in the stone circle?" Ms. Dowling asked sharply.

"She used her magic to hide us," I explained.

That took Ms. Dowling a minute to absorb, and once she did, I was stunned by the emotion that showed on her usually guarded face. I understood she was mad she'd been tricked, but the white-hot fury in her face and her voice knocked me back.

"The stone circle is a conduit to the magic of the land. That magic powers everything at Alfea. Like our electricity. And the Barrier."

It took me a second to put together what Ms. Dowling was saying. Tonight the castle had gone dark. The Barrier had gone down, and the Burned Ones had come through.

I almost couldn't force the words out. "Are you saying Rosalind is the reason the Barrier was weak enough for the Burned Ones to get through?"

She was saying the Burned Ones had come for me, and I'd freed Rosalind and helped them do it. I'd done this. I'd ruined everything, twice over.

Dowling's silence was the only answer I needed. I barely had a chance to process before the terrible, bone-rattling rasp of a Burned One echoed outside the gates. A second rasp issued from outside the canteen. Two more from either side.

Dowling's expression turned into one I'd seen Sky wear often: a soldier's determination.

I had to tell her. "They're after me, you know."

"Yes. I didn't realize that at first. But I do now." Ms. Dowling turned the force of that soldierly determination onto me. "Which means it's my job to protect you."

I didn't want to be protected. I wanted to help. I gritted my teeth, looking around the castle. I could make this right.

"We're going to fight them, right? Rosalind told me how to fight them."

Ms. Dowling's lip curled. "Your actions are the reason the school is in danger, Bloom. I'd say you've done enough."

SPECIALIST

The rasps of Burned Ones echoed through the greenhouse. Riven clamped down on his rising panic as he distilled oils. Distilling had to be done with a steady hand.

Terra would faint if she saw how badly Dane was grinding those herbs.

Riven confiscated Dane's pestle and mortar. He'd do it himself.

"Uh . . . how are you so good with this?"

Dane sounded very surprised. Of course, Riven reflected. Dane didn't actually know a thing about him. He'd only seen what Riven was trying to be.

"Terra and I used to hang out a bunch here. I'll deny saying this, but . . . she's not the worst," Riven admitted. *I'm the worst. She was right about everything.* "I might've led you astray this year."

He'd thought this would be his year. That he'd be cool, and skilled, and surrounded by admirers. No more doubting his place, no more insecurities. Funny to think that Riven had actually been much happier last year. In the greenhouse, surrounded by stuff he was actually interested in, doing what he loved.

Yeah, that was real funny.

Riven poured the oil into the powder. Vapors rose, the correct color. Terra would've been proud of him.

Oh wait, obviously she wouldn't, because he was an evil criminal. Riven placed the concoction next to Beatrix's still, beautiful face.

When Riven glanced around, he saw Dane watching Beatrix inhale with worshipful intensity.

"You didn't," Dane breathed. "Beatrix is special."

Riven stared at Dane, confused more than anything.

Was Dane gay, was he straight, was he just into awful people? If Dane liked girls, maybe Riven could find some way to deliver him to Terra. Dane would be safe then. Riven couldn't be saved. Nobody wanted him back, but perhaps Dane could be all right.

The world was upside down right now and monsters were coming to kill them all, and he wished he had even a shred of certainty.

Finally, he just asked who it was Dane wanted, and wasn't terribly surprised when Dane said, "Screw you."

He was very surprised when Beatrix said archly, "That sounds like an answer."

They both whipped around to see Beatrix stirring, and stretching as she sat up. It reminded Riven of the way she'd wake up in his bed, when he'd thought she was his girlfriend. When he was happy. And deluded.

"No need to fill me in. I could hear everything." She fixed them both with her dark eyes, unusually serious. "You two made the right choice. When this is all over, you're going to want to be on our side."

Riven thought, panic fracturing his mind, *I didn't make a choice!* But he had, hadn't he? He'd helped Dane. He'd helped Beatrix. As usual, he'd made the wrong choice.

Wow, Terra should've tied Riven up with her vines when she had the chance.

MIND

Sam was pouring with sweat and shaking, black veins running under the surface of his skin. Musa watched, Terra beside her, as Professor Harvey injected the oil directly into Sam's forearm. The veins receded for only an instant, then returned like an oil-black tide.

"Why isn't the Zanbaq working?" Terra demanded.

Professor Harvey's brow was knit; Musa could feel his concentration and his worry. "It's a deep wound. There might be something else going on."

Harvey pulled bloody gauze from the wound. As he did, Sam screamed. His pain went through Musa's mind like a second scream, reinforcing the first.

"He's in pain. *Help him.*"

"I'm doing all I can," said Professor Harvey.

He turned his attention on Musa. She felt the weight of his speculation, along with the weight of his eyes.

"But there is something you can do. You're a Mind Fairy. Feeling emotions is only a small part of your magic. You have a connection. You can take some of his pain."

"What?" Musa stammered. "How?"

"Instead of pushing it away? Bring it into you. Try it."

Musa reached out and took Sam's hand, focusing her magic on him. But then Sam screamed. Touching his mind was like touching a thorn. Musa pulled her magic instinctively away.

"I can't. I'm sorry."

Terra exclaimed, "You didn't even try."

"I said I can't, okay?" snarled Musa, overcome with shame, and terror for Sam, and dread for herself. She couldn't do it. She couldn't take it. She wished she could.

As Musa stumbled off, she saw Bloom watching with wide guilty eyes, like Bloom was the one who'd failed.

FIRE

The other Fire Fairies were assembled at the gates, saying that Queen Luna and her reinforcements wouldn't get here till tomorrow. Sam wouldn't last until tomorrow. If the gates didn't hold, none of us would last.

I'd been terribly wrong, but if Ms. Dowling thought I was going to stay still and do nothing when this was all my fault, she was wrong, too.

But I'd learned my lesson about one thing.

I headed away from the Fire Fairies and went to find Sky.

He was trying to carry a huge, heavy piece of timber alone, which was just like him. He paused at a barricaded door, lifting one side a little awkwardly, and I grabbed the other end to hold it in place. Time for truth. Time to be real.

"I should've told you what I was doing at the stone circle. I should've been honest with you like you were with me. I'm sorry."

Sky said, "Thank you."

We reinforced the barricade together. I took a deep breath. Time for even scarier honesty. "And that kiss? Sky, if you thought that was anything but genuine?"

"It's fine, Bloom. Whatever it was—"

He didn't finish. I didn't let him. Instead, I pulled him into another kiss. This one was warm until it was hot, burning like fire, real as magic. After we separated, I finally saw Sky's soldier-boy facade crack with a smile.

"If I say I still don't believe you . . ." said Sky. "Will you do it again?"

I shared that smile and gloried at the feeling of connection restored between us. But that wasn't what I'd come to him for.

"What is it? You can tell me."

"Can I?"

It wasn't a real question, not this time. Right now, at this most desperate moment, all my painful doubts about who I could trust and who I should tell seemed resolved. Everything seemed so clear. Our smiles turned into mischievous grins, troublemakers in this together.

"Whatever you're thinking of doing," said Sky. "I'm here."

But Sky wasn't the only mischief maker I needed in my life.

I went searching and found Aisha and Stella whispering in a corner of the courtyard together. They were talking about me.

"I know Bloom," said Aisha. "She won't sit around and do nothing. Especially if she thinks all this is her fault."

I grinned at Aisha's back. Hey, she *did* know me.

"If only her friend and roommate hadn't turned on her . . ." Stella said with mournful malice.

"Really, you're still doing this?" Aisha snapped, and then sighed. "I feel bad, okay? Is that what you want me to say? I figured the fact that I was coming to you of all people would tell you that I'm sorry. What more do you want?"

Stella seemed to consider what she wanted.

"I suppose I was just enjoying the friendship high ground for once," she admitted. "It's not a view I normally get. All right, then. What do you think she's going to do?"

I decided to make my presence known. "Probably something reckless and a little crazy," I admitted.

The two of them turned to see me, standing in front of them. Not running off by myself.

"But for once," I told my friends, "I'm not gonna do it alone."

SPECIALIST

Sky engaged their lunch lady in conversation about herbal concoctions as Bloom, Aisha, and Stella sneaked by. He nodded at Bloom as she went, her hair the brightest thing in the dark night.

He hoped the nod conveyed, *Good luck, girlfriend!*

Well. Maybe girlfriend. He guessed they could determine the relationship if they survived the night.

He was thinking of how to excuse himself from the lunch lady when Silva said, "Sky. A word."

Sky went over to where Silva was reinforcing a door, and quietly helped him. It had always felt reassuring to him, just being in Silva's presence, accomplishing tasks together. Everything was understood between them when they had to do their duty.

"You think it'll hold?" Sky asked.

"For a while," Silva said grimly. Then, in a voice so soft it sounded strange coming from him, "But I don't know how this night will end, Sky. So . . . I need you to know the truth about Aster Dell."

"Bloom told me everything," Sky assured him.

"Aster Dell is where Andreas died," said Silva.

Okay, Bloom hadn't told him that. In fact, Bloom had never mentioned his father's name to him. Everyone else said it over and over again. *Andreas of Eraklyon, the great hero.*

But how could his father have died at Aster Dell? They'd ambushed their enemies at Aster Dell. Nobody would've had a chance to attack Andreas.

"How is that possible? You said my dad died in battle. Fighting."

"He did," said Silva. "I just didn't tell you who he was fighting."

Silva told him now, in this night of chaos and strange

light. In a slow and halting voice, Silva told how he'd realized what Rosalind was doing at Aster Dell. That the people in it had to be evacuated. He'd needed to tell Ms. Dowling and Professor Harvey.

Andreas, loyal to Rosalind, had stood in Silva's way with a blade in hand. So Silva had cut him down.

Silva had believed he'd be able to warn the others in time. He'd thought wrong.

Sky tried not to let his voice tremble as he said, "You told me my dad was a hero."

Suddenly, he understood better how Bloom had felt, with all the adults around her lying.

Silva answered haltingly, "He saved countless lives before that day. Killed more Burned Ones than any of us. But he was . . . flawed, Sky. We all are."

"*Flawed?*" Sky snarled. "That's the best you can do? He killed hundreds of people and you killed him. And all I get is that you're both *flawed?*"

"Sky . . ."

"What the hell am I supposed to do with that?"

Sky's entire world was collapsing around him. Who was he supposed to be, if he couldn't be his father, and he couldn't be Silva? There was nothing to be proud of and no solid place to stand.

That was why Silva had always mentored him so grimly. It hadn't ever been love, not for Sky, not for his dad. Silva had only raised him out of duty and guilt.

He'd never had anything close to a dad.

Silva's voice was sharp. "You grow up, and you accept it. And you focus on what matters."

As if in answer to Silva, there came another loud rasp, like a huge alligator's scales scraping against the granite walls of the castle. Then there came a slam to the door, with such shattering force Sky wondered if it would break down.

Silva said, "They're here."

EARTH

Musa was sitting alone in a corner of the courtyard, headphones on. Her back to the carnage. As Terra approached, she was reminded of how Musa used to ignore her in their own room, and she got even more furious.

"What the hell?" Terra demanded of Musa's back.

But Musa didn't turn, so Terra pulled her headphones off.

"You can't run away. He's in pain. And my dad is trying, but—"

When Musa turned around, Terra saw the abject panic on her face.

"Please just leave me alone," Musa begged.

Seeing Musa's panic was like a slap in the face, reminding Terra that there were people and pain in the world besides Sam's. But would she really be helping Musa, if she just let her sit here in a corner ignoring the world?

Terra hesitated.

"I know you care about him," she began, gently.

Musa was shaking. "That's the problem! I can't feel it. I can't feel somebody I care about die. Not again."

"What? Musa . . ."

"My mom died last year, Terra. And I was with her. I felt the moment it happened. Felt everything she felt." Musa was fighting back tears as she spoke. "It's why I can't talk about my family. And why I can't be with Sam now. I can't feel it again. Please don't make me feel it again."

Musa seemed on the verge of a full-fledged panic attack. Terra realized this was a dead end. All she could do was be kind to Musa, or not.

"Okay. It's okay," Terra promised.

Terra pulled the smaller girl into a hug, and felt Musa draw in a shaky breath, and then a calmer one.

Into Musa's hair, Terra made another promise. "And I'm not gonna let him die."

Her dad wasn't succeeding. Musa couldn't try. So Terra had to make a move of her own.

Terra patted Musa gently, gave her back her headphones, and then whirled and headed for the barricades where Silva and Sky stood. The castle doors were echoing with the impact of blows. Fairies across the courtyard were clutching their weapons. There was the sound of shattering glass from somewhere, far away.

Standing at the doors, Silva said, "They won't hold much longer."

Great, thought Terra. She had to get to the Burned One

that had hurt her brother, and kill it so Sam would be well. She pulled at the barricade, trying to bring it down.

"Terra!"

Sky grabbed her by her shoulder.

Terra gave him a look of annoyance. "We're hiding when we should be fighting."

"We'll fight when we have to," Headmaster Silva snapped. "We can't put lives in jeopardy."

Terra had heard quite enough out of the adults today.

"They *already are*. The only way to help them is to kill those things."

"That's not as easy as you might—"

Silva didn't get a chance to finish. He was interrupted by a part of the barricade falling inches from Terra's face.

Terra backed up a step and watched as the barricade came apart before their eyes.

All across the castle there were burned arms worming through cracks in the walls. Timber was falling to the ground. The awful rasping was loud as thunder. Through the broken barricades, there were glimpses of Burned Ones, snarling, reaching, their awful eyes glistening. A Burned One's arm burst through the wood, clawed, grasping for them.

There was a crash as the glass roof fell in, a Burned One hurtling from the sky. In another direction, flames cast by a defending Fire Fairy swept the floor in a destructive wave. The burned hand tried to seize Terra.

Then the Burned One's arm was withdrawn. Shadows

skittered at the edges of their vision, and the night went quiet as the rasps stopped. Terra looked around, dazed.

"What just happened?"

A tense stillness settled over the space. Dowling walked to the center of the courtyard. The rasps had almost entirely died away. Silva went toward her, moving fast.

"They're leaving," Dowling told him. "Going outside."

"They're all moving together, like they're following something," Silva reported, his brow furrowed.

Their headmistress's cool control abruptly broke as realization struck.

"*Where is Bloom?*" Ms. Dowling demanded.

LIGHT

Stella, Aisha, and Bloom emerged from the passageway into the cold night air. It felt just like sneaking away from her mother, shivering and alone. One part of Stella wanted to go back to Ms. Dowling, or to wait for her mom and the army, or to cling to Sky, to ask someone, anyone, to protect her and solve her problems.

Only that didn't work.

It was a princess's duty to protect her people, and Stella wanted to be someone who helped and didn't hurt her friends. She wanted Alfea and those inside it to be safe. She wanted to be as brave as Bloom, who was so determined to protect everyone from the threat she might pose.

Bloom glanced back toward the lights of the school, and Stella wondered if Bloom's nerve would break. Stella wouldn't blame her if it did.

"Come on," Bloom told them, brave as a knight. "We have to make sure the Burned Ones are following me."

They headed on into the dark that Stella had always feared, but Stella didn't feel so afraid now. For the first time, Stella wasn't alone in the dark.

EARTH

If the Burned Ones were chasing Bloom, Terra had to go after them and hunt them down. That much was clear. Kat the Specialist grabbed a weapon and nodded to Terra. They moved forward together.

Her dad's voice behind her said: "Terra, do not go out there."

Terra steeled herself to resist his appeal. "I know you want to protect me, Dad, that you think I'm just a kid, but I'm not. I have to do something."

"You're right," her father said, and that made Terra turn, startled. "I need your help."

When Terra saw the fear in her father's eyes, she ran back with him.

It seemed only a handful of seconds before Terra was in a fight, but not the fight she'd anticipated. She was fighting for her brother's life. Sam was screaming in agony. Bloodied lumps of gauze littered the table. Her father picked up and wielded the forceps as Terra threw herself at Sam, desperate to stanch the bleeding.

"I found a splinter near his heart. A piece of the Burned One. That's why it's still spreading. If it gets much farther—"

Her father clearly couldn't bear to finish the sentence.

"How do we get it out?" whispered Terra.

Her dad said, "I'm trying, but if I accidentally tap it . . ."

Her father's hand trembled as he reached the forceps into the wound. Terra bit her lip hard. Every time Sam screamed, her dad shook.

Sam whimpered, "It hurts."

"Dad," Terra urged.

"I need you to fight it, Sam," their dad begged. "Try and stay still for me."

Sam clenched his eyes shut, but even closing his eyes seemed to make pain rip through him.

"*I can't!*" Sam screamed.

Terra shouted over the screams, "Dad, we're gonna lose him."

She couldn't bear to look into Sam's face, so she was staring down at Sam's hand, clenching and unclenching desperately in the air. She kept worrying the hand would go limp.

Then another hand slipped into Sam's.

Suddenly, the thrashing stopped. Sam's eyes opened, and Terra saw his gaze had turned pure violet with mind magic. Musa stood over him, her own eyes glowing vividly. Tears were streaming down her face.

Sam said weakly, "Musa . . ."

Musa murmured to him, "I think maybe it's your turn to get some peace from me."

Musa squeezed his hand, and then gasped in pain. They were sharing it, Terra realized, and shared between two people the pain might be bearable. Enough to let her father do what he must.

"Are you okay?" whispered Terra, almost as terrified as she was relieved.

Musa, so controlled and aloof, was weeping openly. "Just do what you need to do."

With that, Dad dived back in. Sam and Musa seemed lost in their own private world of shared suffering. Terra could see Musa struggling, but she didn't break eye contact.

There was nobody for her dad to turn to, except Terra. He stared at her pleadingly.

"I can't get it," her dad said helplessly.

He sounded as young as Sam, as young and uncertain as she was. But Terra knew how to be certain for other people, when they needed her.

"Yeah, Dad, you can," Terra told him. "I know you can."

Her father drew in a deep breath. His hands stopped. With one final attempt, Sam and Musa both gasped.

The black veins retreated as her father slid out the huge

splinter. They all breathed a sigh of relief, but the relief couldn't last.

Her father said quietly, "He's okay for now. But it's still severe. He won't be out of the woods until the Burned One who attacked him is killed."

FIRE

Aisha and Stella and I made our stand behind the school, in the cleared-out Bastion area. Aisha eyed the shimmering surface of the waters.

"I can use the water from the pond," offered Aisha.

Stella was looking at me with what truly appeared to be concern. "My mom will be here soon. With an actual army. You don't have to do this, Bloom."

This was my fault. My mind was made up.

"She won't be here in time, Stella."

I looked out into the darkness of the forest. A rasp echoed, under the leaves and drifting toward the sky.

"The Burned Ones are after me. They've always been after me."

In the depths of the forest, I thought I could see Burned Ones slipping between trees. Shadows, moving with terrible speed. Headed for their target.

"If I can connect with them like Rosalind said? I can stop them."

I tried to keep my voice steely. But underneath that, I knew both of them could sense my fear.

"But to do that . . ." I swallowed. "I have to draw on more magic than I ever have before. I don't know what's going to happen when I do."

"It's okay," Aisha told me steadily. "I'll make sure we're safe. And that you are, too."

"You won't see us, but we'll be right here," murmured Stella.

Aisha took one of my hands. Stella took the other. Aisha, water to my fire. And Stella, who could hide Aisha away from our enemies.

I looked from one face to the other and found strength.

"Rosalind wants me to believe that she's the person I need to get through this. She's not."

Then, I took a breath and turned to the clearing. Aisha and Stella retreated away from me. When I turned back, by all appearances, they were gone.

I took a few steps into the clearing.

Let it come, then. Everything I was afraid of. Let me be everything I ever feared or desired.

Water swirled from the lake, Aisha's magic pulling it out in a silvery stream that moved in the air like a wind current. It encircled me in a curtain of water, a diamond-bright cocoon that wrapped around me, isolating me from the world. Suspended in there, I felt weightless, as though I could fly.

Water and fire. Oddly, there at the end of my journey, I

didn't think of Rosalind's words or even Ms. Dowling's. I thought of my mom, how we used to play pretend princesses in a castle, and how she would sing me peppy cheerleading songs.

Close your eyes and open your heart!

Okay, Mom. I closed my eyes.

I felt flames come to dancing life at the very tips of my fingers, encircling my hands.

I felt sparks coruscate up along my legs as my feet lifted off the ground.

And out of my back, I felt tendrils of fire escape, unfurling like a flower made of flame.

Finally, I opened my eyes. The water curtain evaporated in front of my gaze, raindrops melting in the air. I burned brightly and felt the night air ruffle my bright wings.

My feet touched down on the ground, and I turned my lambent gaze toward the forest.

The Burned Ones were coming for me. I lifted a finger to beckon them on, and saw a magenta flame spring from the fingertip. The flame seemed to summon an echo of fire in the Burned Ones' chests. I could see a light in each of them, a strange and terrible light. This must be what Professor Harvey had called a Cinder. But why could I see them? Why did the Burned Ones suddenly look so strange to me?

"What *are* you?" I whispered as they leaped through the trees at me. I ran to meet them.

The closest struck out at me, and I lifted my hand. The

fire slipped from its chest to me, and as the Cinder left it, the Burned One's charred shape wavered and changed.

He was dead on the ground, and the other Burned Ones were attacking. They seemed almost slow-moving to me, as though they were out of their element and I was in mine. I lifted my hand and light called to light, the Cinders a trail of torches as their magic came to me.

The Burned Ones fell all around me, like leaves in the forest. Human bodies hit the ground, and at last I stood in a circle of the dead.

The Burned Ones were gone. My school was safe. I'd done it.

I turned and saw Ms. Dowling on the edge of the clearing. She was looking at me the way I'd always wanted her to: with pride.

"Well done, Bloom," she said.

I nodded. But then, faster than my magic had risen, the flames receded. Darkness began to flicker at the edges of my vision, and I felt my knees give way as I toppled over. Ms. Dowling ran across the clearing, and caught me in her arms.

Aisha and Stella rushed up out of the darkness.

"What's wrong?" Aisha demanded.

Stella's voice was fearful. "Is she . . .?"

"She's okay. Just weak." Ms. Dowling looked from Aisha's face to Stella's. "Maybe you girls want to help bring her back to her room?"

As they took my arms over their shoulders, I managed

to look at each of them. Stella, beautiful and haughty. Aisha, tranquil and steadfast. Both of them right here, determined, and afraid for me. Holding me steady, as they had been all night.

"We did it," I whispered.

"Yeah." Aisha's voice as warm and strong as her shoulder supporting me. "We did."

MIND

Musa was sitting curled around Sam, feeling the agony batter at both of them like black waves trying to tear them apart, carry them away and drown them.

Then suddenly, the tide receded.

Musa blinked, trying to clear her vision. "His pain. It's leaving." She started to smile. "I think they got it."

Sam squeezed Musa's hand, gazing up at her. They locked eyes. There was no joking around between them right now. No banter. Just gratitude in Sam's eyes, deep and sweet as the beginning of something true.

"Thank you," he murmured.

Musa nodded, then looked at the Harvey family, feeling the waves of gratitude come at her from all sides. Tears welled in her eyes. Musa blinked hastily to hide them. She wasn't the emotional type. She never had been. It wasn't safe.

Professor Harvey turned to Terra, his face shining with pride.

He said, "Yes. Thank you, both."

Terra glowed, but it was too much for Musa. This felt like another sea trying to swallow her, too many feelings all around. She began to turn away, until Terra put her arm around her roommate, and stopped her.

She held Musa gently in place, for just long enough. The sea of emotions didn't drown Musa, as she'd feared. The relief and joy surrounding them didn't feel like struggling in dark waters at all, but like stepping out into the light.

"Nope," said Terra into her ear. "You have to feel the good stuff, too."

And to Musa's own astonishment, she relaxed into her best friend's arms, and did.

SPECIALIST

In these times of trouble and murder, Riven found consolation in one of his few constants: Messing with Dane's head was fun.

"So wait. 'Fighting like a girl'? 'Throwing like a girl'? 'Running like a girl'?"

"All. Problematic," Dane informed him.

And what about letting killers loose while holding grudges against an innocent girl who really liked you, Dane? Riven thought. *Is that problematic?*

But it was kind of sweet, what an earnest dumbass Dane could be.

From her position by the greenhouse window, Beatrix spoke up, her voice lazily amused. "He's messing with you, Dane. Riven understands contemporary gender linguistics much better than he lets on. A cute act, though."

Riven shot Beatrix a smile. *She got him*, he thought. Nobody else did, but she did. She thought he was smart, and that he was cute. That felt as if she liked him.

Then he transferred the smile to Dane. Yeah, they were kind of awful, but so was Riven. Their weird gang was reunited, and in the midst of horror, it felt pretty good.

When Beatrix spoke, her tone was warmer than usual. "This term . . . It didn't suck, boys. Thanks for that."

The lights flickered on, and the conversation went silent. Riven glanced at Dane.

"We should get back," he said.

"We should," Dane said.

Nobody moved. If they left, it was over. Riven would be alone, with all his fear and all his regrets.

Only then Beatrix said, "Rosalind will be here soon. Hear her out. She and my dad have a plan. You two can be a part of it. This . . . doesn't have to end."

This. So Beatrix thought there really was a "this." It hadn't all been an act. There was something between them.

And that meant there was something to lose.

Dane said, in tones of revelation, "Hang on. Your dad was the one who sent you in here?"

"Technically, he's not my dad, but he'll know what to—"

Then, the door swung open. An older blonde woman stood at the greenhouse's main entrance. She was wearing an unsettling smile. Riven had been a Specialist long enough to recognize an air of command.

Beatrix breathed, *"Rosalind."*

Rosalind. Yay. The mastermind behind the no-doubt-evil plan Beatrix was talking about.

"You remember me," said Rosalind the mastermind. "Good."

She eyed Riven and Dane with a haughty air, all *who the hell are they?* Riven eyed her back, like, *who the hell are you, lady?*

He didn't say it. This lady had intensely unbalanced vibes. Like if she was fifty years younger, Sky would try to date her.

But then Beatrix said, "They're friends. Both of them."

That sounded nice. It sounded real.

Rosalind's eyes glowed, and Riven felt her magic like a torch shining into all the darkest corners of his soul. Eventually Rosalind nodded, as though they passed muster.

Guess that meant Riven's soul was pretty dark.

"Always nice to have friends," said Rosalind. "I bet they wanna know what happens next?"

Rosalind smiled, a slow smile that seemed somehow both warm as sunshine and cold as a snake. Riven wasn't sure he wanted to know what came next at all.

FIRE

As Stella helped me into my room, Aisha pulled down my covers and pointed imperiously. I crawled into bed just in time for Terra to enter with soothing tea. Musa was following behind. She did not have soothing tea.

I had to double-check. "And you're sure Sam is okay?"

Terra beamed at me over the teacup. "Yep. Thanks to you and Musa."

Musa shot her a fond glance. "Please. You should've seen Terra. She'll be operating on all of us in a week. As practice. Even if we don't need it."

"I will say, I'm a bit disappointed I missed the wings," Terra admitted. "They were like full-on, Tinker Bell–style?"

"Much cooler than that."

High praise, coming from Stella.

"*Cooler?* I like Tinker Bell," Terra said wistfully.

"Of course you do," Stella murmured.

My phone buzzed on the nightstand. *Mom and Dad.*

"You rest," said Aisha. "I'll cover. It will be my one allocated lie of the month."

As Aisha grabbed the phone and walked out of the room, I heard her voice go peppy. Mom would like that.

"Mr. and Mrs. Peters, *hey!* What? No, Bloom's fine. Yeah, it's been a rough week. Exams are killer."

I looked around at my friends, all around me. Their faces smiling. They were happy and safe. They were with me. I wasn't alone.

I let my eyes drift shut.

SPECIALIST

Bloom had done it. Sky had known she could.

He just wished he knew what to do with himself.

He sat outside the school, in the grass before the main entrance. The stars moved. The sky lightened. The sun rose. The gold-touched castle standing against the blue sky was the same, he knew that, but it didn't feel the same. Alfea was the only home he'd ever known, but now it was tainted.

His hours-long daze was broken by Bloom's voice. "There you are."

She sat in the grass beside him and leaned in a bit. Letting her shoulder touch his. It would've been nice, if he hadn't felt a million miles away.

"I heard a rumor you went full fairy last night," he said.

"Was it a good rumor or a bad one?" Bloom mused. "Actually, I don't care. Whatever people think, it was the first time I felt like myself. Totally myself." She added, softly, "I belong here."

Sky looked over at her. Unlike his school, unlike the world, Bloom made sense to him. She didn't look lost anymore. She'd found herself, as he'd always been sure she would.

"You do," Sky murmured.

He just wasn't certain he could say the same thing about himself.

Bloom's voice went suddenly sharp. "Are you wearing the same clothes you were wearing last night?"

Her gaze stopped being dreamy. She focused on his face.

"Sky. What happened?"

She'd been so happy when she came out to meet him, glowing like the sunrise, feeling she belonged here. He didn't want to be the dark cloud on her horizon.

"I'm fine. I promise."

Then he motioned up the driveway, where Dowling stood. Providing the perfect excuse.

"Looks like somebody wants to chat."

Personally, Sky was done talking.

FIRE

Another interview in Ms. Dowling's office. I'd slammed my way in here demanding truth so often, it was slightly weird now that we were trying to be polite to each other.

"How are you feeling?" asked Ms. Dowling.

"Bit rough. But I'll live."

Ms. Dowling nodded. "You drew on a great deal of magic. I'm sure you'll be drained for a few days, and—"

That was enough pretending. Maybe Ms. Dowling's punctilious soul would be horrified, but I had to get this out.

"I was a brat. I keep thinking about what I said to you last night."

Without Ms. Dowling, I wouldn't have Aisha or Sky or Terra or Musa or Stella. I wouldn't have Alfea or magic. I wrestled with my guilt at how I'd treated her. I knew now she'd been doing her best. I knew now how hard it was, to do your best.

"You've been incredible to me. You found me when I was lost. Brought me to a place I was safe. Gave me guidance. Surrounded me with good people. And I've been—"

I'd been so ungrateful.

Ms. Dowling looked a little like Rosalind, as though perhaps she'd modeled herself on Rosalind long ago. Maybe that was why I'd trusted Rosalind too fast, wanting her to be everything I'd decided Ms. Dowling couldn't be for me. Ms. Dowling's blonde hair was a shade darker than Rosalind's, her eyes dark instead of Rosalind's intense blue. She wasn't Rosalind, who glittered like costume jewelry. Ms. Dowling was real gold.

Ms. Dowling smiled, sudden and bright and true. As though from now on, we would be true to each other. "It's forgiven."

I believed her.

"Do you . . . can we . . . hug?"

It just came out, an awkward and probably ridiculous request. Cool, aloof Headmistress Dowling would be horrified by me as she usually was.

Only Ms. Dowling nodded, stepped forward, and took me into her arms. The first time I'd seen Ms. Dowling she'd been surrounded by light. She'd looked like a revelation, but the light had been cold. This hug was warm. I put my arms around her and held on tight.

We would understand each other more, and get along better, from now on.

She would be my mentor, and Alfea would be where I belonged, from now on.

Except there was one thing I needed to do first.

FIRE

My home in California was in better shape than the last time I'd seen it. Everything mended, with time.

My dad was very surprised to see me. All he could think to do was yell for my mom.

"*Bloom,*" Mom said as soon as she saw me. "Why are you home? Are you in trouble?"

My mother had no idea of the trouble I'd been in, or the trouble I suspected I'd be getting into in the future.

"I'll explain everything," I declared. "I just need to ask one quick question."

I gestured to my friends.

"Hi," murmured Aisha.

"Hello," Stella intoned regally.

"So good to meet you!" Terra gushed.

"'Sup," drawled Musa.

My parents' eyes went wide.

"Can my friends crash here for the weekend?" I asked.

Mom's face was baffled, but brightening. I could see the *my-daughter-has-gone-demented* worry battling with the *my-daughter-has-a-social-life!* joy. "Um. Sure."

And then I asked my friends to go wait in my room, while I sat down with my parents and told them the truth. About what I was, and what I'd done to them. About their first daughter, whom they had lost without knowing it.

She would have been human, that first daughter. She would never have set fires, or set off for strange lands. But she couldn't possibly have loved them more than I did.

I was too scared to look at my mom. When I finally managed to do so, she was staring down at the burn scars on her arms.

"I'm sorry," I whispered as the tears spilled down my face.

I felt as though I'd been waiting for months to say that. To cry.

And just like every time in my whole childhood, when I cried, Mom was right there. She put her arms around me and held me tight, and I knew I was hers, and I knew I was home.

We talked for a lot longer. And my friends and I talked later, up in my room.

The next morning, I came downstairs, and my parents welcomed my friends properly. Mom let Dad order pizza that evening, and even ate some herself, since it was a special day. Mom had always wanted me to have enough friends to throw a pizza party.

I'd read in poems, back in my old school, that fairies granted wishes, and fairyland was called the Land of Heart's Desire.

All my wishes had come true, even though none had come true in a way I expected. Still, I got to go home, with my new friends. Now I'd embraced the truth of myself, I could have everything I'd always wanted.

Maybe fairyland was the Land of Heart's Desire after all.

SPECIALIST

Sky helped Silva carry weaponry through the shattered detritus of their school. The windows were smashed, the gates torn down, but at least the armory would be in order.

"Where's Riven?" asked Silva.

"Probably getting stoned somewhere with Dane."

That was all Riven did these days. Apparently, that was what he'd been doing on the night the Burned Ones attacked. Bloom and her friends were off being heroes, and what was Sky's friend doing?

On the other hand, Riven had seen how screwed up Alfea was way before Sky had. Perhaps Riven was the smart one.

Silva gave Sky a direct look. Sky had always thought that look of Silva's was so honest.

"One day I hope you see that everything I did was for your benefit. The world is not perfect, Sky. It's not black-and-white. Heroes and villains. Good and evil."

Sky asked, despairing, "Then why did you spend my entire life convincing me otherwise?"

He wanted to ask, *Did you ever love me at all*, but he'd never said anything like that to Silva in his life. He didn't get the chance to ask now. Down the driveway came a retinue of SUVs, and Queen Luna's Rolls.

Silva approached the vehicles with his brow furrowed. "They shouldn't be here. We told them the attack was over."

He strode toward Queen Luna's retinue, confident and fearless as always. Silva stopped dead when the queen's guards all aimed their bows, directly at him.

"What the hell is going on?" Sky demanded.

Queen Luna emerged from the Rolls. "Saúl Silva, it's with a heavy heart that I must place you under arrest."

Her heart might be heavy, but her voice was light as bells.

"For what?" Silva asked roughly.

"The attempted murder of Andreas of Eraklyon," Luna responded.

One word, and it was like a stone thrown at Sky's whole life. Overturning everything.

"Attempted?" Sky repeated.

The door of a truck opened, and a man climbed out. Sky knew his face from a hundred pictures, knew him from a hundred stories Silva had told.

"Hello, Sky," said his father.

There wasn't much chance for an emotional family reunion. Luna ordered her soldiers to enter Alfea and put matters to rights.

One such matter was Silva. Sky's Specialist Headmaster seemed still in a daze when they snapped the handcuffs on his wrists, and Sky was ordered to stand down with the rest of the Specialists.

Sky had to watch as soldiers flooded his home, reorganizing everything. He had to watch as they took Silva away in cuffs.

And the whole time his father stood there. His father was alive, and he'd never bothered to contact Sky once.

Beside Andreas, leaning in toward him as though Andreas was *her* father, stood Beatrix. The girl who'd killed someone and fled the school. Now Beatrix was giving Riven and Dane a smug smile.

Though shock made everything seem very distant and unreal, Sky managed to think, *Bloom. I'm so glad you're not here. Don't come back. Alfea isn't safe. Not anymore.*

Perhaps it never really had been.

THE HEART
GROWS OLD

When Rosalind came to find her, Farah was burying the bodies that had once been Burned Ones. How noble. But that was Farah all over. So noble, it made her ultimately ineffective.

"The story behind the Burned Ones is a doozy," Rosalind told her former mentee. "Trust me."

It seemed Farah didn't. How sad. Rosalind patted the bench beside her, inviting Farah to sit, but Farah wouldn't even move a step toward her. Farah had never been personable. It was a serious flaw. Rosalind found her own ability to make people warm to her extremely useful.

Just to tease, she let Farah know that the Burned Ones had once been soldiers in an ancient war, soldiers who were transformed by the magic known as the Dragon Flame. This same flame burned inside little changeling Bloom.

Farah said angrily, "You let Burned Ones into the school to test her. Risked the lives of countless students . . ."

Yes, yes. And what was Farah's point?

"There's a war on the horizon. Burned Ones are nothing compared with what's coming." Rosalind came to her own point. "I fear you lack the composure to lead the next generation into it."

Farah's mouth twisted in a wry smile. "And there it is."

"Don't get me wrong, you've done a lovely job," Rosalind told her condescendingly.

Farah—Headmistress Dowling, what a joke—observed, "I had a choice. Continue your methods or learn from their shortcomings."

She really seemed to believe it. She seemed sure. Rosalind didn't remember Farah Dowling as sure of herself. Once, she'd only been sure of Rosalind.

"Look at you," Rosalind murmured. "All grown-up."

Farah looked down her nose at Rosalind. "Once I stepped out of your shadow, I saw a world filled with light. It turns out this place isn't miserable. It was just you."

Rosalind said sweetly, "If only Queen Luna agreed with you."

She hadn't even had to blackmail Luna into thinking Alfea needed new management. Apparently, Luna was cross with Farah about something to do with Luna's daughter. That was Farah, so silly, always making enemies.

Luna was eager for Rosalind to change the school. Ben

Harvey would fall in line, for his precious son and daughter's sake. And Rosalind was rather delighted to inform Farah that her precious Silva was being carted off to prison. For the *attempted* murder of Andreas of Eraklyon.

Andreas was taking back his son. And Rosalind was taking everything. Her castle, and Bloom.

Farah turned away, trying to hide how shaken she was at the sudden ruin that had descended upon her. But of course, Rosalind knew Farah too well. She didn't need to see. She knew the despair Farah must be feeling. And she loved it.

"So now we just have to talk about you. I thought it'd be best if you took a sabbatical. Head to the mountains. Take a break. You've worked so hard, Farah."

Farah's voice rang like drawn steel. "I am the headmistress of Alfea now. And there is no way I'm leaving the school in your hands."

"I know that," murmured Rosalind. "But the rest of the world might believe it."

Dear Farah, always too honorable. She'd thought they were having a civil discussion. Farah turned now, drawing her magic to her, but Rosalind's magic was already let loose. It only took a wave of her hand to snap Farah's neck. Almost too easy, really.

Farah Dowling's last thought was that she should have warned Bloom, safeguarded her, taught her more. Taught her better.

But it was too late.

All thoughts ceased for Farah Dowling. The light died behind her eyes, and the earth rose to claim her. Seven new graves, instead of six for the lost Burned Ones.

Rosalind made sure flowers grew in vivid profusion over the disturbed earth. The new blooms were gorgeous. It looked like this was shaping up to be a beautiful day.

Oh, it could all have ended very differently, Rosalind supposed. But it hadn't.

There was only room in her dear Bloom's life for one mentor.

FIRE

As my friends and I strolled up the driveway of Alfea, chatting and giggling, the sunlight caught the towers and casement windows of Alfea and made it resemble more than ever an illustration from a gilt-edged book of fairy tales. The sight was so familiar by now, it made me smile. The castle looked like home, and it was a beautiful day.

We passed through the gates, Aisha and Stella and Musa and Terra and I.

Then all talk and laughter ceased, amid the dust and ruin of Alfea. Stella's breath hissed out between her teeth as she stared at her mother. Alongside Queen Luna stood a man I'd only seen in pictures, a man with Sky's face. A man who was supposed to be dead.

And standing in the center of Alfea as if she owned the place, smiling her sweet devil's smile, was the woman I'd freed.

"Welcome back, ladies," said Rosalind.